Julie Bozza

# The Apothecary's Garden

LIBRAtiger

Published by LIBRAtiger 2017

ISBN: 978-1-925869-19-4

First published by Manifold Press 2013

Text: © Julie Bozza 2013
Proofreading and line-editing: F.M. Parkinson
   Any remaining errors are the sole responsibility of the author.
Editor: Fiona Pickles, Manifold Press
Print format: © Julie Bozza 2017
Set in Adobe Caslon

Cover design: © Tiferet Design 2017 | TiferetDesign.com



libra-tiger.com | juliebozza.com

*Is not old wine wholesomest, old pippins toothsomest, old wood burn brightest, old linen wash whitest? Old soldiers, sweetheart, are surest, and old lovers are soundest.*

John Webster, *Westward Ho*

# One

Once upon a time … Well, it was the autumn before last, actually …

Once upon a Thursday one recent autumn, in that part of England where the corners of Wiltshire, Hampshire and Berkshire meet, there dwelt a man who had passed a longish yet uneventful life. His name was Hilary Kent, and until five weeks before this story begins he had lived in London, having been born there and then rarely leaving it but for occasional trips to the Brighton seafront.

It was not in his nature to be discontent, and that had proved truer than ever since his move to the outlying reaches of the village of Nether Bedwyn. The only astonishing thing that had ever happened to him had brought him here.

One day, a few months before retiring from work at a London borough council, Hilary had opened his mail to discover that a long-estranged cousin had left him his property, a small old place called Riverside, on the banks of the Thames in the country. Once he'd retired, Hilary had broken the habits of sixty-five years to sell his home in London and move, sight unseen, despite the understandable scepticism of his acquaintances. Not that anybody knew him very well, or gave him more than a thought or two once he had gone, for Hilary was used to keeping himself to himself.

He hadn't regretted the move for one moment, though, and he was quite happy to live alone, as he had done for decades. He was already contentedly developing new habits that suited Hilary himself, for he had no one else to mind. For instance, each afternoon, just as today, he would leave the old round stone tower by the front door, and turn to walk back along the outside of his high garden wall, along the verge of the field stretching away to the west. He ducked under the foliage hanging down from the wall as he went and detoured around clumps of ivy, before turning to take a thoughtful constitutional along the riverbank.

The waters were flowing fulsome on that autumn day. As Hilary watched, he imagined the river bearing the fallen rain between fields and through towns, winding east between chalky cliffs and soft green hills, then past Hilary's former home on the southern bank of the Thames, and eventually down to the sea. The salty heaviness at the river mouth would be so very different to the clear autumn day Hilary was enjoying now, with the air as crisp as an apple, and the trees just beginning to turn, reds and golds beginning to glow amidst the green. Hilary watched them, noting the changes each afternoon, surprised at how eagerly he, an urban man, awaited what would happen next.

The sun set quite early here; this nook of land was sheltered by hills to the west. A shiver ran through Hilary as the air chilled, and he turned for home again, his new home, though he wasn't in any hurry. He pushed his hands into his cardigan pockets, and quite contentedly strolled back along the same path by the riverbank.

Hilary was a solitary man. And so it was with a tinge of resentment rather than either pleasure or alarm that, as he rounded the corner of his long garden wall, he saw a bicycle propped against the overgrown hedge that ran along the far edge of the gravelled area just off the road – and a young man sitting on his front steps. A young man pale and slim with dark brown hair, who immediately broke into the most engaging grin – a little sheepish, perhaps, but happy and at ease. As if it were perfectly natural for him to greet strangers so warmly.

"Hello!" the young man cried, standing up – and up. He was tall, and being on the second step added several inches to his height, so he towered over Hilary for a moment before jogging down to the level ground – and still he was half a head taller. Certainly six foot, and with a relaxed yet confident bearing that made him seem more. "Hello, Mr Kent. I'm Tom," he said, holding out his hand to be shaken.

"Hello," Hilary replied, shaking that hand and looking with wary curiosity into a pair of clear sky-blue eyes.

Striking, the man was striking, and it soon dawned on Hilary why. It wasn't that he was particularly handsome beyond the usual attractions of youth, but that honest grin shone from Tom's eyes, and his whole face was alive with candour. Hilary liked that. Very much. It was a rare thing to find – but he took a step back, and simply asked, "How may I help you?"

"I'm here about your room."

"My room – ?"

"Marjorie – at the store? – she said you might have a room to let."

"Oh, that blasted – !" Hilary closed his mouth before he could utter the whole angry epithet. He turned away for a moment, until he thought he could speak without cursing. "I'm sorry. Is Mrs Flanagan a friend of yours?"

"Oh, no." Tom was still grinning, all irreproachably wicked humour. "It's all right. Everyone knows she's a frightful meddler."

"I told her I didn't – It was all her idea, and – I told her it wasn't necessary."

The humour was fading now, though Tom was gamely trying to hold onto his smile. He seemed surprisingly disappointed. "Pity."

"Is it?"

"Yes." It was Tom who turned away for a moment now. But then he asked, very directly, "Look, could I come in? Please. There's something I want to talk to you about. I mean, something else."

"Oh! Oh, well –"

"I'm a grad student, from the university." Tom gestured somewhat in the direction of the old market town to the west. "My name's Tom Laurence. Anyone there would vouch for me." He chuckled under his breath. "Even Marjorie wouldn't have sent me here if she thought I'd do you any harm."

And Hilary didn't really have a good reason why not, other than habit and solitude and – Well, it was time for a cup of tea, so why not do the decent thing and offer one to this young man as well?

"That would be grand," Tom said, and his happy grin was back in full force as he followed Hilary inside.

Tom seemed a bit jittery as he sat waiting at the kitchen table while Hilary put the kettle on. His hands rested calmly enough on his narrow thighs, but he was holding himself stiffly upright in the chair, and his feet seemed as if they'd detach themselves at any moment and start tap dancing around the room. Hilary thought an effort might be called for, and so he put aside his own jitters and endeavoured to make small talk. "What are you reading? At the university."

"Medieval history."

A pause lengthened, which Hilary had assumed Tom would fill with chatter about his studies. Apparently not. All right. He could manage the next obvious question. "How long have you lived in the area?"

"Four years. I'm from Colchester."

"Is that home, then?"

Tom sketched a smile. "Not any more! My parents live there, but I won't be going back. Not to live, anyway."

Hilary frowned over this, and ventured, "I would have thought that would be an ideal home for a student of medieval history. Isn't it supposed to be one of the oldest towns in Britain?"

"*The* oldest, they say, and there's heaps there. It was a school trip to the Norman keep that got me into all this. But I was ready … to find somewhere new. Somewhere that's my own."

"I see." Hilary found himself stalled. He measured out the tea – Earl Grey at this time of day – while trying to think of another question that wouldn't make him seem to be prying. Unfortunately it wasn't as if the small talk had worked. Tom hadn't relaxed at all. He was obviously restraining himself from saying something in particular. Hilary thought the edginess didn't suit him so well as the candour, and yet the transparency of his feelings was rather wonderful.

Eventually Tom asked very tentatively, "How exactly were you related to old Mr Kent?"

"We were cousins, on my father's side. I hardly knew him, though. We hadn't seen each other for years. Decades."

"Oh …" was the only response.

"Did you know Evelyn?"

"Sorry?"

"Evelyn Kent. My cousin. Did you know him?"

Tom grimaced. "Well, I met him a couple of times. You could say we … didn't exactly hit it off."

"I see."

The grimace turned apologetic. "It's not that I did anything, or anything bad happened."

"Of course not." Hilary took the teapot over to the table on a tray already loaded with cups, saucers and spoons, a jug of milk, a pot of sugar and a plate of biscuits. The jug and the pot were full, while the provisions on the plate looked very scanty. "I'm sorry there aren't many biscuits left. I'm afraid it's the wrong end of the grocery week."

"No, it's great. I mean, look at all this! Anyone else making me tea, they'd have just handed me a mug with hot water and a teabag dumped in it."

"Ah …"

"This is really great!" Tom picked up a biscuit and started wolfing it down, as if to demonstrate his enthusiasm.

"About Evelyn ..."

"Mmm?" Tom prompted around another mouthful of biscuit. Heavens, and they were only the plain sort, as well. Not even a nice digestive.

"You don't need to assume I'd necessarily take his side in any disagreement. I really didn't know him; he was twelve or fifteen years older than me for a start, and our fathers had a falling out – oh, *years* ago. Apart from which, Evelyn and I were each the kind of man, I think, who likes to keep himself to himself."

"He left you this place," Tom countered, with a gesture indicating the tower and its surrounds.

"I suppose I was the nearest relative still alive," Hilary observed. As he poured the tea, Hilary prompted, "What was it you wanted to talk about? The room ... ?"

And Tom immediately blurted, "No, it's about your garden."

"My garden!" Hilary glanced towards the windows, though one could hardly see through the thickly undulating old glass, and he'd only opened one of the two sets of curtains that morning. "I hardly think it qualifies for the term. It's nothing but thickets and wilderness these days, I'm afraid."

"I know, but ... it used to be quite something. A priest lived here – Do you know much about the history of this place? The local priest usually lived in the village – the current vicar still does! – but Thaddeus lived here. This is about four hundred years ago. He had some kind of friendship or connection with the squire's family at the Hall, and they let him live here. And he created a physic garden, you see. An apothecary's garden."

Hilary was rather surprised, to say the least. "Heavens!"

"Interestingly, the squire's arms include a leaf from one of the old medieval medicinal plants – though I haven't quite worked out why. So there's another connection for you, between the garden and Bedwyn Hall."

"How do you know about the garden? Did you talk with Evelyn about it?"

"No. Oh, no." Tom's eyes slid away for a moment, but then he re-engaged. "I've been reading up on it in the local library, searching through the old town planning records, parish maps, whatever I could find. Only things that were available to the public," he added reassuringly. "I wasn't prying … I'm just interested."

"You're interested in physic gardens?"

"Yes, from a historical perspective. I mean, obviously he was working in the Jacobean era, but he was following medieval precepts. This is a great example of what they would have done. And the thing is … no *actual* medieval gardens have survived, so this is kind of the next best thing."

Hilary took a moment with that, glancing again at the windows, where twilight was greyly misting. He lifted his hands hopelessly. "But if it's been overgrown all this time –"

"Not *all* the time. From what I can make out, people looked after it, even if it was never quite as grand as when it started. I think for a long while there was this tradition that the gardener from the manor house lived here – from up at Bedwyn Hall. It's only been the past fifty or sixty years it's been really let go."

"I see." Hilary thought that was roughly equivalent to how long Evelyn had been resident.

"I don't mean to criticise …" the young fellow began.

Hilary waved off any apology. "There's no need to be polite for my sake. Honestly, I scarcely knew the man."

Tom nodded. And then seemed to wait expectantly, as if hoping Hilary would make the next leap.

But Hilary could hardly guess at what Tom might want with the place. "You want to explore the garden … ? You might need a machete! And you should probably take a packed lunch."

Tom laughed, and the delightful chime in his voice echoed in his bright eyes. He seemed relieved. "If I could … explore it, yes. And I was thinking – " Tom sat forward, leaning his elbows on the table and jabbing at it with a neat pale finger. "I was thinking – there may be papers, stored away in here. Planting records, plans, a journal perhaps. Who knows! There could be all sorts of things, if – Well, if there are any old papers around here. Maybe your cousin cleared everything out … ?"

Hilary sighed, thinking of the upper floors of the tower, into which he'd hardly dared even poke his nose. "There might be nothing of interest," he warned, "but I doubt that Evelyn was the clearing-out type. More the opposite! It's been all I could do to create a bit of elbow room in the bedroom."

Tom was shining with the possibilities of Hilary's answer – and his smile had a wicked twist to it. "Need a bit of elbow room, do you … ?" he asked, with the loveliest hint of innuendo. But then he smoothly continued, "If you find anything like that, anything about the garden at all, would you mind if – ?"

"Of course I wouldn't mind," Hilary replied. "If you're really interested. Were you planning to write an essay on physic gardens?"

"My thesis. For my Master's."

"Ah!" That sounded like a rather serious matter. Well, it wasn't as if it didn't all need sorting out at some stage. "I could start looking through things. What sort of time-frame did you have in mind? If I find anything, I'd be happy to call you –" But even as he started happily anticipating making tea again for this engaging young man, Hilary came to a halt, for it was obvious that Tom still hadn't told his whole tale.

An apologetic grimace was offered, and then Tom said, "I was wondering if you'd let me actually work out there – in the garden, I mean."

"Oh, I couldn't ask that! It's an utter mess, I'm afraid. Quite beyond redemption."

"*I'm* the one who's asking."

"I could hardly even make my way down the steps to ground level, it's all so overgrown."

"But I can help you with that."

"I don't think you understand how much work it would be just to clear a path down to the river … I've come to think of it as quite impossible."

Tom was looking at him with an odd combination of patience and eagerness. "But," he slowly repeated once Hilary fell quiet again, "I could help you with that."

"I couldn't ask –"

"Like I said, I'm the one who's asking, Mr Kent. You'd be doing me an enormous favour."

Hilary considered him for a long moment, trying to find the right balance between caution and cooperation, reason and generosity. "Well, let's not hurry into things. Of course you must use the garden for research, Tom, in any way you can, and I'll be happy to look for any papers for you. But why don't you come back again and see the place in the light of day? I find it all quite daunting out there – and there is a *chance* that you might, too."

Tom was grinning at him. "All right. Thank you. I'd love that. But I have to warn you, I've been itching to work on that garden for four years now."

"Well, then. Come back when you can, and we'll see what we can agree upon."

Hilary finally drank the rest of his tea, and instinctively reached for a biscuit – only to find the plate empty, and Tom suddenly pausing mid-chew with an expression of dismay. "I've eaten all your biscuits!"

"Oh, there's no harm done."

"I'm sorry! I was thinking about the garden."

"It's not a problem." Hilary poured them each more tea. "It's almost dinner time, anyway."

"You're hungry," Tom concluded, sounding wretched. "Um, look …"

"Never mind," Hilary reassured him, afraid that Tom was going to offer him the half-eaten biscuit still neatly held between the shapely fingers of one lovely hand.

"Look, the fish-and-chip shop here in Nether Bedwyn, it's the best in the county." Tom cast him a half-wary, half-daring glance. "I always have my dinner there when I'm around. Why don't I ride down there, get us two cod and chips, and bring them back here?"

Hilary couldn't repress a smile at such a delicious plan, though of course he demurred along the lines of, "Please don't trouble yourself –"

"It's no trouble." Tom was already standing, and gathering himself for the short journey. "Is there anything else you'd like while I'm there? Something in particular to drink? Or a pineapple fritter, maybe … ?"

Hilary grinned at that. "How decadent!"

"All right, then. And we can watch telly, or something," Tom added, almost at the door already.

Which was when Hilary remembered: "*Midsomer Murders*!"

"That's right," Tom agreed. "They're showing the whole thing again, aren't they? Right from the beginning. Starting tonight!"

"Go on, then," Hilary said, walking over to shoo him out the door. "Ride carefully, but don't take too long! You don't want to miss the start!"

And the young man hopped on his bicycle and rode off down the lane into the gathering twilight, the glow from his lamp just visible along the tops of the hedgerows. Hilary watched until even the faintest hint of light was out of sight, and then turned towards the front room. He started tidying it up, and he turned on the television to warm it up, with a giddy little flutter in his heart. He wasn't used to company. And he certainly wasn't used to keeping company with such intriguing young men as Tom Laurence.

Tom apparently wasn't the sort to talk through a show, for which Hilary was grateful, so they'd eaten their dinner and shared their reactions to 'The Killings at Badger's Drift' in relative quiet. Towards the end of the episode, however, Tom's silence took on a disgruntled note. Once the credits started rolling, Hilary turned the sound down, and cast a careful glance at his companion. He wanted to ask what was wrong, but seeing as the plot had resolved in sibling incest and a murder-suicide pact, it was hard to know quite how to broach the matter. Hilary finally settled for, "What did you think … ?"

A half-irritable shrug. "I'd forgotten what these shows were like. As soon as you find a love that's not the norm, you find the bad guys."

"Yes," Hilary tentatively agreed, "I suppose."

"I just think it's a pity that a forbidden love should always mean they become so amoral as to be murderers."

Hilary pondered that for a moment. "Should these two have been allowed to be lovers, then? Sister and brother?"

"Yes. Maybe." Tom shrugged, and offered him a hapless grimace. "I don't know. But there's other sorts of love that society doesn't approve of, and I don't like the idea that they should all be driven to amorality."

"No doubt," Hilary murmured.

They sat there in a silence that threatened to become awkward, before Tom settled his hands on his thighs with a muffled clap. "You said yes about the garden, didn't you?"

Hilary laughed in surprise at the young man's audacity. "I said you'd better come back and see it in daylight before you decide."

"Tomorrow, then? Is that all right? I'll come by around ten in the morning, or maybe eleven."

"Tomorrow!"

"Told you I was keen," Tom said with a grin.

"So you did. All right, then. Tomorrow." They stood, and Hilary used the remote to turn off the television before accompanying Tom to the front door. "Will you be all right?" he asked, thinking about the bicycle and the distance and the late hour. It was a clear night, and the moon was up, but still. "Hadn't you better …" Although he wasn't sure what he was going to suggest. Hilary didn't own a car, and it was far too late to hope for a bus.

"It's only five miles, I'll be fine," Tom assured him, already organised and ready to be off, the ball of one foot braced against a pedal. "See you, Mr Kent!"

"Goodnight, Tom!" he called after the figure, which soon vanished between the hedgerows.

He stayed out there for a few minutes, soaking in the absolute peace of the countryside at night. It had taken Hilary a little while to get used to it, but already he was starting to rather like it. The night felt … open, somehow. Full of possibilities. And the stars shone their bright blessing on everything below.

It was cold, however, and a shiver soon sent him inside. Hilary took his time closing up and tidying away, before heading up for bed. He'd thought after all the excitement that he'd have trouble falling asleep. But as it was, he hardly had time to start pondering his memories of the candid blue-sky eyes of his new acquaintance, those lovely eyes as clear as a cloudless holiday, before the night's peace flowed through him and took him away.

# Two

Hilary walked downstream towards the village early the next morning, in the opposite direction to his afternoon constitutionals. After a ten- or fifteen-minute walk, the river broadened, and then branched off into a canal. Hilary crossed the footbridge at the lock, and headed off up the towpath. There were recently built houses at a respectful distance all along this stretch, and then the small parish church and churchyard. A few minutes later, he was in the heart of the old village, and turning past the preserved façade beyond which Marjorie Flanagan kept her modern grocery store.

"Morning, Mr Kent!" she cheerfully cried as he walked in and collected a basket.

"Good morning, Mrs Flanagan." Hilary paused by the desk, as she wasn't serving anyone. She seemed to be sorting through a stack of invoices. "I wonder if you could help me with a recommendation."

"Of course."

"What would a young man like in his sandwiches, do you think … ?"

Marjorie didn't forbear to smile smugly. "So, you took him in, did you?"

"No, I did not. But he's coming back this morning to look at the garden, and he may well need the consolation of a good lunch. Really, Mrs Flanagan," Hilary added in mild rebuke, "you had no business suggesting he might lodge with me."

"You don't really want to live in that awful old place all by yourself, do you?"

"My cousin did, for decades!" A thought occurred to him. "Perhaps you tried to set him up with lodgers as well."

"No," she said, unrepentant. "But you're a kinder man than old Mr Kent. He wouldn't even give Tom the time of day."

"And it's your business because … ?"

"Just being neighbourly, Mr Kent!" As if to prove her point, she came out from behind the desk, and beckoned for him to follow her. "You'll be wanting this wholemeal loaf; it has a nice malted flavour. These gherkins – no, in the sweet vinegar. Slice them up for the sandwiches, or put one or two whole ones on the side of the plate. Then these slices of roast beef, and Gouda cheese. Perfect!"

"I see." He looked down into his shopping basket, a little wide-eyed with wonder, not to mention juicy-mouthed with hunger. Maybe he should ask for Marjorie's recommendations more often. "That does look rather good."

"You've got yourself the makings of a nice hearty sandwich there," she said. "Was there anything else this morning, Mr Kent?"

"Oh, just some digestives for now," he replied as they headed back towards the till. "I'll think about my weekly shop later." Hilary collected a pack of the nicer digestives on the way – which Marjorie promptly swapped for the same brand but coated with dark chocolate. "Mmm," he muttered, permitting this indulgence. It was for Tom's sake, after all.

"You should think about having him stay with you," Marjorie commented as she rang up his purchases. "You could spare him a room and a study, and you still wouldn't know what to do with the other half of that old pile."

"There's really no question of it," Hilary said – before finding himself explaining, "I've lived alone my whole life. It's too late to change such habits now."

"It's never too late for any of us," Marjorie replied, though she kindly didn't push any further. Between them they'd packed the groceries into the old canvas satchel Hilary used for carrying things back and forth. "Will you be all right with those? You weren't expecting the gherkins in that heavy glass jar, now, were you?"

"I'll be fine. Thank you, Mrs Flanagan!" he called over his shoulder as he left.

"Have a nice day with that young man, Mr Kent!" she called back.

The impertinence of the woman! At last he was free to walk back home in the blessed silence.

Tom, of course, was keen to get out into the garden just as soon as he could, and wouldn't even wait for a cup of tea. "I'll have one when I've done something to earn it. If I may."

"Of course you may."

The young man started unpacking the various items he'd brought in his backpack. He'd at least planned ahead to the extent that he'd brought a sturdy old canvas coat to wear. "I'm not sure what to expect, really," Tom said while shrugging it on, "but it won't matter if this gets destroyed in the process.”

“And what about your hands?” Hilary asked.

“I brought gloves as well, don’t worry.” While he drew first one on, and then the other, Tom smiled at Hilary. “It’s nice of you to think about my hands.”

“Well, they’re nice hands,” Hilary said. And they were. Neat and lovely and unblemished. It was a pity to see them disappear into the thick old gardening gloves, but at least that meant they would emerge the same way.

“Thank you. I like yours, too,” Tom declared with the smile sparkling from his guileless eyes.

“These old things … ?” Hilary held them out and peered at them curiously. They were as sturdy and as worn as Tom’s canvas jacket.

“They’re great! Large and strong. Nice and virile, you know?”

There was a wink in Tom’s voice, but Hilary wasn’t game enough to discover if the wink was real as well. He suspected he was blushing. He let his hands fall again, and then tried to hide them away without making it too obvious.

Tom took pity on him, and started lifting some wrapped tools out of his backpack. “I brought a small axe and a bow saw, but I won’t cut down anything without your permission, I promise.”

“Oh, you must do whatever needs doing. There’s no point in it staying the way it is! If you can clear a way in, that would be marvellous.”

“It’s just that I have to get in there somehow to be able to work out what can be done. But I’ll try to only chop down the dead wood, at least to start with.”

“No, that’s fine. That’s fine. You’ll be able to judge far better than me what can be cleared, and I’ve heard that all good gardeners need to be ruthless.”

Tom grinned at him, and then swept a hand towards the back door. “Lead the way, then, Mr Kent!”


There was a stone terrace of sorts just outside the back door, with steps against the wall leading down to the left. Plants that probably should have remained shrubs had grown tall here, right up against the tower’s feet, with gnarly branches looming aggressively towards the doorway, reaching even over Tom’s head. Hilary had only ever ventured out here once before, and had very soon retreated back inside.

Tom, however, seemed undaunted. In fact, he seemed positively cheerful. "Well, this won't do, will it? I'm glad you said that about being ruthless, because this lot will have to go."

Hilary managed to say something fervent about his undying gratitude.

"In the meantime, I'm going to see how far I can work my way through from the bottom of the steps," he announced. "There might be a relatively open area in there."

"You'll be careful, won't you … ?" Though Hilary was at a loss to describe what he feared might happen. Perhaps he was imagining that Tom would get stuck as if in a briar patch, and Hilary wouldn't be able to follow him in and bring him back out again.

"Of course I'll be careful," Tom reassured him with a grin. "I'll start clearing a path, if it's any use, but what I'll definitely do is cut back some of those bushes right up against the paved area there. You should at least be able to see out!"

"Oh!" said Hilary, not knowing what he'd ever done to deserve this. It was true that the kitchen and living area at the back of the tower were rather dark rooms, even though they faced to the south; sometimes he didn't even bother drawing the curtains in the morning. The idea of getting some more light into his home was wonderful. "Thank you, Tom."

"Don't mention it!" Another wink as the young man reached the bottom of the steps – and then with a twist and a wriggle, Tom disappeared into the dark foliage.

Hilary took a breath and held it, his heart picking up an extra beat in every moment that he couldn't see or hear or somehow *sense* Tom's presence.

"Interesting!" came a muffled exclamation at last.

Hilary relaxed a little. "What's that? What have you found?"

"Think I can make a path through here –" There was a bit of determined rustling, and then a satisfied breath. It seemed that Tom had emerged on the other side. "Oh, Mr Kent! This is –"

"This is what?" he prompted after a moment, raising his voice a little.

"This is lovely. It's just lovely! Look, I'm going to cut these shrubs back so you can get through." Tom's voice seemed to float around a little closer, as if he were circling round to near where Hilary waited on the terrace. "I think they're mostly rhododendrons gone wild. Old Thaddeus wouldn't have planted these … To be honest, we'll probably need to get rid of them altogether, but for now I'll cut them right back – *severely*. But it's too early to make decisions that we can't undo, you know?"

"It's perfectly all right!" Hilary called in response. "Do whatever you think best."

"All right! I'll make sure to save the wood, too. We'll be able to use it for other things."

"Is there anything I can do … ?" he asked, feeling rather useless.

Tom's voice drifted back from where he must have first emerged. "Cup o' tea is gonna be very welcome, if you don't mind!"

"Right." And as industrious sawing noises began, Hilary headed back inside to put the kettle on.


By the time Tom reappeared to stand by the kitchen table, the tea was growing cool, but he refused to let Hilary make a fresh pot. Instead, Tom took the opportunity to drink down two cupfuls very quickly, and then said, "Come on, I've got something to show you."

Hilary was perfectly happy to follow the young man out the door again, and down the back steps. Tom had cut back enough of the shrubs to form a man-sized tunnel into the garden.

"D'you see?" Tom said, pointing into where the branches were thickest. "You can cut away just about everything, except the primary branches. There's usually two or three of them at the heart of the thing. You can cut them right down, too, without doing the plant any harm. Though it might take a year or two to flower properly again."

"I don't mind about that," Hilary assured him.

"There'll be plenty of foliage in the meantime. Careful where you step," Tom said, reaching to take Hilary's hand, and then backing away before him to help lead him through. Hilary had a sense of light around Tom's tall lean silhouette – and then they emerged.

"Oh!" Hilary cried in surprise. The garden was wild and overgrown, of course, but there was something elementally beautiful about it, and there was a feeling of openness and space that he hadn't expected at all. "Oh, Tom! Thank you."

"Well, don't thank me yet," Tom said, watching him with a smile. "A lot of this is gonna have to go. All that ivy, for a start …"

Ivy covered almost everything in a vibrant dark green, through which an assortment of living and dead plants struggled. Further down towards the river, the ivy created a canopy across what seemed to be a double row of trees.

"It's almost like a magical glade down there," Hilary said.

"It is, isn't it?"

"I hardly had the first idea … My bedroom window looks over the garden, but it's the same thick glass as downstairs, almost opaque in places. I think it might be rusted shut, because I haven't been able to open it at all."

"We'll both have plenty to discover, then. It's probably good timing, too; I think we're seeing it at its best. But the ivy's just going to kill everything else, and eventually it will even destroy the garden walls if you let it go. You don't want that, do you … ? Or do you?"

"No, I agree it has to go. But the trees …"

"They should be all right. I think they're all oaks. Pretty sturdy, anyway, and they look okay from here. Once they're left to their own devices, hopefully you'll get the same kind of shade from their leaves as from the ivy. You'll have a lovely walk down to the river, that's all your own!"

"At the moment," Hilary observed, "it looks like the walk would go on forever." It must be some trickery caused by the greenery, but the large tunnel formed by the trees under the ivy seemed to continue on far beyond where he knew it must come to an end. "Can we walk down there now?"

Tom laughed happily at his eagerness. "Not yet. I don't think it would be wise to yet. And you'd better be careful if you come out here exploring. There is – or was – an old water feature running down the middle there, with a pond up here near the tower. If it's still there, it's all hidden under debris now, and if you go tumbling into that, you might be in trouble. You're pretty isolated out here, aren't you?"

"Yes. Yes, I am."

"Apart from which, physic gardens always had a separate section for poisonous plants, the ones they grew for medicine. I have no idea where that would be, if it wasn't all destroyed years ago, but any protective fencing or whatever will be pretty flimsy by now. You don't want to go accidentally walking into all that either."

Hilary had turned to look at his young friend. "You must promise me you'll be careful, too, Tom. You won't be reckless."

"I promise," the fellow easily agreed. "What I thought," he continued blithely on, "was that I'd fetch you a chair from the kitchen, and you can sit out here and watch while I cut back some more of those rhododendrons. Then at least you'll be able to look out over the garden from your back door."

"Wonderful!"

"We'll leave the rest for now – see how they're planted all along the foot of the tower? If you want to keep them, we can prune them properly later."

"You're very good to me," Hilary said.

"Oh, but I have ulterior motives," Tom reminded him with another wink.

Hilary felt a bit deliciously self-conscious, though he knew well enough what Tom's real motives were. "Tom," he said, halting the other man on his way back inside. "You won't do too much today, will you?"

"No, just what I said about the shrubs. Then I'll show you the one map for the garden I was able to find. It dates back a while – though not far enough! – but it'll give us an idea. We can start working out a plan of attack."

Hilary nodded his agreement, and turned away again to contemplate his newly revealed treasure while waiting for Tom to fetch the promised chair.

It was certainly a pleasant way to spend the rest of the morning, though Tom's cheerful chatter quietened after a while, lost in concentration and effort. Once the back terrace was fully visible from the garden, Hilary headed inside and made the sandwiches – as close to Marjorie's specifications as he could. Then he went back out to call a halt to work for the day.

Tom, thankfully, was still quite able to direct a happy grin towards Hilary. "That's great timing," the young man said, shucking off his gloves and jacket. Hilary was able to stand on the terrace with his hands grasping the old iron railing, and look down into his garden, and watch. It was quite the luxury. Soon Tom was in nothing but a t-shirt damp with virile sweat, snug jeans, and his boots. "I'll wash my hands," Tom commented as he headed for the steps. Already the tunnel was gone; Hilary was almost sorry for that. "I hope I don't whiff too high!" Tom added as he reached Hilary's side. He heeled his boots off, with one hand on the railing for balance. "Maybe I should wash properly."

"That's really not necessary," Hilary said. "Though of course you may take a shower if you like."

"I'm all right. I was worrying about you."

"But I'm all right, too." Hilary really didn't mind. If anything, the young man's scent was intoxicating. It had been far too long since Hilary had experienced, even second-hand, the heady results of honest labour.

"Give me a minute, then. Oh, lunch looks great!" Tom exclaimed as he headed in through the kitchen, padding across the stone floor in his socks. "Thanks, Mr Kent!"

Hilary followed after him, beaming. "It's my pleasure," he murmured, though Tom had already slipped away into the downstairs bathroom.

Tom loved the sandwiches. Hilary sat there, pleased as punch, demurring at Tom's compliments but somehow failing to give Marjorie the credit she was due. Then, with another pot of tea to hand, Tom brought out some papers in a plastic sleeve, and laid them on the table between the two of them. "I made copies for you of what I've found – which isn't much." He drew out a map which seemed to be enlarged just to the point of graininess. "This place used to be part of the old estate, of course. You can see it here. The fields round here have all changed over the years, a lot of the old hedges are gone, but you can make out the tower and the garden here."

"Yes, I can see the long walls! I thought this one was a bit skew." Hilary had got the impression that the eastern wall sloped outwards, though only by a few yards, so that the garden was narrowest by the tower – and it seemed he was right. "And there's the river, of course."

"This is from about two hundred years ago. The river used to be wider, but I think that mainly affects the further bank. Here you can see the pond I mentioned; it was rectangular, at this time anyway, and I'm pretty sure it was part of the irrigation system, though it was probably also ornamental. Then water runs down this channel, or maybe up it, between that avenue of oaks …"

"What's that by the river?" Hilary pointed to a darkly hatched area along the foot of the garden. It was too regular not to be a structure of some kind, but far too wide to be only a wall.

"I'm not sure. Some kind of boundary, maybe even a defensible wall. It has to have at least provided mooring for a boat or two belonging to the manor house, but it could serve any number of purposes: part of the irrigation system, another terrace, shelter for something; it could be any or all of those. We'll have to get in there and solve the mystery."

Hilary traced a curious finger along the slow curve of the river. "Have you tried exploring it from the water? Or looking at it from the other bank?"

Tom turned a bit self-conscious. "Well, I did happen to hike along the far bank one day … accidentally on purpose. Didn't see much, though! That ivy just covers everything. And if that's been left to grow, it might have already destroyed some of the stonework."

"I wonder if I could find a boat to borrow … Just a rowing boat, I mean. Perhaps someone in the village would be willing." Hilary looked at the young man, wondering if he was asking too much. "Would you take me out? On the river, I mean."

"Of course!" Tom looked delighted. "Messing about in boats, eh? It doesn't get much better than that! It's a date."

Hilary found himself smiling too much to say anything.

"But …" Tom's brightness dimmed a little. "I won't be able to come by at the weekend. I've got to – I've got plans. Then I've got classes on Monday morning, but I could come by in the afternoon. We need to work out what to tackle first – though ripping out the ivy won't ever be a bad idea, and there's plenty of that to be done."

"What sort of time-frame were you thinking?" Hilary asked, hoping for a few weeks at least of Tom's company.

"There's no hurry. Some things we can't do until spring, anyway. We'll take it slow and steady through autumn and winter, eh? If you can be patient."

Not weeks, but months! Hilary was smiling again, but this time he managed to say, "Oh, I can be very patient indeed."

# Three

After a weekend which seemed to last far longer and be far quieter than most, Hilary started watching for Tom's arrival as soon as the clock turned twelve. When he heard a car coming down the lane and slowing for the turn the road took by the tower, he dismissed it as irrelevant – until he realised the car was actually stopping on the gravelled area out the front.

Hilary opened the door to see a tall man emerging from the driver's side – and what appeared to be Tom's bike attached to a rack on the back of the car, a promise fulfilled when the passenger door swung open and Tom climbed out.

"Hello, Mr Kent!" Tom called with a smile and a wave.

"Hello, Tom!" Hilary called back in welcome.

The other man locked the car and followed Tom over towards Hilary, who had time enough to take in not just the tall and well-proportioned figure but a handsome face, a fall of golden-brown curls, and a virile prickling of stubble. Ah. And the whole was topped off by a genial smile. Hilary sighed. There was so very much to dislike about the man.

"Mr Kent, this is Justin, my tutor. Um, actually Dr Ware. He's supervising my thesis."

"How do you do, Mr Kent?" the man said in easy tones, shaking Hilary's hand. "I hope you don't mind me showing up like this unannounced, but I thought I'd better see if we need to head Tom off at the pass before he gets too enthusiastic –" A pause, and a glance at Tom with the slightest hint of fondness, with the tiniest softening into intimacy around the mouth and crinkling round the eyes – before Ware chuckled and corrected himself: "Before he gets *even more excessively* enthusiastic about your garden."

"I see," said Hilary. "Well, I can assure you that Tom is very welcome here, and I am already glad of his attentions to the garden."

"Of course," Ware murmured agreeably, though it was obvious that wasn't enough to satisfy him, and he wasn't going away any time soon.

Hilary bowed to the inevitable, for Tom's sake. Ware would be only the second visitor to cross the threshold since the removal men left. "Won't you come in, then?" Hilary said, politely enough. "I'll make us a pot of tea."

"Thank you."

Tom walked in happily and headed through to the kitchen. As Hilary ushered Ware in and shut the front door after him, he heard Tom exclaim, "Oh, that's such an improvement, isn't it?"

And it was. It truly was. The kitchen and its living area were south-facing rooms, so to have the light unencumbered by anything other than the old glass of the windows made all the difference.

"It's marvellous," said Hilary, leading the way through. "Tom, why don't you take Dr Ware out on the terrace, so he can see what you've already achieved?"

"Sure," said Tom, and he beckoned to his tutor. "Come on, Justin. You'll see what I mean about it being magical!"

Hilary smiled to himself as he filled the kettle, thinking that probably no one would see the beauty of the garden better than Tom. He heard Tom chattering away out there, with Ware's occasional murmured responses. The two of them came back in just as Hilary was carrying the tray over to the kitchen table. Tom obligingly moved a chair out of Hilary's way, and then they were all settling, with Hilary in his usual seat, and Tom to his right at the head of the table, and Ware opposite Hilary.

They were quiet for a while, as Hilary offered biscuits and poured the tea, saying no more than was necessary for them each to have his tea made the way he liked it best.

Eventually, once he'd taken his first mouthful and offered his compliments, Ware said, "Tom tells me he's asked you to search for any paperwork, any historical records relating to the garden."

"He has, yes." Hilary turned an apologetic gaze to Tom. "I'm sorry I haven't found you anything yet. I did start looking during the weekend, but it seems that everything I pick up or turn over here only leads to further confusion. Or cleaning. I'm sorry. It can be very distracting, but I'll try harder this week —"

Tom was looking horrified. "No, you mustn't apologise. You're doing me the most enormous favour. I don't want you to feel you *have* to do anything."

"No," Ware smoothly agreed, "I didn't mean to put any pressure on you. I was just trying to get a feel for your understanding of what Tom is after."

"Well, as you say: any papers relating to the garden. I'm more than happy for Tom to have the use of them — if indeed there is anything. He should have whatever he needs for his research."

"And the garden itself … ?" Ware asked.

Hilary turned to Tom, wondering what he should answer for the best.

"I already told Justin I'd love to help you restore it," Tom said.

"And did you tell him I protested that it was far too much for you to offer … ?"

"Yes," Tom said, with his candid grin sparkling in his eyes. "But Justin knows how insistent I can be."

Hilary huffed a laugh.

Ware softly snorted, but then said very seriously, "Of course the experience would provide solid, practical material that may well be useful in Tom's thesis, but I must make clear that it's really not *necessary*. This is supposed to be a purely academic, research-based thesis. So, if you have any qualms about that side of things, Mr Kent –"

"No, of course it's fine. As long as Tom doesn't try to do more than he should."

"There'll be expenses –"

Hilary sighed, and sat back. "As long as we're careful," he said to Tom, "I should be able to fund the project." He'd inherited no debts or mortgages from Evelyn relating to Riverside, and he'd sold his home in London for an amount his parents couldn't have even imagined back when they'd first bought it. His day-to-day needs were simple enough to be met by his pension, such as it was. The tower could do with some improvements, but it wasn't about to fall down round his ears. There were funds. Hilary turned back to Ware. "I wouldn't expect anything from the university, if that's what you're concerned about."

"I have a few concerns." Ware was sitting back in his chair, and he took a moment now to finish his cup of tea, then waited while Hilary poured him more. "For example," he finally continued, speaking very directly to Hilary, "you'd do far better with an archaeology student or a botanist, rather than a history student."

Tom seemed to pale a little at this, though he didn't offer a protest or even seem to disagree.

"I'm perfectly happy with Tom, for as long as Tom has reason, time and inclination to help. He's already proved that he knows what he's talking about, as you'll have seen for yourself with those rhododendrons."

Ware nodded. "May I enquire, then –" He glanced at Tom, as if knowing he was running into troubled waters. "May I ask why you were reluctant to take Tom on as a lodger?"

"Justin!" Tom cried out. "I told you not to get into that!"

"Does it indicate," Ware persisted, "some discomfort or wariness about Tom? A lack of trust? Because if he's going to work on the garden, he'll be spending a great deal of time here."

"Justin, *please!*" Tom cast Hilary an appalled look. "I'm sorry, you made it perfectly clear that you didn't want – And I would never have asked again, honestly I wouldn't."

Hilary looked from one to the other of them in bewilderment. And recalled Marjorie's persistence about the matter. "Why is this such an issue? Mrs Flanagan as well. Almost as if there's some kind of conspiracy –"

"No!" Tom cried, reaching out to grasp Hilary's hand where it lay on the table. "Nothing like that."

"There's rather a crisis this year in student accommodation," Ware smoothly explained, ignoring Tom's impulsive gesture. "There was repair work scheduled for one of the halls over summer, and it's only uncovered further structural problems, significant ones. And it's a heritage-listed building, of course, a Grade Two Star, so that slows everything down. In any case, it's uninhabitable for at least a term, and that situation has put pressure on the accommodation available in town. And then Tom –"

"The place I've been staying," Tom chipped in, "the house in town that I'm sharing, it's being sold. And the new owners want to live there themselves. So," he concluded, with an apologetic shrug, "I'm kind of stuck at the moment."

"He's been searching for alternatives, of course," said Ware.

"That's what I was doing this weekend," Tom explained.

"But so far there's nothing available."

And at last they both fell silent. Hilary took his hand from Tom's, and sat back in his chair, gazing woefully at where his hands cradled each other in his lap. He couldn't. He just couldn't. He cleared his throat, knowing he owed Tom an explanation. "I've lived alone all my adult life."

"Of course. Of course. That's fine."

"And it's so very isolated here! I don't mind, though I'm used to the city. In fact, I've come to appreciate the peace. But it's hardly appropriate for a young man –"

"*That* wouldn't matter. But you don't have to say anything," Tom assured him. "You already said no, and that's that." He cast a glare at his tutor. "Justin shouldn't have mentioned it."

"But he raised the issue for a reason," Hilary rallied himself enough to say, "and that was to ask whether or not I trust you. And I do. Of course I do. My decision really isn't anything to do with your suitability as a house guest, but only mine as a host."

"*Please*, Mr Kent, don't say anything more. It's all right." Tom reached for him again, and grasped his shoulder. "I'm sorry. I'm really sorry."

Hilary turned to Ware. "I trust Tom, and I'm happy for him to work in the garden. So, I hope there won't be any obstacles from the university."

"I shouldn't think so, no." Ware got up – and up. He must have been well over six feet tall, perhaps even six feet four. "Well, I won't intrude any longer. Tom, would you like a lift back to town?"

Tom looked at Hilary for a long moment, and then said, very quietly, "May I stay for a while, Mr Kent? Please."

"Of course you may."

"Only if you don't mind. I'll just be out in the garden, so I won't be any trouble."

"You're perfectly welcome."

Tom smiled at him, and then said to Ware, "I'll go and get my bike."

"Thank you," said Ware, shaking Hilary's hand in farewell. "I know this will mean trouble and expense for you, but your support means the world to Tom. If it's any help, I can assure you that Tom's thesis will be excellent."

"Will it? How do you know?"

"It's what I've come to expect from him. He's quite an extraordinary young man." Again there was the hint of languid softening around the mouth and in the eyes this time, too, before the man recalled himself. "Thank you again, Mr Kent." And Ware followed Tom out the door and was gone.


Hilary pottered about a bit, clearing the tea things and enjoying having his home to himself again. Tom must have headed back through into the garden without Hilary noticing, for he could hear Tom rustling about out there, remaining discreetly out of the way by default or by design.

Once Hilary was settled again, he made a fresh pot of tea, took the tray of tea things out onto the terrace, and then came back for a chair on which he could sit and wait. He took the opportunity to look out over the garden, and consider what kind of furniture he might have out here on the terrace, or if it would prove too small for such an arrangement. Perhaps it would be just as convenient to carry out a kitchen chair whenever he wanted, as to have anything that remained out there – which would no doubt get in the way of Tom's comings and goings. Maybe once the garden was in a better state. There was plenty of time to decide on such things.

Tom eventually appeared – rather unexpectedly – from Hilary's left, pushing his way along the tower wall beneath the straggly growth of the remaining old rhododendrons. "Hello!" he said with a smile when he saw Hilary there waiting for him.

"I've made some more tea," Hilary said, leaning down to start pouring. The tray was on the stone floor of the terrace, though, and Hilary no longer bent in two quite as pliably as he'd used to.

"Here, I'll get that," Tom offered, not making a fuss, but simply folding down to sit on the top step, and taking the teapot, his hands wrapped around Hilary's for a moment, while Hilary's hands were still wrapped around the knitted cosy made warm by the tea. Hilary withdrew carefully, and Tom poured. He already knew how Hilary liked his tea, so a moment later he was lifting Hilary's cup towards him, and again their hands brushed as they transferred the cup from one to the other. Hilary was made a little shy by all this interaction, but Tom seemed completely comfortable. And Hilary knew already that he could trust Tom to honestly display whatever he was feeling.

A notion soon proved as Tom looked up at him, wrinkled his face in a charming grimace, and declared, "I'm rather embarrassed at wanting to spend your money for you. I'll do what I can myself, of course, but you know us students; I'm on rather a limited budget."

"You'll do nothing of the kind," Hilary immediately replied. "If it's for the garden, then I am happy to invest my resources. Within reason."

"Don't know that it'll be much of an investment. D'you think it would have that much effect on the property value?"

"Well, no doubt it will have some effect. But I was thinking more about my own enjoyment, I'm afraid. This is my home now, and I'll be living here for years. Decades, if I'm lucky. What you've done has already made such a difference."

"I guess …"

"In any case, you are already investing something of far more value, for very little return." When Tom turned a quizzical look on him, Hilary explained, "You're devoting a great deal of time and effort, when there isn't even a practical component to your thesis."

Tom's face cleared. "Oh, but to *really* understand something you have to get your hands dirty, you know? It can't be all about libraries and paperwork. I mean, that's fine, too, and I love reading, but to have the chance to really *do* something with what I've learned – and to learn more by doing so, and then doing something with *that* … Well, that's marvellous, to me."

Hilary smiled at the young man, understanding exactly why Ware was so fond of Tom.

"Anyway," said Tom, "I was going to ask if we could hire a skip. We're going to need to deal with a lot of waste for a while. Some of it we can keep and use, like the rhododendron wood, but some will just need to be hauled away."

"Of course."

"I can look into it, find somewhere that recycles or composts garden waste, that kind of thing."

"Of course, Tom, that's fine."

"I'll get some quotes and stuff, yeah? And tell you about it. Before making any bookings, I mean."

"I appreciate that," Hilary said smoothly. In many ways, he'd be happy if Tom just went ahead and made such decisions, but he supposed there was the potential for that to result in complications or misunderstandings. It was probably better that they negotiate these things between them, and that Hilary had the final say. "I'm sure it will be fine."

"Can I come back tomorrow, and do some more work, then?" Tom put his empty cup down, and gestured towards the corner from which he'd appeared. "I'm pretty sure there's a gate in there, under the ivy. You know that bit of the wall that faces the road, to the side of the tower? It isn't original, like from Thaddeus's time, but there was a large double gate put in later, so they could move things in and out. It doesn't show on this map, but I'm pretty sure I've found where it would be."

"The ivy needs to be cleared away, in any case," Hilary agreed.

"Exactly. Then we could have the skip out there, and take stuff out through the gate, yeah? That is, if you don't mind a skip sitting in front of your home for what could be weeks."

"Tom, my dear, that is a *long* way down the list of things that I mind."

They were quiet for a moment then. Until what he'd said caught up with Hilary, and he paled. The endearment had slipped out all too easily for an old man who hadn't been really close to anyone since his parents had died – and even back then, their familial affection had been expressed in deeds and in quiet glances exchanged rather than in words.

Hilary looked carefully around at Tom, who was sitting there with a warm and untroubled smile on his face. A smile that encompassed those eyes as clear and deep as a summer sky. Eventually Tom said, "Thank you, Mr Kent."

"Yes," was all that Hilary could say.

"Well, I'd better get on my bike!" Tom collected Hilary's cup, and picked up the tray while he stood all in one smooth movement. "I'll be back tomorrow, then. Probably ten or eleven, if that's all right. And I'll bring lunch for us both, eh?"

"Oh, that won't be –" Hilary protested as he followed Tom inside.

"Yes, it will!" Tom had put the tray down on the kitchen table, and was slipping into his jacket and swinging his backpack over his shoulder and walking towards the front door – like any young person, Hilary supposed, always doing three or four things at once if possible. Well, either that or nothing at all. "So, I'll see you tomorrow, all right?"

"All right!" Hilary called, still following along in Tom's wake.

"Bye, Mr Kent!" Tom called.

"Bye!"

And the door swung robustly closed, and Tom was gone.

Hilary took a breath, and sat down at the kitchen table. He suspected that he had some thinking to do. But instead of facing that rather alarming prospect, he decided to do some more searching through the various piles and drawers of paperwork that Evelyn had left behind. It was the least he could do under the circumstances. And why it should suddenly feel like such an urgent task was another thing that Hilary didn't want to think about either.

He was soon distracted by the mundanities of his cousin's life. He sent up a little prayer of thanks for that.

On the Tuesday afternoon, while Tom was in the garden clearing a way through to the putative gate, Hilary realised he'd been misdirecting his search. It had been quite obvious when he'd first come to the tower that Evelyn had been living – or existing – solely on the ground floor for some while. The solicitor had even explained that there'd been a filthy old single mattress in the corner of what was otherwise the reception room at the front. She'd had the place cleaned, and the mattresses and linen taken away – not just the one downstairs, but those on the two beds on the floor above. However, all the rest of the detritus of a long–lived hoarder remained.

And Hilary could hardly claim to have ventured much further than Evelyn. He'd reclaimed the larger bedroom on the first floor, at the back of the tower, though even that had involved a rearrangement of goods and chattels rather than a proper clean-out. He had briefly poked around the second floor, been repelled by the dust and disarray – and hadn't even dared set foot on the stairs that spiralled steeply up into the attic.

But it belatedly occurred to Hilary after sorting through myriad receipts and random faded newspaper clippings that it was no use looking through Evelyn's belongings. He needed to dig further into the past. And perhaps that would start on the next floor up.

Hilary cautiously opened the door to the smaller bedroom on the first floor, and looked about. There were books – shelves and piles of books – which was an excellent thing. Sorting through them could be his reward for clearing the rest of the room. There were a couple of boxes of outdoor playthings, such as a croquet set, with the mallets propped up and gathering cobwebs in the far corner of the room; they must predate Evelyn, and perhaps went back to the Edwardian era. There were other oddments: a broken oil lamp, a few framed pictures leaning against a wall, a few small boxes that might contain trinkets, some board games, and a stack of linen which looked as if it had been neatly folded a century ago and would now crumble apart the moment he touched it. But more importantly for Hilary's current quest, there were larger boxes which might well contain papers and files.

The three-quarter sized bed was made up with clean linen, so Hilary fetched an old sheet to protect it from dust, then hauled one of the boxes over to start looking through it. The contents weren't very exciting. More receipts – what was it with people keeping all their receipts? – old photographs though unfortunately none of the tower or the garden, old theatre tickets and programmes, church newsletters, correspondence from Inland Revenue and the Marlborough town council. All very dull.

In the third box, however, Hilary at least found some receipts that related to the garden – though as they only dated back to the early 1900s, before the First World War, he didn't suppose that Tom would find them of much interest. Still, he took them down with him when he went to make a mid-afternoon pot of tea.

"No, these are great," said Tom as he looked through the receipts. Again, he was sitting on the top step of the terrace while Hilary was in a kitchen chair, and the tea tray was on the stone surface between them. Hilary had been about to bring out another chair when Tom declared it wasn't needed, and Hilary supposed that a supple young man could make himself comfortable anywhere.

"You're humouring me," Hilary observed. It wasn't even a complaint, really.

"I'm not, though!" Tom shot him a grin, as candid and honest as ever. "See," he added, holding the relevant sheet of aged paper towards Hilary: "they've itemised the plants they bought, though just with the common names. That's really useful!"

"But you're interested in the original physic garden, and these only date back a hundred years."

"But some of these were obviously continuing the same practices. See here? Comfrey, pimpernel, lavender; you'd find all of those in medieval physic gardens."

"I see," said Hilary, feeling rather *too* heartened. It pleased him to please Tom, he knew that already. It was one of the things he wasn't thinking about right now.

"Anyway, what we're interested in depends on what you want to do with the garden."

"What do you mean? I thought it was understood that you want to restore it."

"Yes, but do we try to recreate what old Thaddeus was trying to establish? We can give it our best shot, but it'll never be exact. Some plant varieties just aren't available any more. Others, we'll have to find through specialist nurseries. This comfrey, for instance –" Tom brandished the papers again. "Given the time period, they might have been buying Russian comfrey. It was imported around then, so it would have had novelty value, if nothing else."

"What kind of comfrey would Thaddeus have known?"

"Common comfrey – *Symphytum officinale*. We might find some growing in the wild around here; if not, there's a nursery in Hampshire that would probably stock it." Tom sighed. "The thing is, if we find any Russian comfrey in the garden, or any hybrids, do we tear it out and replant with the common variety? It's not like comfrey is a bad thing to have in the garden, no matter what variety. It grows fast; it makes great compost." Tom glanced at Hilary, for once looking a bit self-conscious. "It's all great, but I think the Russian comfrey is particularly pretty."

"It does sound lovely," Hilary agreed.

"The flowers are bell-shaped, in creams and purples, or blues and purples."

"*Really* lovely." Hilary paused for a moment, and then asked, "So, what is the alternative approach to the garden? What you just described: I assumed that's what you wanted to do. Recreate what the priest first created."

"Yes, but that was four hundred years ago, it's not like we even have his plans or anything – and even *he* was doing something that his contemporaries would have thought old-fashioned. Then there's been a lot of history in between. Gardens have history, too. They evolve. Different owners want different things from them over time. So, you can take all that into account as well when you're restoring a garden, you can let the history be reflected in the garden. Like, not just take it all back to one particular era – whichever that might be – but include something of everything that's happened here. Or even just pick and choose which things you like best!"

Hilary the city dweller felt he understood the general idea and could probably apply it well enough to buildings, but was stumped on the specifics when it came to gardens. "Such as … ?"

Tom scrunched his face up in thought before he came up with a good example. "Such as, what if the Victorians devised some really efficient irrigation system? You know, something that used their knowledge of engineering or whatever. Do we strip that out, and take it back to the medieval system? What if that meant you had to start fetching buckets of water from the river, and hand-watering? Maybe the Victorian system is better for the garden – not to mention better for you.”

“I see! Absolutely, I see.”

“And it’s not just that kind of infrastructure. Those rhododendrons: Thaddeus wouldn’t have had anything like that in his garden. But they’re a low maintenance shrub, attractive all year round, and they’re just magnificent when they’re in flower. So, maybe you’d want to keep them, simply because they’re beautiful.”

Hilary thought about that for a moment. “Physic gardens were very practical, though. Weren’t they all about providing medicine?”

“Food and medicine, yeah, absolutely. They were all about being self-sustaining, growing what you need. Especially if you were a long way from the nearest market town – not that we are, here, it’s only five miles away. But there was always room for beauty as well. The classic thing was to include lily of the valley, because its beauty and its scent are their own justification. You could, you know, think of the rhododendrons in the same way.”

“Yes. I do see.”

“Though, interestingly, lily of the valley is quite poisonous! I think the medieval gardeners enjoyed that kind of duality: beauty and toxicity, roses and thorns.” Tom trailed off, perhaps feeling he was talking too much. Another moment passed. Then Tom kept his face averted while he asked another question, as if he didn’t want to prompt Hilary’s answer. “What sort of approach would you like to take, Mr Kent? To restoring the garden, I mean.”

And Hilary felt flummoxed again. “I think that should be your decision, Tom.”

“It’s not my garden, though.”

“I doubt that I’d ever have even thought to start this project without you, Tom. And I want it to be of use to you in your studies.”

“Either way would be of use. It’s all good research!”

A silence stretched for a while. Hilary thought that if it really was his decision alone, he’d have probably gone for the second option, and not tried to recreate whatever might have been the priest’s intentions of four hundred years ago. However, he suspected that Tom would prefer the more purist approach, and Hilary didn’t want to prematurely cast what Tom would consider a deciding vote.

"Anyway!" Tom eventually said. "I've uncovered that gate in the wall."

"Oh! So you were right about the gate. Well done!"

Tom grinned at him in appreciation. "You're a good friend, Mr Kent. Very encouraging! D'you want to come and see? Not that we're gonna be able to open it or anything; I think the hinges have pretty much rusted solid. I'm gonna have to work out what to do about that. But come and see!"

Hilary stood from his chair and – even though Tom had held Hilary's hand when leading him through the rhododendron tunnel – he chose to interpret Tom's outstretched hand this time as simply an invitation to follow him. They skirted around some of the wild shrubs, pushed through some knee-high grasses, and then turned in past a pile of ivy stems and other cuttings.

"Ah!" said Hilary in surprise. The gate was rather large for something he hadn't even suspected existed before now. It was a double gate, as Tom had predicted, made of rather heavy-looking planks of wood. While the two halves of it sagged askew, the hinges did indeed seem solid with rust and debris. There was no light coming through the gaps – presumably due to the ivy and perhaps also the overgrown hedge on the far side – and the gate was in shadow on this side of the wall, so Hilary had to draw quite close to examine the detail. Layers of paint of various colours had faded and flaked away over the years, leaving a random and oddly attractive pattern.

"The wood seems fine in itself," Tom observed, giving it a rap with his knuckles; the deep knocking sound added to the impression of sturdiness. "I'd try taking this right back to the wood, and varnishing it. It'll need to be rehung, of course, but I don't think the gates themselves will need to be replaced for decades yet."

"Excellent," said Hilary. "That's really excellent. Thank you, Tom."

"Oh!" Tom flushed a little. "That's all right. I mean, it's my pleasure."

"I'm glad."

They were both a bit self-conscious now. Hilary tried to think of something to say that was of some use or held some meaning.

"Well, I need to be getting back," Tom eventually said. "Can I come again tomorrow?"

"Please do," Hilary said, even while Tom was still asking the question.

Tom chuckled. "I'll clear away the ivy and stuff round the front of the gate. And I'll do some research tonight about how we're going to sort out the hinges and things. I don't know … Some things, I'm just not gonna be qualified to do. Or I won't be able to do on my own."

"I'll ask Marjorie," Hilary suggested, "if there's a local tradesman or landscaper. Or someone who'd be able to help, with some time on his hands. She'd know."

That earned him another grin. "She *would* know, yeah. Thank you, Mr Kent." Tom reached to shake his hand. "I really do appreciate this."

"I suspect I appreciate it more," Hilary observed, taking Tom's neatly formed hand into his own large hand, and allowing himself to enjoy the gesture for what it was, no more and no less.

And moments later, Tom was gone, the poor fellow, having to cycle five miles back to a home that wouldn't be his for much longer.

Hilary didn't want to think about any of that, though, so he headed upstairs, and started sorting through more boxes in the spare bedroom.

# Four

"I can't believe it's only been a week!" Tom declared that Thursday.

"I can't either," Hilary said, rather stunned by the realisation. It seemed as if he'd been living an entirely new life since meeting Tom – for some reason he'd experienced an even greater sea change than when he'd retired and moved from the city to the country.

They had settled on the sofa in front of the television with the cod-and-chip dinners Tom had fetched from the village – he had once again indulged Hilary with a pineapple fritter – and the second episode of *Midsomer Murders* was about to start. It had the rather promising title of 'Written in Blood'. In sum, Hilary felt that he could ask for nothing more.

Two hours later, however, as the credits rolled, Hilary muted the sound with a sense of foreboding. "You didn't like it," he observed.

"I was enjoying it well enough until the resolution!" Tom quietly cried out. "So, one murderer was a gay transvestite, who dared to have an affair with a married man, off in some exotic location *years* ago – and the other murderer killed him in disgust! It's just like last week: find any love or sexuality that isn't the norm, and you find who did it. I mean, even if you don't mind that, you'd think they'd manage to come up with some different motivations every now and then."

"It is a bit much," Hilary cautiously agreed, "two episodes in a row."

"Apart from which, it all started with the gay guy being sexually abused as a child! What a horrible old cliché *that* is. Abuse doesn't *cause* homosexuality or transvestism, and they're not the inevitable *effect* either!"

"No, of course," Hilary murmured.

"Apart from which, we don't all get killed by people who think we're disgusting." Tom paused for a moment there, and considered this bleakly. "Well," he added, a little calmer, "the vast majority of us don't, anyway."

When the young man didn't continue, Hilary ventured, "I don't mean to justify the show, or even defend it, but maybe you'd agree that at least Tom Barnaby seems open-minded in his approach to these matters."

Tom grimaced and essayed a shrug. "Yeah, he's all right. So I guess the writers aren't complete idiots."

It only belatedly occurred to Hilary: "Your name's Tom!"

"Thank God it's not Troy!" Tom returned, referring to Barnaby's sidekick, Gavin Troy. "He's a right git, isn't he?"

"Oh, I suspect he's just ignorant. You can cure ignorance."

"Huh," said Tom, apparently unwilling to commit himself on that issue. "Well," he said, clapping his neat hands to his thighs, "I suppose I'd better be off! Thanks for a nice evening, Mr Kent. I'm sorry if I spoiled it."

"You did nothing of the sort." Hilary was rewarded with such a softly honest smile that he finally dared to say, "I wish you'd call me by my name. By my given name, I mean."

Tom turned solemn, though the gentle honesty remained. "Hilary," he said, tentatively.

"Most people have called me Hil – my colleagues and acquaintances, that is – though I would prefer Hilary if you can say it with a straight face."

"Of course. Thank you, Hilary." Tom hadn't moved, but he was focussed very closely on Hilary. It wasn't *quite* unnerving. "I appreciate that."

"And I was wondering if," Hilary managed to plough on – "given that you'd only be coming back here tomorrow morning – if you would care to stay the night. In the second bedroom."

"Oh!" said Tom, obviously surprised.

"I'm sorry, I should have mentioned the idea yesterday, so you could bring a change of clothes. But I wasn't entirely –"

"Sure. You weren't sure."

"No."

Tom was silent for a horribly long moment, considering Hilary. "Well," he eventually said, "I kind of have a change of clothes. Mostly. There's the gear I wear out in the garden, and then there's this." He plucked at the denim over his thighs. "So I *could* …"

Another pause. Nothing more was forthcoming. "But you don't want to," Hilary concluded. "That's perfectly all right. Of course we all like to be in our own beds when we can."

"It's not that so much as … what changed? You like keeping yourself to yourself, remember? I totally respect that."

"I know you do." Perhaps that was what made this possible. "I found that … I couldn't face the thought of you having to cycle all the way home and back again for no purpose."

"Well," said Tom, still not committing himself, "I would *like* to …"

"Then you shall," Hilary concluded. "The bed's already made up. You haven't been upstairs before, have you? I'll show you the room, if you like, and then I'll make us some tea before we settle. I always have a cup of Assam in the evenings."

"If you're really *sure*," Tom said, even while he stood and followed Hilary to the stairs.

"I'm sure!" Hilary replied. He was breaking the habits of a lifetime. It was enough to make a man giddy with delight.

Hilary lay awake that night, unable to sleep. Not because he felt insecure or anxious – surprisingly enough, he didn't – but because he was happy. He was *happy*. It struck him as a rather marvellous thing that he had a home, and that his home should shelter his friend.

He heard Tom rummaging around in the other bedroom for a little while, and couldn't quite decide if Tom was searching through the books or leafing through the box of papers in which Hilary had found the garden receipts. He didn't mind. Tom could have it all, if he wanted.

Then there was quiet for a while, an alive kind of quiet, with occasionally the rustle of a page turning. Hilary imagined Tom reading, with those candid eyes drinking in every word, and that clever mind cutting right to the heart of it.

But then soon enough, as if the young man were more tired than he'd thought, there was the sound of gently snuffling snoring for a few minutes – silence, and the pages were rustled again – and then the snoring for a few minutes, until finally the light switch was clicked off and Tom settled down into the bed.

Hilary lay there as the moonlight poured in through the opaque glass windows, listening to the peaceful rhythm of his friend's breathing. It really was rather marvellous.

The morning brought the cold light of day, of course. Tom had already risen when Hilary finally woke, and when Hilary poked his nose through the open door into the other bedroom he saw that the bed was already made. The room was tidy, and seemed empty again, as if perhaps it had all been a dream.

But no, Tom had obviously found a bowl and a spoon, cereal and milk, the toaster and bread and butter, a plate and a knife. He'd rinsed the crockery and cutlery, and stacked them neatly on the draining board ready to be properly washed, but still. Hilary really wasn't used to this kind of thing. Tom had left a fresh pot of tea sitting there warmed by two cosies – but he'd used the wrong kind of tea. Hilary always had English Breakfast first thing in the morning. Not that Tom could possibly know that, of course, despite the name being rather a giveaway. He'd chosen the tea Hilary had served him during the mornings and afternoons: Earl Grey. Which was perfectly reasonable of him, really.

Hilary sighed. Maybe he was too old a dog, but he should be able to get used to sharing his mornings, shouldn't he? Maybe this was his one chance to learn how.

He poured two cups of tea, and took them out to the terrace. It seemed that Tom was clearing and widening a passage through to the gate – but as soon as he saw Hilary, he smiled and waved, and then came over once he'd finished wrestling a long stem of ivy into submission. "Hey, thanks," Tom said as he took the cup of tea.

"Thank you for making it," Hilary countered.

"Oh, that's all right. I hope you don't mind –"

"Not at all," Hilary smoothly lied. Or, rather, told what he wanted to be the truth. There should be a special term for that. It should have positive connotations. "I hope that you slept well."

"Like a log!" Tom said with a happy grin. "Thanks. I really do appreciate –"

But this was all too much first thing in the morning, before he'd had more than a mouthful of tea. "It's perfectly all right," Hilary murmured, taking a step back, and turning to look out into the garden.

Tom took the hint, and obligingly fell quiet. They stood there, near each other but not too close, and enjoyed the autumnal morning sunshine.

"I think there's enough," Hilary said once they were done, "for another small cup each."

"I'd like that."

Hilary went back in and poured the rest of the tea, and then came back out to find that Tom was sitting in his accustomed place on the top step, with his back against the tower wall. His eyes were closed as he soaked up the sunshine, but they opened again a moment later. Hilary handed him both cups of tea, and went to fetch himself a kitchen chair.

"Are you really all right?" Tom eventually asked, rather quietly. "With me staying over, I mean."

"Yes …" Hilary tentatively agreed. "Perhaps … Perhaps on Thursdays –"

"What I was going to ask was –"

"No, I know. When will you need to move out – ?" It was beginning to seem that they were already on the inexorable path that led towards Tom lodging with him.

"No, I mean, Justin offered –"

"Justin!" Hilary blurted, hoping to God that Justin wasn't offering to share his home with Tom. It would be highly inappropriate, to say the least.

"Dr Ware, yes." Tom paused for a moment, so they weren't talking over each other. "He suggested we ask for volunteers from our three classes –"

"*Your* classes – ?"

"Yes, I'm his teaching assistant. Um – volunteers to help clear out the ivy and any other rubbish that we find. Only once we've got the gate working again, of course, so they don't even have to come into the tower, they can just –"

Hilary had blanched. He could feel himself turn pale and cold. God knows what he looked like –

Tom was scrambling, verbally at least, and sitting up to reach a reassuring hand towards him. "No, that's too much, isn't it? I have no idea how many would actually volunteer, but even if it's five or ten – I should have known it was too much. I'm sorry, Mr Kent."

"Hilary," he corrected in a very small voice. He suspected he was being rather pathetic.

"Hilary. I'm sorry, I should have known, but Justin is trying so hard to be helpful. He knows we're imposing on you – and he's just as insistent as me, I'm afraid, and far more persuasive!"

Tom had finished with a glint of appreciative laughter in his eyes, which didn't make Hilary feel any better. He turned once more, shifting on his seat, to look out at the garden. The thought of it occupied by a riot of students, led by the persuasive Dr Justin Ware, was rather alarming. On the other hand, as he imagined them frenetically tearing into the undergrowth, Hilary realised that perhaps he was being unreasonably selfish. Perhaps Ware was right.

"Of course you need the help," Hilary said rather diffidently. "No one could expect you to clear this place by yourself. I will exert myself a little more, I promise, but even so I won't be very much use to you. Of course you must have the help."

"No, don't worry about that. We have plenty of time. Months! In fact," Tom confided, crossing his legs, and swivelling towards Hilary – "in fact, I was looking for a reason to tell Justin no myself. The thing is, we can't just have people in here randomly ripping things out – if they don't know what we're likely to want to keep."

Hilary puzzled over that. "But surely it's obvious how much clearing has to be done."

"Yes, but if the ivy is hiding a plant that we want to keep, then we need to be careful. We need to nurture it, and shelter what remains – not just rip everything out every which way, and leave what's left exposed. So in many ways, I'd rather just do the lot myself."

"You would … ?"

Tom's smile began dawning again on that candid face. "I would. Partly because I'm an independent sod, it's true. But partly because then I can work out what we've got here as I go."

"I see …"

"And we've got the rest of autumn and all winter. There's no point in making wholesale changes or decisions until we see what comes up in the spring. So there's no harm in me taking my time. And meanwhile we can get the gate sorted, and try to work out what to do with the irrigation and drainage – that kind of functional thing. We'll be fine."

*We'll be fine …* Hilary stared at the young man. "About you lodging here –" he began.

"Ah, don't worry about that," Tom said, sitting back again but looking perfectly cheerful.

"But if you –"

"Hilary, it'll be fine. I'm sure I'll find something in town."

He almost felt disappointed. "Well, on Thursdays, then," he said.

"Yes," said Tom, apparently quite content. "I'll stay over on Thursdays."

And that would have to do.

# Five

Of course Marjorie knew exactly whom Hilary should ask to help them fix the gate. There was a man in the village, recently made redundant from his job at the town's hardware superstore and now trying to make a go of it as a carpenter and craftsman – or general handyman if there was no work more skilled available. And so Sam Reynolds came to visit Riverside on the Monday afternoon, and spent some while pondering the task before him, while Tom and Hilary tried not to hover too obviously. Then Sam took a few steps back and pondered the tower itself.

Finally Hilary couldn't resist any longer. "What do you think … ?"

Reynolds nodded. "We'll have these shipshape for you, don't you worry about that, Mr Kent. The first thing to do is source some new hinges. I was just looking at your door fixtures elsewhere on the building. This is heritage-listed, isn't it?"

"Yes, but it's only a local Grade C listing."

Tom scrunched up his face. "But all that means is that you're asked to keep it unaltered."

"As far as possible," Hilary agreed.

"It's not even enforceable!"

"No, it isn't – and the tower has become such a hotchpotch over the years, the solicitor seemed to imply I could honour that in the spirit rather than to the letter. Such as it is."

Reynolds offered, "I'm thinking black, cast iron – sturdy obviously, they have a job to do. But do you want a simple style such as on the back door, or more decorative such as on the windows?"

"Oh!" No doubt he was very slow, but this was a question Hilary hadn't even thought about asking let alone answering. Still, even a clueless old man such as himself could see the difference between the long straight no-nonsense hinges that held the door in place, and the hinges and latches on the windows and the few remaining shutters, which had more of a curve and a flourish. "I suppose the windows have the more authentic fixtures," Hilary said.

"Yes, they do," Tom agreed.

"They're very like the style up at the big house," Reynolds observed.

Tom was nodding. "This place started as a sort of gatehouse and landing place for the manor. But it's centuries since it needed to even pretend to be defensible."

"So we should try to match the original style," Hilary concluded. "Or at least work with it rather than against it."

"No, you can go with your own tastes," Tom argued. "Like you said, this place is a hotchpotch of its own history. All the changes it's seen. You're part of that history, too, Hilary. I reckon you can pick and choose, and make it your own."

Hilary considered the young man for a long moment. "I thought you'd want to put things back the way that Thaddeus had them, as much as we can. I thought you'd be more of a purist."

Tom shook his head, though it was more a refusal to be drawn rather than a negation. "It's your garden, Hilary. You should choose the hinges that make you happiest."

Hilary let out a rather undignified guffaw, and glanced at Reynolds, wondering what he made of all this – but the man was deep in contemplation again, perhaps of the sky or the passing wisps of cloud. And maybe it wasn't so odd after all, to be discussing the varying degrees of happiness to be found in gate hinges.

"Mr Reynolds," Hilary eventually announced, "I am a simple man, but I appreciate elegance. So if you could find such a hinge that wouldn't look out of place beside the current mishmash of hinges, I would be in your debt."

"Right you are, Mr Kent. A curve, perhaps, or a tapering line, but nothing so fancy as a fleur-de-lis."

"Exactly. I am obviously in good hands."

Reynolds nodded in affable acknowledgement of the compliment, though he wasn't necessarily agreeing. "I won't take the gates down until we have the hinges sourced, and anything else we need. Then it will be a matter of a few days to sand and stain them, before rehanging. We can block off the hole in the wall while we're working."

"Excellent."

"I'll let you know, then," Reynolds promised, before farewelling them both with a shake of the hand. "Mr Kent. Mr Laurence."

"Mr Reynolds."

It was all happening. Hilary smiled at his young friend, who grinned back happily, and announced, "I've been looking into skips …"

Determined to be true to his word, and to make up for the lack of help from Tom and Justin's students, Hilary began spending two or three hours out in the garden each day. He might only be collecting rubbish, and ferrying things back and forth in the new wheelbarrow they'd had delivered from the hardware superstore, but at least he was contributing in a small way. And he couldn't deny that it was pleasant to keep company with Tom, and to watch the fellow while he worked and thought and felt his way further into the garden.

Thursday was rainy, and for a little while Hilary feared the worst – but Tom rode over anyway, and once he'd changed into dry clothes, they took the opportunity of the bad weather to search through the remaining boxes of paperwork and other oddments on the first floor, those in Hilary's bedroom as well as in what he was already thinking of as Tom's room. They didn't find anything of great relevance, but the hours passed together were warm and congenial, and Hilary began pondering the notion that there might yet be a depth and breadth of contentment that he hadn't even guessed at.

That evening they settled into the sofa together with a pot of Assam to watch the third episode of *Midsomer Murders*, titled 'Death of a Hollow Man'. For a while contentment fled, as Tom's growing irritation set Hilary himself on edge. There was a gay couple on the show, and the slightly older man of the pair was all that was stereotypical about gay characters. He was camp, and fussy, and while he might be forgiven for owning and running a bookstore, he was also the set designer for the local theatre troupe. And yet again, the couple seemed to have secrets – kept from each other as well as from the village – and they became suspects …

The tension eased towards the end when it became clear that the only real secret kept was that the slightly younger man had been having an affair – with a woman. Faced with threats of blackmail, he did the decent thing and confessed all. The last view of the couple was of the older man sobbing disconsolately in the younger man's encompassing arms, while the latter reaffirmed his commitment in plain and simple words. It was an honest love, even if it hadn't always been a loyal one.

Tom was silent as the credits rolled, though it was a more thoughtful silence than had been the case before. He seemed to be contemplating his own hands where they lay loosely on his lap. Hilary hardly dared speak, though he muted the sound of the television before the ads began. Eventually Tom cast him a glance, and said, "Well. I can't really complain about that, I suppose!"

"No …" Hilary agreed, though with enough doubt that he might be easily refuted and not take it amiss.

"That turned out to be a real love, didn't it?" Tom looked at him. "I mean, we were meant to assume they'd be all right together, weren't we? That they'd get past this?"

"Yes, I think so," Hilary said with somewhat more certainty.

"Good," said Tom. And he lapsed back into silence.

After a while of neither of them speaking but not moving either, not calling an end to the evening or heading for bed, Hilary very tentatively asked, "Tom. Forgive my nosiness. Are you, er … ?"

"Yes," Tom answered with a smile. "Yes, I am, *er* …" The smile broadened, as if he couldn't resist his own mischief. "Gay. I'm gay. If that's what you're asking."

Hilary nodded quietly, and wondered to himself why he was intruding. He'd known or at least guessed this about Tom for almost as long as he'd known the fellow, and he knew what would happen, too. One day in the not too distant future, just as soon as Tom had finished his thesis, just as soon as it was no longer improper, then Dr Justin Ware would declare his long-invested interests, and surely Tom was too fond of the man to refuse. Even if there was more love on one side than the other, perhaps that was inevitably how these things worked.

"Hilary … ?"

"Mmm?"

Tom was tugging gently at Hilary's hand – and there was something about his tone that indicated he was repeating himself when he asked, "What about you?"

The meaning was no doubt plain enough, but meanwhile Hilary had been overcome by the feeling of his hand wrapped up in another's. Tom had only done it to regain his attention, of course, but it felt kind and it felt deft despite the shared aches and pains and calluses of their gardening work.

"Hilary. Are you, er … ?"

He regathered himself, and offered with a soft smile, "I haven't been anything much, for such a very long time."

"But *were* you," Tom persisted, "even if it was a very long time ago?"

He took a moment with that, and then slowly began, "When I was your age, homosexuality had only just become legal. I was twenty-one in 1967."

"I don't want to be wrong about you. Not about *this*."

Hilary huffed a laugh, wondering if it mattered most to the young man that his gay radar, or whatever they called it, wasn't malfunctioning.

But Tom hadn't let him go yet, and his fingertips were exploring the back of Hilary's fingers when he said, "You've got great hands, you know."

"Do I … ?" Hilary peered down at the large clumsy things, made larger and clumsier by the contrast with Tom's neat perfections. "Well. You've said so before."

"Yes. I love watching them make tea, and handle fine china. Carry a tray so perfectly steady. Or tug a weed out of the ground, and then grasp the wheelbarrow's handgrips. They're competent, and they're strong … and they've seen life."

"Well, maybe not quite so much of life as you suppose," Hilary admitted.

"Tell me," said Tom. "You know I'm just going to pester you until you do."

Hilary laughed again, aloud this time. If anything was going to illustrate the two-generation chasm between them, it was this issue of homosexuality; it was Tom's openness and curiosity, and Hilary's insecurity and discretion. It was Tom's experience – for Hilary assumed the young man could hardly have failed to take full advantage of the more accepting environment he'd been born into – and it was Hilary's reticence.

"Well, then," Hilary finally said. "There may have been an encounter or two … before the law was so obliging as to offer permission, as well as after."

Tom was grinning at him, which was reward enough. "You rascal, Hilary! You rebel! It makes me wish I was breaking the law, too!"

"No, it doesn't," Hilary replied rather severely.

That candid face fell again. "No, it doesn't," he agreed. After a moment, he asked, "And more recently … ?"

Hilary gazed down at their joined hands. "Don't enquire too deeply, my dear, or you'll realise what an uninteresting person I am. I've led a rather quiet life, you know."

"That's all right," Tom reassured him in a murmur, his hands never ceasing in their movement as they stroked and caressed Hilary's.

"Until recently, I thought the most astonishing thing that had ever happened to me was inheriting this place from Evelyn. Since then, I've realised that has been well and truly eclipsed –" he had to draw a breath for courage – "by your friendship."

"Oh …" Tom sighed, as if enchanted.

"Though I also realise that you only care about me for the sake of the garden."

That earned him a great guffaw of laughter, and Tom jostled his hands for a moment before finally letting go. "Such a tease!" Tom accused, his eyes merry, before he started collecting the tea things onto the tray, and then he stood to take it through into the kitchen. "You really had me going for a moment there!" he called back.

*Well*, Hilary reflected. Unlikely as it all was, Tom had really had Hilary going as well!

Hilary had the most perfect night's sleep that night, and woke exhilarated. Tom was already in the kitchen when Hilary went down, putting the kettle on to boil. Dear Tom, dressed in long striped pyjama bottoms and a blue t-shirt, barefoot, and his usual bright candour softened by sleep, gentled by dreams. Hilary measured the English Breakfast tea into the pot, though what did he care what kind of tea they drank? Indeed, he should break out the special black tea with ginseng and vanilla that he saved for the odd occasion when he felt adventurous. What odder or more wonderful occasion could there be than this … ?

They took the tea out onto the terrace, and settled in their accustomed spots, Hilary on a kitchen chair and Tom on the top step, both so comfortable. They hadn't even spoken yet, except through shared smiles, glinting glances. They were so perfectly in accord.

And there was no reason on earth why Hilary shouldn't enjoy this year to come, this academic year, as they worked on the garden and Tom wrote his thesis. Next summer would come soon enough, and Tom would have worked his miracle and then moved on. That was for the future. For now there was *this*, there was this almost euphoric contentment, and it hardly needed saying but Hilary said it anyway: "You must move in, my dear. You know the second bedroom is already yours."

And Tom was smiling like the sunshine itself, and shaking his head, but he wasn't denying Hilary, he was only reflecting as Hilary himself was: *Only two weeks since we met, only two weeks, and see how far we've come?*

Of course such giddiness could not sustain itself, and neither should it. But Hilary, still marvelling at how comfortable he felt at sharing his home with Tom, wasn't discomforted by the presence of Sam Reynolds either. The man's careful, considered thoughtfulness couldn't disturb the peace of Hilary's home or garden, even if Hilary did retreat behind a protective layer or two.

Reynolds had brought a couple of samples of cast-iron hinges, but it was immediately obvious that the one he recommended was the right choice to make. They agreed he would begin work on the gate on Monday, but in the meantime Reynolds and Tom took the chance to really clear the area in which he'd need to work.

More protective layers were donned when a car pulled up outside. Hilary wasn't surprised to find that it was Justin, no doubt come to see Tom, but at least offering the relatively plausible excuse of talking to Hilary about the possibility of Justin's students being drafted to help in the garden. Hilary managed to put him off for now, though it was apparent that Justin was reluctant to take no for an answer.

Instead, seeing that Tom had finished with the area around the gate and was now starting to dig into the decades of detritus that had filled in the pond, Justin offered to pitch in. He fetched his wellies from the car, shrugged his jacket off, and was soon working alongside Tom. Hilary carted the rubbish off in the wheelbarrow, and Sam Reynolds helped him to make a new pile of it. The skip couldn't arrive soon enough, at this rate. They'd probably fill it within a day!

Meanwhile, Hilary tried not to notice Justin noticing Tom looking surprisingly virile in his sweaty t-shirt. Hilary knew – he *knew* how this would end, and he knew he had no right to anything other than Tom's friendship – but Hilary found to his disappointment that he wasn't above feeling the sourness of jealousy, the burn of resentment. The worst of it only lasted for a little while, though – until he regathered the acceptance, and at least glimpsed again his usual contentment.

Any peace of mind was thrown, however, by yet another car pulling up out the front, along with Sam's van and Justin's car. This time, Hilary was astonished to see the squire from the manor house clamber out of the driver's seat. They hadn't met, but Marjorie had pointed him out to Hilary once a few weeks before.

"Good morning," Hilary said politely, standing on his doorstep in a manner he hoped combined a cheerful willingness to talk while not welcoming anyone in any further. Hilary had surely been challenged enough with visitors for one day!

"Morning!" the man cried, walking towards Hilary with what seemed a sense of implacable entitlement. "Mr Kent, is it? Old Evelyn's cousin?"

"Yes." He offered his hand to shake, if not his first name.

"I'm Sir James Archard, from the big house."

"Yes," said Hilary. "I know."

A pause as Sir James waited with his hands in the pockets of his tweed trousers. Eventually the man prompted, "Just wondering what all the fuss is about."

They'd piqued his curiosity, had they? For, squire or not, the man had no real business here. Not any more. Hilary said, "A young friend of mine is helping me with the garden. His friend from the university and a man from the village are helping us today."

"Used to be quite the thing, this garden," Sir James commented.

Hilary had no real idea of how old the man was, but he risked asking, "Do you remember it? From when you were a child, perhaps?"

"Oh, no, not really. Bit before my time. But people used to talk about it. Pity it was let go."

Hilary felt like retorting that the Archards shouldn't have sold off the land if it was so precious, but he belatedly remembered that Tom might appreciate this man's goodwill. "My friend is hoping to restore the garden," Hilary said. "Perhaps you've met him already? Tom Laurence. A graduate in medieval history at the university."

"Ah. Can't say as I've had the pleasure. But I'd heard he was looking at the old records."

Hilary smoothly ignored the suspicious tone. "Perhaps there are records up at Bedwyn Hall? Planting plans, seasonal maintenance. Even a drawing, a painting, would be of use." Tom had mentioned some possibilities.

"Perhaps a sketch done by a lady of the house working on her accomplishments? Anything like that might illustrate something useful."

"Oh, I wouldn't think –" Sir James spluttered a moment. "That is, I'd have to search –" Eventually he said, curiosity apparently overcoming all else, "Perhaps, if I saw it, my memory might be jogged."

Well, Hilary reminded himself, it was for Tom's sake. "Of course," he said. "Won't you come through?"

Hilary escorted the squire through to the tower's back door as briskly as he could, and then led him down the steps. The other three men paused in their work while Hilary named them each to the squire. "You know Mr Reynolds from the village, I assume." After offering a nod no more or less respectful than he'd given any of the others, Sam returned to work. Hilary indicated Justin. "That's Dr Ware from the university, helping us clear what used to be a pond." Justin considered Sir James and Hilary curiously, but simply seemed to appreciate the opportunity for a break, leaning on his shovel and taking deep slow breaths. "And that's Tom Laurence, of course." Tom, as transparent as ever, watched Sir James with a turbulent scowl.

They couldn't yet explore very far, so Hilary's guided tour only took a few moments, and most of it involved him pointing out possibilities and vaguely discussing theories on which Tom had a far better grasp. And perhaps Sir James had been as aware of Tom's disquiet as Hilary had, because once the tour was done the two of them seemed to quite naturally gravitate towards him.

"So, you're young Laurence," the squire observed.

"Yes," said Tom, in an oddly belligerent tone. Justin quietly cleared his throat, but it was towards Hilary that Tom glanced before adding a slightly more respectful, "Sir."

"You've been asking for access to the records up at the Hall."

"Yes, sir," Tom acknowledged.

"Young man, let me give you a word of advice. You pestered my housekeeper until she swore you'd only cross the threshold over her recumbent corpse."

Tom, strangely, quirked a grin at that – though Justin gamely tried to leap to his defence. "No, surely there must be some misunderstanding –"

Sir James stopped him with a lifted hand, not even deigning to shift his gaze towards him. "The trick to getting what you want, young man, is knowing whose favour to curry. If you thought the matter was entirely up to me, you were wrong."

"Yes, sir," Tom said, quite agreeably now.

"Well, we'll see about you paying a visit." Sir James glanced at Hilary. "Perhaps you'll ask Mr Kent to accompany you, to guarantee your good behaviour."

"Yes, sir. Thank you, sir." The grin was in full evidence.

Hilary ventured, "Sir James, I understand there's an old medieval plant on your family arms; a medicinal plant. I wondered if you knew anything about that."

"Ah, yes. It's called Silverseal."

"*Hydrastis argentum*," Tom supplied.

"Quite. Signifies purity, d'you see," Sir James explained a bit self-consciously. "Seems a bit of an old-fashioned notion to you young people, I suppose!"

"No, that's cool."

"The plant used to be quite common around these parts – that's my understanding – but it died out a hundred years ago or more."

"Over-harvested," Tom explained. "And the purity thing: Silverseal was known for its cleansing and purifying properties, so that totally makes sense! I bet Thaddeus grew it here in this garden."

Unfortunately the momentary accord was soon broken. "Did you ever find out what happened to old Thaddeus?" the squire asked in a tone that somehow managed to be both jolly and aggressive.

"No," said Tom, scowling once more.

"Why?" said Hilary, looking from one to the other. It was the first he'd heard of any of this. "What do you mean?"

"Old Thaddeus," said the squire, "disappeared in the midst of some scandal or other."

"He *left*," Tom pointedly corrected, "under a cloud of some kind. No one knows for sure what happened."

"These monks and priests and what-have-you always were a rum old lot. The man was probably queer; felt up the wrong fellow, and got his skull smashed in for it. Justice could be swift and quiet in those days …"

They were all staring at the man in an appalled kind of silence – including

Sam, who had a wife and children, and therefore presumably a somewhat less immediate interest in these matters than the other three. They all stared, hard, until at last the antipathy dented that lordly assurance.

"Not a popular sentiment these days, of course," the squire concluded weakly. "And rightly so … rightly so."

He wasn't fooling any of them.

"Get out."

Hilary looked around in surprise to find that he himself had spoken – though it was so quietly that no one else seemed any surer about the matter than he did. Except that Tom was looking at him with fierce approval. And of course it was Tom and his research that Hilary wanted to put first – but Tom nodded firmly, and that gave Hilary not only permission but the necessary courage.

"Get out of my house," Hilary said to the squire, in clear and simple tones, though he felt rather pale.

"Now, now! Don't take it like that."

"Get out of my garden, get out of my house – and take such horrid thoughts with you."

"Now, *really*, Mr Kent …" The man seemed to want to bluster through this, but he was already backing away towards the tower. Perhaps he wasn't used to such direct confrontation. "Why must you people be so *sensitive*?"

*"Get out!"*

"Well, all right …" The man was strolling towards the back steps now with his hands in his pockets, as if trying to amble, as if he'd have been leaving anyway. "Yes, farewell, then …"

Hilary followed him, dogged on his heels, pushed him along with the force of his will – they passed through the ground floor of the tower even more briskly now, and then the squire was out the front door. Hilary closed it behind the man, and fastened the locks for good measure. He heard a faltering step or two – but then the gravel crunched underfoot with a more determined purpose, and the car was kicked into life before drawing off down the road in the direction of the Hall.

He took a deep breath, and headed back out towards the garden – only to be met on the back terrace by Tom, who took Hilary into a vigorous hug. Hilary was almost too startled to even register let alone enjoy the moment, but then his head was tucked in against Tom's shoulder, and his hands had come up to clasp Tom's neat waist – and Tom was saying, "You were incredible! Fuck! How good was that!"

Justin was looking up at Hilary with a smile that wavered between concerned and impressed. "Are you all right?"

"Yes, yes, I'm fine," Hilary said. Though he clung fast to Tom, until at last Tom pulled away and danced down the steps with a whoop.

Sam gave Hilary a very respectful nod as Hilary slowly followed his friend down into the garden again, one hand firm on the railing. "All right, Mr Kent?" Sam asked.

"Yes, really, I'm fine," he said, though he did feel a little bit shocked by what he'd just done. "Thank you, Mr Reynolds." Then Hilary was standing there near where Tom and Justin had been working, and Tom was still dancing about like a mad thing. "But, Tom –" Hilary began. "Tom – just as he'd agreed to you visiting the manor house …"

"Oh, don't worry about that," Tom sang out, hands swooping and soaring dizzyingly through the air. "*Fuck*, that was great! You really told the old bigot, Hilary. You really –"

A moment dragged oddly.

"Justin," Tom said with calm authority, "get a chair from the kitchen. *Now.* Sam, fetch some water, a glass of water." One of Tom's hands had taken both of Hilary's and the other was firm at the small of his back, holding him in place. Whether Hilary was still upright or not, he couldn't really say. "Hilary, stay with me here," Tom continued gently. "It'll be all right, Hilary. Stay with me."

He was being lowered to sit in one of the chairs, and the world started tilting back into focus, starting with Tom's dear face. Sam helped Hilary take a mouthful or two of water, and he murmured something reassuring about having put the kettle on, but Hilary only really cared about Tom kneeling at Hilary's feet, leaning on Hilary's knees as if grounding him again, propping his chin on his own hand and gazing up at him with rueful fondness.

"Hilary … ?"

"Yes?" he managed.

"Are you all right? *Honestly?*"

Hilary found a smile for the young man. "Yes, I'm fine. Honestly." And he was. He really was. Already the world had settled back into its accustomed time and place, and Hilary was clear-headed enough to declare, "I've never done anything like that before in my life!"

"You were very brave," Tom said fervently, cutting off the reassurances of the other two. "You were *incredible*, seeing him off like that."

"Yes, you were," Justin chimed in.

"You were *heroic*," Tom insisted.

"Oh dear!" Hilary said with a laugh. "Not such a hero that I didn't have a turn immediately afterwards."

"Can't blame a man for that," Sam offered. "I'll make the tea," he added, heading off inside again.

"And guess what else, Justin?" Tom said.

"Tell me, then."

"Hilary said I could move in with him! He just asked me this morning. Isn't that great?"

"Yes, it is," said Justin, standing there with his hands wrapped up together, and starting to knot into an anxious tangle.

Tom seemed oblivious to the fact that Justin's delight in this news was a little forced. Apparently deciding that Hilary was recovered now, the young man sat back on the ground and let his head fall back with his eyes closed as if to soak up the sun. "What a day!" he quietly exclaimed.

Hilary took the chance to really consider Justin – who looked back with something a little lost in his eyes. Hilary had no idea if Justin had picked up Hilary's frequency on his gay radar, but Hilary offered the man a nod of acknowledgement. Reassurance. It was hardly as if Justin had anything to fear from Hilary; the man was probably just mourning the fact that Tom would be moving five miles further away, and there would be fewer chances of accidentally running into him on the high street.

Still, of course Justin was ready to put a good face on it. "I'll help you move your things, Tom. Will the car be enough, do you think? If you have furniture, we could hire a trailer, perhaps …"

"Thanks, Justin! Just the car, I think. Probably won't even need two trips!"

"And when, do you think … ?"

"Hilary?" asked Tom.

He stirred himself. There was no point in putting this off. And in fact – in fact, he was even looking forward to it! "This weekend, if you like."

"Sunday would suit me better," Justin said. "Though I could change my plans for Saturday if you needed –"

"No, Sunday will be fine," Tom replied, looking blissfully smug, as well he might with these two men each falling over themselves to make him happy.

Hilary found that he couldn't resent the fellow for that, not even a smidgen.

Tom looked thoughtful. He was drying up while Hilary washed the tea things, and they seemed to work together well in quiet harmony. Hilary was smiling a little. It was his natural state these days. He should try to remember to be discreet, not only for Tom's sake, but because they still had company: Justin was in the bathroom, tidying up after his exertions in the garden. He'd be leaving soon, and no doubt taking Tom with him.

It seemed that Tom was ruminating on the very same topic, for the young man eventually observed, "I'd better leave you in peace. Let you enjoy your last couple of days here alone."

"You probably need to pack," Hilary agreed. "I'd never realised how much time and effort it takes to move!"

Tom grinned at him. "Ah, but you'd been living in the same place all your life, hadn't you? And you would have had your parents' stuff to deal with as well as your own. Me, I'm pretty streamlined by now, with all this moving back and forth. I have plenty of books, but a lot of the ones I need are on my Kindle these days."

"Oh! Oh, yes, I've heard of Kindlings –"

"Kindles," Tom corrected with a happy guffaw.

Hilary smiled at him. "Kindles. A woman I worked with had one, but she kept it all very secret … Heaven only knows what she had on there! Perhaps, if you have a harmless textbook or two on yours, you wouldn't mind showing me one day."

"Of course I will." Tom added with a wink, "And you can see the not-so-harmless stuff, too, if you like!"

They shared a chuckle even though Hilary really wasn't sure what to expect there – he was only happy that Tom hadn't yet refused him *anything*.

"Anyway, with the packing, I'm pretty organised already. I knew I'd be moving soon, so I never really unpacked when term started, and since then I've got most of the other stuff boxed up already …"

Which seemed to smoothly lead to Hilary asking, "Would you rather stay here tonight, then?"

"Yes," Tom immediately replied – and they shared a grin. "Do you really not mind me living here … ?"

"No, I don't mind at all." They were done with the washing-up now, so Hilary occupied himself with wiping down the sink and work tops. "Or not yet!" he offered. Tom laughed, which was lovely, before Hilary continued a little more seriously, "I know you realise what a change this is for me, and I can hardly tell you how it came about – except that you've been a good friend to me, Tom, and a very enjoyable companion."

"That is so cool!" Tom said in a low, almost awestruck voice.

A happy silence blossomed – but when Hilary looked up, it was to see that Justin was there across the room, watching them with that lost expression on his usually equable face. And of course, in many ways that was utterly ridiculous: Justin could have absolutely nothing to fear from an old man such as Hilary; and though Justin didn't know it, Hilary had no interest at all in scuppering the man's plans. Justin would make a fine partner for Tom, once their relationship could be above board. But all of that was beside the point, at least for now. Justin was hurting, and it behoved Hilary to treat him considerately.

"Dr Ware," said Hilary, "would you like to stay for dinner? You've certainly earned it with all your hard work today."

"No. Oh, no … Thank you, Mr Kent, I couldn't impose – But you're staying, are you, Tom? Well, if I accept Mr Kent's invitation, it would mean that you don't have to ride home in the dark …"

"No, I'm staying over," Tom cheerfully announced. "I'll head back tomorrow afternoon to finish off the packing, so I'll be ready for you on Sunday."

"I see," said Justin.

"You're very welcome to join us," Hilary said.

"No. No, thank you. I won't impose." And within moments he had gone.

Tom pottered about, helping set the table for dinner, apparently quite oblivious of Justin's feelings for him – but Hilary supposed he shouldn't mind about that. Hopefully it meant that Tom wasn't aware of Hilary's feelings, either.

# Six

Hilary was in love. If he hadn't quite acknowledged that to himself before, it was so very clear to him now. And what a wonderful sensation it was … He felt as if he were floating six inches above the ground, and his smile just wouldn't stop … He must look rather daft, but Tom would care even less about that than Hilary did, so he simply wallowed in enjoyment of it all.

He supposed he should endeavour, for both their sakes, to pretend he felt nothing more or less than friendship, but occasionally that was rather difficult. On that Saturday morning, for instance, while they were sitting on the terrace in the sun, and once they were well into their second cups of tea, Tom observed, "We haven't talked about rent yet." To which Hilary's instinctive response was, "Oh, there's no need to worry about that."

"Sorry, what?" was Tom's confused reply.

"Well, I just mean –" *Please live here with me. That's all I want and more than I could ever ask. What care I for rent, when I have your dear company?* Which wasn't at all appropriate.

"Of course I'll be paying you rent, Hilary."

The counterargument was obvious. "But you'll be working in the garden. More than enough to earn your bed and board."

"No! No … Come winter I won't be able to put the hours in, not like I am now – and once I get properly into the thesis, that will take up my time, too. Anyway, we already have an agreement about the garden, and how we're both getting something out of it. Me living here is something else again."

"I'm perfectly happy for you to –"

"No, Hilary." Tom sat up straighter, and laid it on the line. "My budget's all worked out, with the loan, and what my parents give me. I've allowed a hundred pounds a week for rent, four twenty-five per calendar month, which includes bills. That's how much I've been paying in town. You should have that, and of course I'll put in half towards the groceries as well, or give you a flat rate towards food, if you'd prefer –"

Hilary was flabbergasted. "No, that's all far too much!"

"But –"

He supposed he had to accept something. Even if he kept the money separate, and – and, yes, put it towards whatever Tom wanted for the garden, or treated him to a particularly special present when he passed his thesis. Perhaps a significant gift of some kind when Tom finally moved in with Justin. Something to remember that daft old man by …

"Hilary … ?"

"Yes?" After a moment, he realised he hadn't heard whatever arguments Tom had just put forward. Instead, Hilary went with a counteroffer: "Fifty pounds a week, and you buy the cod and chips on Thursdays."

Tom was considering him with rueful fondness. "And a pineapple fritter, too?"

"Done!" Hilary cried.

Tom just shook his head. "This subject is not closed. It is simply on hold for now."

Well, Hilary could live with that.


In order to avoid any further discussions about rent over lunch, however, Hilary raised a topic he knew would interest Tom far more. "What do you think really happened to Thaddeus?"

"Well … we just don't know. There's this mention of him in the council records, which loosely updated goes something like, 'The shadow cast over his name has not been dispelled, and the man who might best illuminate matters has not been seen for many a month.' And that's it. I guess they were doing him a favour, being tactful about whatever the problem was – and they're not even actually accusing him of anything. Just saying there was some kind of issue they wanted to hear from him about. Which means the whole thing is up for interpretation."

"I suppose," said Hilary, "whether we think him guilty or innocent says more about us than him."

"Exactly! And what sort of problem it was. It might not have been a crime, after all, either legal or moral. And did someone deliberately cast the shadow? You know, was there an attempt to set him up, or report him for something, or was it more about appearances and misunderstandings?" Tom sighed. "I guess we won't ever know."

"There aren't any other records that mention him?"

"None that we know of. And I'm not the first person to have looked, over the years. There's been a few historians, amateur and otherwise, who've given it a go."

Hilary contemplated this for a long moment, and then asked, "What do *you* think happened, Tom?"

"I don't know," the fellow replied with a shrug.

"I won't test you on your sources! You must have a theory or two by now."

"Well, I don't like to make assumptions. I try to keep an open mind. The truth is," Tom added with a sigh, "the answer is usually rather banal. You know? It's so ordinary a thing that no one thinks to write it down. So chances are that Thaddeus simply returned to his family in Kent, and lived in a quiet way."

"You don't think he was murdered?"

"I doubt it." Tom looked to Hilary as if appealing for reason. "People make the mistake of underestimating the law and order in those times. That would have been quite something to get away with: killing a village priest with connections to the local manor house? His family weren't exactly poorly off, either, though they were merchants rather than wellborn."

Hilary nodded. It made sense to him. Though he had to wonder: "Why is Sir James so keen to make so much of it all?"

"I have no idea," Tom replied flatly. "But unless he knows something he's not telling –"

"It says more about him than Thaddeus," Hilary concluded.

"Exactly."

And so Tom settled into the tower and Hilary settled into sharing his home as if neither had ever known anything else. When Hilary watched Tom ride off into town on the Monday morning for his classes and other academic commitments, it was with a sense of utter contentment for he knew that Tom would return that afternoon, full of chat and cheer. It was such a luxury to have someone who'd make the tea as often as not – and if they had to wash his favourite teacups more frequently because the formerly solitary Hilary had only a limited amount of good crockery, that was a chore performed with goodwill as well.

For now Hilary was too much in love to mind about the toilet rolls being changed around so that the paper hung under, against the wall. He would smile, and patiently change them back again, the proper way, with the paper over – and next time he was in the bathroom, he'd find that the roll had magically reoriented itself again. They never said anything to each other, but

Hilary thought he spied a wicked smile on Tom's face sometimes, and it became rather a good-natured game.

It didn't matter that Tom preferred the television turned louder than Hilary did, despite the younger man obviously having better hearing. It only mattered a little that Tom liked channel-hopping during the commercial breaks, while Hilary would wait through them patiently, attention focussed elsewhere. Commercial breaks were a chance to ruminate, Hilary thought, about important matters such as whether he should buy more crockery. About whether there were toilet roll holders that were … multidirectional.

On the Thursday night, as they waited for the next episode of *Midsomer Murders* to begin, Hilary was pondering whether he needed to purchase a larger sofa to replace this one, or a second sofa or an armchair to supplement it. The two men had managed well enough so far on the two-and-a-half seater that Hilary had owned for over a decade. It was wide enough that they could each sit there comfortably without touching or getting in each other's way. But perhaps it wouldn't do in the long term. No doubt Tom would prefer to have his own space; while he'd seemed happy to shift about restlessly between sitting upright and slumping down so far that his torso was nigh on horizontal, the young man would probably like to move around laterally as well. The fact that Hilary accepted and even wanted to aid all this fidgeting about was further proof that he was in love, of course. It might have proved unbearable, otherwise.

Hilary glanced at the clock, which he knew to be correct. "It's almost time," he said quietly.

"I know," Tom replied in almost exactly the same tone. He aimed the remote control at the television, and switched it to ITV, then firmly put the remote aside. Perhaps during *Midsomer Murders* he would restrain himself from the channel-hopping; on previous occasions they had used the commercial breaks to discuss what they thought of the story so far, and where they thought it was going. They were each right about the latter about as often as they were each wrong.

This episode, 'Faithful Unto Death', portrayed a pair of lesbian lovers, Simone and Sarah, in what appeared to be a sympathetic manner. 'It's not a crime to love someone, is it?' seemed to be the theme that night.

"This is more like it," Tom declared in satisfaction – though whether he meant the television show, or the fact that he'd now stretched himself out sideways and was leaning his head against Hilary's shoulder, wasn't clear.

"Mmm," Hilary agreed, rather pleased by both developments. Tom had always seemed quite at ease with expressing physical affection; he'd had no qualms in taking Hilary's hand, or gently touching his shoulder to gain his attention. In fact, now that he thought about it, Hilary had probably been touched more in the past three weeks than in the past three decades put together! Still, the only time they'd ever hugged or anything like that was on Friday, after Hilary had seen off Sir James. And that had been about Tom's exuberant celebrations. This current arrangement spoke eloquently of comfort …

If comfort it could be called, with the young man's legs bent and hanging over the sofa's armrest, and his head propped up heavily at an awkward angle. Well, obviously the young man was more flexible than Hilary, but surely they could manage better. Hilary was afraid of doing anything that might end this innocent pleasure, but at the next commercial break, Hilary stirred a little.

"Oh!" said Tom, rolling his head back to look up at Hilary. "Is this okay? Or – ?"

Hilary mumbled, "I just thought you might be more comfortable if –" And he shifted, lifting his arm once it was free – and Tom seemed to quite naturally fit in against him, under Hilary's arm with his back against Hilary's side, his head obviously far better off, resting against Hilary's shoulder.

"That's nice," Tom murmured happily. Then he asked, "This is okay with you?" twisting around and tilting his head back to meet Hilary's gaze with his own unmistakeable candour.

"It's lovely," said Hilary.

And then the show started again.


Just as Hilary was feeling complacent about Tom not finding anything at which to take offence in this episode, it turned out that the lovers were two-thirds of the episode's villains. Tom groaned and grumbled a little, but that wasn't so bad while the older woman was taking full responsibility and pleading guilty for the sake of letting the younger woman walk free. It was noble, this self-sacrifice, and all for love …

Then the twist at the end was that the women each betrayed the other, and both their lives were destroyed. Which made bitter mockery of the episode's title.

Tom's groan now was gut-wrenching. "'Faithful Unto Death'," he complained as the credits ran. "They think we can't be. They think we're amoral at best, criminals at worst – and we turn on each other. We have no faith, no trust. We don't even have the 'honour among thieves' thing going for us!" He pulled away from Hilary's embrace, straightened up and sat there with his elbows on his knees and his face in his hands. "I'm not like that," he said, muffled.

"No," Hilary quietly replied, "I don't suppose you are."

"And you're not, either."

"I hope not," said Hilary.

"You're not," Tom insisted, turning his head to shoot a vehement stare.

After a moment, Hilary offered, "I only quibble because no one has ever required my faith of me. I grew up in a time when it was all too likely that people would be on their guard, and put their own safety first."

Tom shook his head. "I can't imagine you even doing me a bad turn, let alone betraying me like that."

"Well, to be honest, I can't imagine that, either."

Tom grinned – and then shook himself, as if a body-long shudder would rid himself of any remaining distasteful notions. "Come on, then. Let's play some music, and snuggle some more until we feel better again."

"Oh," said Hilary, who was actually feeling fine, but didn't think it worth his while mentioning the fact. "All right. Your music or mine?"

The grin grew more genuine. "Yours. Something nice, yeah? Something soothing."

And so Hilary directed him towards a beautiful compilation of Bach pieces titled *Contented Rest*, and Tom curled up beside him on the sofa and snuggled in close. This time Tom was facing Hilary, and he wound both arms around Hilary's waist, while finding the perfect place just below Hilary's shoulder on which to rest his head. Hilary turned into the embrace a little, and let his arms encompass his lovely young friend – and reflected that there were certainly degrees of contentment that even a contented man might never before have had cause to guess at.

# Seven

There was no proper desk anywhere on the ground or first floors of the tower, and Tom said that the one he'd used at the house in town hadn't been his, so he set up his laptop and notebooks on the far end of the kitchen table; they drew an imaginary boundary halfway down its length so his studies wouldn't interfere with meals. Hilary found an old standard lamp tucked away in what might have otherwise been a broom cupboard, which helped to illuminate that corner of the room, and Tom created a set of free-standing shelves along the exterior wall from old bricks and boards, that served well enough for his books.

If there were nothing else demanding his attention during the day, Hilary would sit in his usual place at the table and read, dwelling in the comfort of Tom's company. If Tom happened to walk past him on his way to fetch something from upstairs or to make tea, he'd ruffle Hilary's hair as if Hilary were the youngster of the pair.

On three days a week, and occasionally four, Tom would cycle off into town to participate in his classes, discuss his thesis with Justin, and use the university library. Hilary would watch him go, and watch for him to return, hardly even conscious of the notion that he might enjoy the time alone.

In the evenings they sometimes watched television together, but as often as not Tom would study. Hilary got the feeling that the garden had taken up rather too much of Tom's time and attention during the first few weeks of the autumn term, so Hilary was careful not to distract the young man now. No matter what the provocation.

One Wednesday evening, for instance, while they were both reading on the sofa, Tom decided to stretch out a bit. Without taking his eyes from his book, he swung around and lay back along the sofa with his head propped against Hilary's thigh. His feet – in bold red socks – were braced against the sofa's armrest, with his knees bent so that his lap cradled his notebook upright. He always read with a pencil tucked behind an ear, so now he'd reach for the pencil, roll his head a little to see past his book, and then scribble some notes, lost in another time and place – while Hilary sat there staring at his own open book, and if his eyes managed to scan the words, his brain rarely actually registered them. It was enough that he take in the warm weight of Tom's head against his thigh, and how that warmth spread like tendrils of ivy to insinuate themselves about Hilary's person. There was no denying … that Hilary Kent was slowly stirring back into life.

And yet he would not do anything about it. It was not his place to take action. Such a thing would not be seemly or proper. If he allowed himself to bask in Tom's instinctive affection – well, that might be understood, that might even be forgiven. If he asked for anything more, no matter how subtle and undemanding the request, that could not and would not meet with anyone's approval.

Hilary remained content. He had more richness in his life, after all, than he had ever looked for.

On their fifth Thursday – not that Hilary was deliberately counting, but his whole life now seemed to revolve around Thursday the sixth of October 2011, the day he first met Tom Laurence –

On the fifth Thursday, the skip finally arrived. Perhaps to make up for the tardiness, the driver helped them fill it full to brimming over with garden waste, and then drove it off. He was back within the hour to deposit the emptied skip by the gate, promising to return on the Monday to take away another load.

That evening, of course, there was another episode of *Midsomer Murders* to watch. 'Death in Disguise', it was called. Other than one brief untoward remark from Troy – easily shrugged off – there was nothing to disturb the peace in that night's viewing.

Tom sat there as he'd done the previous week, nestled under Hilary's arm with his back against Hilary's side and his head resting against Hilary's shoulder. This time, however, he quite deliberately took Hilary's hand and placed it with the palm and fingers flat against Tom's narrow belly, and then he cradled it in both of his hands, or stroked gently at it. Towards the end of the show, in the last ad break, Tom tilted his head back to say, "You really do have nice hands, you know."

And Hilary didn't quibble any longer, but simply murmured, "Thank you."

Once the credits rolled, Hilary muted the sound. But they didn't actually move from the sofa for a long long time.

The following morning found Hilary gazing pensively into the mirror, standing close enough to carefully examine his face and his skin and his hair. He hadn't used to be a *bad*-looking sort, though his face had always been a bit too long, and the general impression had always been of confusion as to which feature – each inoffensive on its own account – was the one which undermined the attractiveness of the whole. It was a long while now since he'd wondered if any of that inoffensiveness remained to him, or whether his ability to please had been smudged irretrievably by age.

His skin wasn't bad; still mostly pale and smooth, with pink splotches on his cheeks that might pass for bonhomie, and wrinkles that might speak of a stronger character than was actually the case.

His hair was completely white now, which he didn't mind, and it had always been plentiful and thick – though receding rather high in front. Perhaps the scholarly Tom would take that latter feature for a mark of intelligence. Hilary had been letting his hair grow, so his face was framed now in short waves of white. Apparently his hair had a mind to not be entirely straight, for which he should probably be grateful. However, it was no doubt time to have it cut properly, rather than settle for a shaggier version of his regular old cut.

Perhaps Marjorie could direct him to the sort of hairdresser who might update him with a more modern style while not making him ridiculous … Perhaps she would even do so with a minimum of teasing about him wanting to look attractive for his new lodger. Because that wasn't really the point, though Hilary knew he was laying himself open to suspicion. It wasn't that he thought Tom would ever actually think him attractive. It was more that, with the way things were going, Hilary didn't want Tom to be absolutely horrified when it finally became clear that Hilary was in love with him. Hilary would do what he could to encourage a more philosophical reaction; perhaps a wistful 'Ah, if only you were twenty years younger!' Hilary could live with that, and he suspected that Tom could, too. Though, to be honest, anything this side of 'Oh God! No fucking way!' would be acceptable.

Yes. It was time for a haircut. And maybe – Hilary took a couple of steps back and considered the larger matters – a new item of clothing or two. He didn't think his chinos and button-down shirts were too awful, but perhaps a colourful sweater to see him through winter, or a cheerful woollen waistcoat. His coat was smart enough, but no doubt it could be improved by a bright scarf and hat so that Tom needn't be embarrassed to introduce him if they met anyone he knew while in the village or out walking.

Yes. It was time Hilary brought himself into the twenty-first century – before the second decade of it got any older!

# Eight

Hilary had a hearty minestrone soup ready for lunch on the Thursday for when Tom got home from his classes, but no sooner had they sat down to eat than a few spots of rain suddenly turned into a downpour.

"Bugger!" Tom cried, standing up and making for the back door, where he urgently wriggled his feet into his wellies.

"What's wrong?" Hilary asked, standing up as well, and moving to help with he knew not what.

"Wanted to clear the last of the muck out of the pond before it filled with rain!" Tom was already halfway out the back door. "I'll get it done now. Don't come out," he poked his head back in to add. "No point both of us getting soaked."

And so Hilary watched from just inside the open door, hovering anxiously while the determined Tom made short work of three or four barrowfuls of dirt and debris. Even so, by the time he was done he was standing in enough water to splash about as he moved. He took a last look around the large rectangular pond to make sure it was as clear as possible before propping the shovel against the tower wall in a relatively sheltered spot, and then dashing up the steps.

Hilary had gone to fetch a towel, and waited there impatiently for the young man to heel off his wellies on the terrace before Tom at last came inside again.

"Whew!" Tom hooted from under the towel, and he chuckled as his own hands and Hilary's scrubbed his face dry and made a start on his hair.

"You're wet through!" Hilary exclaimed, looking at Tom's sodden jumper and jeans, and the growing pool of water on the kitchen floor.

"Sorry," Tom said, taking the towel away from Hilary, and peering down. "I'm making a mess."

"Don't worry about that. You, er …" Hilary feared he was blushing, but he forged on regardless. "You get undressed in the bathroom, and I'll fetch you some fresh clothes. Is there anything in particular … ?"

"Thanks, Hilary! Anything will do." Tom scampered off to the bathroom, making a few more hooting cries as if he was exhilarated by the whole adventure, while Hilary climbed the stairs to Tom's bedroom.

Hilary returned a few minutes later with underwear, jeans, a shirt and a jumper – to find a very pale Tom standing there on the bathmat completely naked. "Oh …" said Hilary, having prepared himself to cope with finding the young man in only his briefs.

Tom cast him the hint of a cheeky wink, and Hilary had a moment in which to register that Tom was rather *more* than neatly endowed despite the fact he must be cold, his cock and balls plump and slightly purplish against the dark virile hair – before Hilary realised something more important at this juncture. "Your hands!"

"Must have been too cold to feel it at the time!" Tom was gazing dispassionately at the grazed knuckles on his left hand, and the raw but mostly unbroken skin on the ball of his right thumb. "Bit stupid of me."

"You forgot your gloves," Hilary concluded, cursing himself for not thinking of the gloves while Tom was wrestling on his wellington boots.

"Ah, well …" Tom sounded philosophical, and let his hands drop as if he wouldn't have given them a second thought.

Hilary wasn't having any of that. He put the fresh clothes down on top of the laundry hamper. "You change into these. Carefully! And then come out to the front room. I'll see what I can do by way of first aid."

In the end, all Hilary could do was clean the wounds with disinfectant, and then gently apply antiseptic cream. He didn't have any kind of bandages that would suit, but only the sort of Band-aids that would wrap around a finger. He sat there pensively, Tom's hands resting on his knees, wondering what more he could do.

"Hilary …" Tom eventually whispered.

"Mmm?" He looked up, to find Tom shockingly close. Somehow it had made sense to sit Tom on the sofa, and to perch himself on the sturdy old coffee table so he could cradle Tom's poor hands in his lap. Which meant they were now face to face and knees to knees, and holding hands or as good as. And Tom was so very close now, and he had no barriers at all; Tom was always an open book, and Hilary felt utterly unprotected.

"You've forgotten one very important step," Tom said.

"And what might that be?" Hilary asked evenly enough.

"You have to kiss me better."

"Ah. I see." He sounded grave, he knew he did, and was in danger of making something far too serious out of what was no doubt intended by the younger man as a piece of harmless fun. But Hilary carefully lifted Tom's left hand, and bent his head to whisper a kiss against the back of it. And then he lifted Tom's right hand, and – in a moment of daring intimacy – pressed a kiss to his palm.

He was rewarded a moment later by Tom swooping in to smack a light kiss against Hilary's cheek – and then the young man was up, and dancing happily about with more whooping noises, heading in the general direction of the kitchen. "Come on, let's finish lunch before it gets cold! You make such great soup, Hilary!"

And he was gone.

Hilary took a moment to rest careful fingertips against his cheek, reliving the sense-memory of Tom's lips against his skin. He thought that, if he were especially careful with it, if he nurtured it and didn't wear it out, that moment might see him through decades of loneliness.


"You're not thinking of going out in the garden again, are you?" Hilary asked as they cleaned up the lunch things. "It sounds as if the rain has set in for good!"

"No, I won't. Not this afternoon, anyway."

"And your hands … You deserve a rest."

Yet Tom was still looking wistful about something.

"What is it?" Hilary asked as he hung up the damp tea towels to dry. "You should probably get on with your studies, shouldn't you? Is Justin pleased with how your thesis is shaping up?"

"Probably. I mean, yes, he is – and yes, I probably should." Tom looked at him imploringly for a moment, and Hilary ruefully chuckled to himself. He'd never be able to say no to that face. "But, Hilary, seeing as it's raining, could we maybe have a bit of a look around the second floor … ? For plans and journals and such. I know there wasn't anything much on the first floor, but I'm still kind of hoping –"

"Oh! Of course we can. Of course." An afternoon of rummaging around with Tom, making discoveries, seeing his eyes light up … What could be more delightful?

"It's just … Well. We haven't done much about looking for papers and things. I thought maybe … maybe you'd changed your mind. I mean," Tom continued, overriding Hilary's confused objection, "I know it's plenty to be dealing with, having me here. Even having me in the garden! I thought maybe me poking about as well was crossing a line."

"Not at all." Hilary was honestly flummoxed. "I was following your lead. Forgive me if I've misunderstood; we can chalk it up to a few senior moments, nothing more. But I thought you were so distracted by the garden itself …"

"I guess I was making the most of the weather. Figured it would start tipping down on a regular basis any day now; looks like it's finally started that."

"Let's make the most of it, then." Hilary filled the kettle and put it on. "I'm going to make a thermos of tea to take with us. We're going on an expedition!"

It seemed that no one had really used the two rooms on the second floor since well before Evelyn's time, and even then they'd been mostly storage rooms. Hilary was beginning to wonder quite how far back the general accumulation of junk dated. Still, he supposed the earlier the provenance the better from Tom's perspective.

They spent a couple of hours looking through whatever was there. Tom was quite focussed, of course, while Hilary got distracted now and then by curiosities or items that might potentially be useful. Neither of them could resist trying to sort and organise as they went, though, at least to the extent that the cramped conditions allowed.

Towards the end of the afternoon, Hilary heard – or at least sensed – a hush. Tom seemed to have stopped breathing. He was sitting cross-legged on the floor under the window, making the most of what light there was, working his way through a box of what seemed to be random papers. And he was staring hard at the neat pile he'd made of papers he'd dismissed.

"Tom … Have you found something?" Hilary made his way over there, almost alarmed at how still the young man had become. "Tom? Look at me. Let me hear you breathe!"

Obligingly Tom looked up, and visibly drew in a breath. "I think I've found something," he said, somewhat redundantly.

"What is it?" Hilary was there now, and leant down to peer at an old square of paper. He was only a layperson in this regard, of course, but he would have called it parchment.

"I'm not going to touch it again – without protection, I mean. I think it's the real thing."

"About the garden?" Hilary was frowning down at the thing, trying to make out the faded lines of ink.

"No, but it might be addressed to Thaddeus. It starts with 'My faithful T', and it's signed 'Lady B'."

"I see …" And he could indeed make out the large swooping B towards the bottom right.

"Lady Bryony was wife to the squire back then, and Thaddeus had some kind of particular connection with the family at Bedwyn Hall, yeah?" Tom laughed a little peal that verged on the hysterical. "I always wondered if he liked her, because he would have appreciated her name."

"Bryony?"

"He probably grew White Bryony in the garden."

Hilary wasn't quite flexible enough to be sitting on floors any more, so he straightened up instead. "Can you read what it says? Or do you want to bring it all downstairs?"

"I don't think it's going to be anything important; it's only a few lines long." Nevertheless, Tom very carefully lifted it back into the box, by the simple expedient of picking up a few papers immediately beneath it. "I didn't even notice it at first. Someone's scribbled on the back, used it for something else." Tom scrambled up and then bent to effortlessly pick up the box. "Come on! Let's get it into the light. And then we can see what else is in here!"

Whether it was due to the lady's handwriting, or Jacobean script in general, Hilary couldn't at first make out anything of the note other than what Tom had already deciphered for him. Tom, however, must be used to reading such things, for once they had settled at the kitchen table in good light, he effortlessly read,

"'My faithful T – There is no peace here, all goes ill, and it seems there is not a single room in the house that is mine to command. I will come to you tomorrow instead, if you will allow it. I beg you do not refuse a quiet harbour to a troubled soul. – Lady B'."

Tom sat back with his hands gripping the table edge on either side of the note. "Wow!" he said, in a marvelling tone.

Hilary looked at him. "You're not disappointed?"

"What? No! How could I be?"

"It's nothing to do with the garden!"

Tom smiled rather dazedly. "No, but it's like – these few words, they're so full of life, aren't they? It's like we just got to peer through a little window into the past. Into their lives! Don't you think that's awesome?"

Hilary couldn't help but smile a little himself at Tom's enthusiasm. "Yes, I suppose that it is."

"So, I guess they had a regular appointment together up at Bedwyn Hall – they must have both been involved in the community, pastoral care and all that, or maybe she liked to have his personal counsel, or both! But the place was overrun with house-guests or whatever, everything was chaos. So Lady Bryony wanted to escape and visit Thaddeus here instead. I wonder if they sat in the garden …"

Hilary was grinning by now. "You certainly have a vivid imagination, Tom!"

"Oh!" Tom seemed rather put out by the remark, though Hilary had intended no harm by it. "Oh, I don't think I was extrapolating *too* far … Well, only about the garden, but that was consciously done – and it might have been more proper, actually, for them to sit in the garden. He never seems to have married. She would have had a maid or companion with her, but indoors can still be seen as hidden away. Anyway, we know Thaddeus had some kind of relationship with the family, and they did let him live here, and –"

"Tom," Hilary broke in, "I didn't mean to make you justify yourself."

"Well –" Tom looked a bit self-conscious. "Oh! Well, I'm a scholar, you see. Not a novelist."

"I understand. I spoke thoughtlessly. I only meant that you brought it all alive for me, just as the note brought it alive for you. That's all. I wasn't questioning the basis of your conclusions."

"Of course not. Sorry." Tom was actually a bit pink about the cheeks now, which was rather endearing. "Should have known you weren't interested in an academic tussle!"

Which promptly drove any words from Hilary's mind other than things that were entirely inappropriate and tussle-related.

After a silent moment, Tom winked at him, and then smoothly changed the subject. "Do you have a large envelope I can slip this into? Just to keep it safe for now. Next time I'm in town, I'll get a proper storage box and tissue paper from the uni. Acid-free, you know."

"Of course," Hilary managed to say. But before he went off to do that, he prompted, "You said there was something written on the other side of the parchment?"

"Oh yes!" Tom turned over the note, again using two other bits of paper rather than touch it directly. And he read in a deadpan voice, "'Burgeon & Grow potting mix, three shillings a bag'."

"Seriously?" Hilary asked after a moment, wondering at this sudden descent from the sublime to the ridiculous.

"Seriously," Tom replied. "What a scandal … Costs at least five quid these days!"

Hilary huffed a laugh, and went to find an envelope. It did nothing for his peace of mind when he heard Tom chuckle a bit filthily before he was quite out of earshot.

That night they settled in to watch 'Death's Shadow', which Tom announced was the first episode of *Midsomer Murders'* second season.

"The second season already?" Hilary quietly protested. How awful to feel there was an end in sight, even if it wouldn't be for a while yet. "How many seasons were there?"

"Oh, only about a hundred," Tom reassured him, adding a cheeky wink for good measure. "And they're still making them, too!"

"That's good," Hilary murmured, relaxing again as Tom turned to snuggle back into his embrace, as they'd done the week before and the week before that.

The story drifted by in a happy blur. After a while, as Hilary listened to Tom's remarks during a commercial break, he dared to turn his head a little towards Tom, so that Tom's thick dark hair tickled and teased against his cheek, and he could inhale the already familiar apple scent of Tom's shampoo. When Tom didn't seem to notice or at least didn't mind, Hilary pressed a little closer, feeling the spring of that thick hair give before him and then push back a little as if flirting with him. He wondered how curly Tom's hair would be if he let it grow out …

Tom gestured towards the screen at one point, and made a tart comment, but Hilary simply mumbled something agreeable, and a moment later Tom settled again, his hand returning to cradle Hilary's hand against the warmth of his flat stomach. Tom might even have wriggled back a little further into Hilary's arms, unless that was Hilary's wistful imagination … It had to have been his imagination. As was the feel of Tom gently rolling his head against Hilary's shoulder, as if revelling in the contact. He probably just had an itch or something. And when Tom shifted, he certainly wasn't turning within Hilary's embrace, he certainly wasn't intending to push in further still … to wind his arms around … to kiss …

"Oh, for fuck's sake!" cried Tom, sitting up on the edge of the sofa, and throwing an irritable gesture at the television.

"What is it? What's wrong?" Hilary's breath was short with need or panic. They weren't touching any more. Tom sounded disgusted.

"Look – Didn't you see that? They just found the creepy old guy – I mean the middle-aged guy, sorry, but he's *well* creepy – and he's fucking with the young guy, Charles, the nineteen-year-old. And paying for it! Why does the secret always have to be something like this?"

Hilary sat there staring dry-eyed at the television screen while the man portrayed upon it acted out Hilary's embarrassment. No, more than that.

"All that self-hatred!" Tom was bitterly complaining. "God, listen to him! He 'hates these urges' that he has … No one should have to hate themselves for who they love!"

"No," Hilary murmured, mainly to ensure that Tom didn't seek any more engaged a response. "Quite."

At least the gay man didn't turn out to be the murderer this time, but was only guilty of stupidity and selfishness. Thirty years ago, when the man was a child, a prank had led to an accident, a boy had lost his life, and this man had had to live with his mistakes ever since. Barnaby was content to let it pass, and therefore so must the viewer.

Tom remained disgruntled. "So why did the secret have to be that he was gay? Or bi, anyway. Okay, so these investigations have to uncover secrets, and he had to seem guilty of something – but why does it always have to be *that*?"

Hilary muted the sound once the credits started running, and tentatively offered, "It wasn't the only secret."

"Yeah, so there'd been an adulterous affair, and an illegitimate child,"

Tom grumbled – "which again had bad consequences!" He turned to face Hilary for the first time, to plead, "Sex isn't *always* bad. Even when it's 'illicit' by their narrow definition …"

"Quite," Hilary said again. "You're correct, of course."

And then Tom at last *looked* at Hilary, and his gaze wandered in concern over Hilary's face and demeanour, while Hilary tried to convey rather more sturdiness than he was actually feeling. "I'm sorry," Tom eventually offered in truly humbled tones. "I'm really sorry. You shouldn't have to suffer through my tirades."

Hilary found a genuine smile somewhere. "I envy you your sense of righteousness, Tom. There's no need to apologise for it."

"My righteousness? My loudness, you mean!"

"I don't mean that at all, and you know it." Hilary added, "It's not that I disagree with you. I suppose I envy you for being of a generation that need know nothing of the … the secrets … and the shame."

"Oh, Hilary!" It sounded as if Tom's heart was wrung by what Hilary might have suffered in the lamentable past – and for one astounding terrifying moment he seemed to be going with an impulse to surge back into Hilary's embrace. But Hilary carefully didn't lift his arms in welcome, and Tom checked himself, and the moment passed. Nevertheless Tom offered, "I'm sorry. I spoiled the evening, didn't I? This lovely evening we were sharing. I love our Thursday nights, you know," Tom declared with his candid eyes softly glowing. "So tell me you'll forgive me, and we can go back to doing it properly again next week."

If anything of Hilary's heart had remained untouched before, then it was a lost cause now, and Hilary couldn't regret that for a moment. "Of course I forgive you," he said. "There can be no question about that."

"We have a date next week … ?"

"And for the week after," Hilary responded cheerfully, as if this really didn't mean the world and the moon and the stars to him. "And for as many weeks after that as we need to watch the whole hundred seasons!"

"Good, then," Tom said, reaching to grasp Hilary's nearest hand, and give it a friendly shake. "That's the best thing I've heard all day."

# Nine

The following week passed in a blur of all their new, happy habits. When Tom wasn't studying, he divided his time between the garden – at least when the rain wasn't torrential – and helping Hilary sort through all the discarded gear on the second floor. They didn't make any new discoveries, but it still felt as if progress of a sort was being made.

Meanwhile, Hilary was discovering the pleasures, rewards and occasional annoyances of keeping house for not only himself but his dearest friend. With Marjorie's prompting, he was becoming more adventurous in cooking lunches and dinners, and rather more health-conscious, too. The real turning point came that week, when she finally picked out the cookbook that best matched Hilary's style and Tom's taste.

Tom's gaze was warm with satisfaction and affection as he sat back after eating a beef casserole one evening. He'd liked it so much, he'd sopped up the last of the sauce on his plate with the bread, and eaten that, too. "Hilary," he said, "that was *amazing*."

"I'm glad," Hilary returned, "because there's enough for tomorrow night as well. If you can bear leftovers."

"Fantastic!" Tom was all but rubbing his hands together in glee.

Hilary couldn't help but laugh. "So it's true what they say about the way to a man's heart …"

Tom patted the stomach in question, and grinned. "It's in my interests to agree with you about that – but I think you'd already found a more direct route!"

That brought a blush to his old cheeks, so Hilary took refuge in clearing the table.

"Anyway, it's not leftovers if it's one of the things that actually tastes even better after a day or two."

Hilary chuckled, and couldn't find it in himself to quibble with the man.

They spent a quiet evening together on the sofa. It wasn't like their Thursday nights, which had somehow become something special – even if Hilary was convinced that he'd only been imagining things last week when he'd felt that their snuggle was fast becoming rather more intimate … Their Thursday nights were different, in any case, though there were plenty of innocent pleasures to be had on other evenings.

That night, for instance, Tom was lying back along the sofa, as he often did, with his feet propped up on the sofa's armrest and his head against Hilary's thigh, reading a new academic book he was all worked up about. And it seemed enthralling. Hilary left the television on quietly, but didn't change the channel so as not to unduly disturb the young man; he paid as much attention to Tom as to the programmes. When Tom was particularly involved in a passage, he concentrated so hard that his breath became audible: long slow pants of breath that might well drive Hilary a little mad.

Tom was tired, however, and who could blame him for that? Around ten, as he finished a chapter, he folded the book closed with his finger marking his place, and cradled the volume over his heart. "That's fuckin' magnificent," the young man could be heard to murmur, before his head tilted towards Hilary, and he drifted off into a nap.

After a while, Hilary indulged himself with a few – only a few – light caresses of that thick dark brown hair. He watched the play of light against the shifting strands, finding an infinite variety in the rich warm colours that evoked delicious things such as chocolate and dark toffee and ginger cake.

After about half an hour, Hilary was pondering the fact that he would have to get up soon, but he didn't want to disturb Tom. He was coming up with a plan which involved him carefully reaching for a cushion from the nearby chair and then carefully substituting it for Hilary's thigh – when Tom stirred, and then provocatively stretched.

"Hey, Hilary," he said with a sleepy affectionate smile. "Sorry 'bout that. Is it time for a pot of Assam?"

"Yes, if you would like it."

The smile became a grin, and Tom rolled off the sofa and up onto his feet in one fluid move. "I'll put the kettle on."


Hilary's imagination seemed to be working overtime that Thursday night, as a *Midsomer* episode called 'Strangler's Wood' unfolded on the screen. There were too many delightful distractions for Hilary to pay much attention to the story, other than keeping a wary ear open for anything that might offend Tom's sensibilities. So far they were safe – though that's what he'd thought the previous week, too, and it had suddenly all gone very pear-shaped.

Instead Hilary was paying far more attention to the young man who was snuggling up close to him. Hilary would have been hard-pressed to describe exactly the ways in which that night's snuggling was different to any other. Only that it was. He was almost certain of it. Perhaps it was *qualitatively* different, for Tom was sitting back against him as usual, Hilary's arm was embracing him as usual, with Hilary's hand flat against that firm warm stomach and Tom's hands cradling his as usual. Tom had brought up his bent legs a little closer perhaps, so that he was curled up in a lovely warm bundle as if cocooned around Hilary's arm. And his breath was slow and slightly louder than usual, as it got when Tom was paying close attention to one of his books. Except that Tom wasn't paying that much attention to the television, he just wasn't, and his head was turned in against Hilary, if he was looking at the screen it was from the corner of his eye – and what else could there be for him to be so caught up in … ?

Hilary hardly dared to believe, but the way Tom was stroking gently down Hilary's forearm, it was almost as if he wanted to draw Hilary closer, almost as if this was the quiet expression of a wish that would become a demanding tug if only it were permitted. And the way Tom was rolling his head back against Hilary's shoulder in occasional restlessness, the way in which he nudged and pushed catlike into the hollow beneath Hilary's collarbone … It must be imagination, or Hilary reading too much into too little, for surely Tom couldn't possibly want …

What Hilary wanted, what his every instinct was clamouring for him to do, was to turn further, to bring his other arm around Tom and cradle the young man against his chest. To express all his affection for Tom in an innocent yet warm embrace. To cherish him. That was all. In those moments that would have been heaven on earth to Hilary Kent.

But no matter how innocent his intentions, at the heart of it was an inappropriate love, and at the core of it was an illicit desire, and he mustn't give in, he mustn't – he mustn't search for an excuse to shift his stance, to turn in and protectively encompass, to reach for more, he mustn't even lift a hand to rub at Tom's arm in a friendly manner.

He mustn't – he mustn't – but even as he thought that, he groaned a little, and shook his head as if shaking off dreams – and his lips brushed against Tom's thick hair, and when he found himself pressing a kiss to the precious head that rested against him, there was an answering moan from

Tom which did not protest. He did not protest. So Hilary stayed there, Hilary let his cheek and his mouth rest against Tom in turn, and Tom was kind enough to let him.

Eventually the programme finished with nothing to disrupt them, thank God, nothing to disturb Tom's peace of mind. Hilary was barely aware of it, but then the news came on, and that would hardly be conducive to this peace continuing – not that it *should* continue, Hilary really should force himself to get up and make the tea, pretend that this was just any other evening – but he couldn't bear that. He couldn't bear it. So he muted the sound, and hoped that Tom might just doze off for a while, and gift Hilary with a few more minutes of this profound contentment …

But no, it was over. Cold air froze him all down his side when Tom lifted away, as he must do, of course he must. Hilary indulged himself in a bereft sigh, then struggled to compose his face into a proper expression, whatever that might be.

Then Tom was back, and resettling. Passing him the remote for the compact disc player. "I put the Bach in," Tom said huskily, curling up again against Hilary, and surely there could be no mistaking it now. For whatever reason there might be, Tom wanted to cuddle, and obviously his only option in that moment was Hilary – who was nothing loath. No one would ever understand, of course, but surely they might cuddle here in private, these two gay men, these friends, these consenting adults …

Hilary managed to turn off the television with one remote and then press the play button on the other, and the sweet plangent strains of music swelled through the room. Then he let himself follow his instincts, he turned towards Tom, and encompassed him in both loving arms – and Tom moaned a little, and wriggled back closer still. He was so warm, Tom was, he was radiating heat, though that didn't entirely explain Hilary's own state, so flushed and roused. Hilary held the young man for long long minutes, for an eternity, for no time at all, and he knew that he would never have more than this in his life and yet he would die complete and happy.

"Oh, *Tom*," he murmured against that thick dark-toffee hair. "Tom, my dear friend …"

"Hilary …" Tom murmured in reply, sounding rather contented himself – then he stretched and twisted within Hilary's arms, pushing back against him, lifting one arm to run a hand back over Hilary's white hair – while

Tom's other hand pushed down, taking Hilary's hand with it. "Hilary," the young man said in hushed tones, even while that hand boldly insisted, "would you touch me? Please. I want you to touch me …"

Hilary was hardly in a state to deny him anything, but he tried to resist a little. His hand was already beneath the waistband of Tom's jeans, but he managed to stall there. Which didn't put Tom off, who instead fumbled one-handed at the button and zip.

"I love your hands," Tom was muttering more urgently. "Your great strong hands, Hilary. I want them on me!"

"No one would understand," Hilary protested in a wretched agony of wanting and not wanting. But mostly wanting. "No one would forgive!"

"Fuck 'em," said Tom – and he took Hilary's hand in his again, and together they plunged down –

And Hilary, who hadn't touched anyone other than himself for so many years, for so many decades, found himself with a deliciously hard cock in his hand, and Tom's own hand wrapping round his, encouraging him to grasp and explore quite shamelessly. Tom pushing back, arching back, with his other hand curling round Hilary's nape now in a broad echo of shapes.

"Oh God," Tom was importuning him in guttural tones, "oh God I need this, please God I *need* this –"

Soon Tom had set a strong rhythm, driving Hilary on, while Hilary tried to hold onto the details – the precious delicate skin he wanted to treasure, shifting over the stunningly rampant flesh – and Tom was uncut, and so very hot in every sense of the word – and there was a way he rocked and rolled his hips as if pivoting around his core which might have sent Hilary wild if he were a younger man and if this were permitted to be a more mutual thing … All these details he grasped onto and printed in his mind, to be played and replayed like the gift they were for all his years to come.

It was all too much, too hard, too driven, of course, for it to last. Tom needed relief, and he would have it. Hilary was aware of every little thing and every large thing, too, as Tom's focus narrowed down, his holds intensified, the pressure of his every touch – as his quietly grunting breaths suddenly became pleading moans, and Hilary remembered enough to not push him along, to resist Tom's will, to simply keep going and let it all unfold in its own time – and soon enough the desperate pleas became triumphant cries, and Tom was coming, his seed splashing over his own belly and

Hilary's hand – and Hilary held on, and still kept going, only starting to gentle now, but he kept going and going until Tom was reduced to a warm satiated weight in his arms, almost mewling in the aftershocks, and his cock was soft now but still precious still beloved …

And then at last Hilary stopped, and carefully let the man go, and simply held him.

They were quiet for a while, and then Tom chuckled, and stirred himself to twist around and look up at Hilary with bright eyes. "God, that was fuckin' fantastic!" He laughed again, in delight – not laughing at Hilary, thank heavens, but only bubbling over in delight. "That was so fuckin' good! God … Hilary! Thank you. I mean it." He pushed up to press a kiss to Hilary's cheek. "*Thank you.*"

"To say it was my pleasure would be somewhat redundant," Hilary remarked, having managed to gather himself. He had to handle this just right. He mustn't let such a perfectly wonderful and perfectly unlikely circumstance be spoiled.

Tom chuckled again, and pushed further round so he could snuggle in under Hilary's arm but facing him. One of his lovely hands settled over Hilary's heart, which must be skipping along at a rather higher rate than usual. His hand settled there for a moment, and then started slipping a little lower down Hilary's chest. "And now you," Tom said, as if there were no question about it.

"Oh no," Hilary murmured, stopping that hand by laying his own over the top of it. Firmly. "No, that's really not necessary, my dear."

Tom frowned up at him, and then couldn't help but glance down, where it was probably fairly obvious despite his chinos that Hilary was in much the same state that Tom had been not so long ago. "What?"

"There's no need, my dear friend. I feel all the blessing of what we've already done." And he lifted Tom's hand to his mouth, and pressed a kiss to the lovely skin, to a sticky patch of Tom's seed, to Tom's tender palm.

"But that's not fair," Tom grumbled in protest. Then he glanced down again, and when he looked up at Hilary again, his frown had become confused. Tom tentatively asked, "Not because you can't … ?"

"No," he agreed. "Not because I can't."

The frown was fast becoming a scowl. "Not because you don't want to."

Which was more a certain statement than a question, but Hilary replied, "Not because I don't want to, no."

"Then it's because you won't!" Tom pulled away, and sat there not touching Hilary – *not* touching Hilary – and his eyes glittered with angry tears.

"My dear fellow," Hilary said softly, with all his love laid bare for Tom to see if he wished to. "Your friendship is by far the best thing that's ever happened to me. You're the best thing in my life, Tom, and what you've granted me this night has made me happier than I can ever remember being. Don't let's spoil it by arguing."

"Hilary –"

He overrode the young man quite effortlessly. "You must know that nothing more can ever come of this, my dear. Let us … enjoy what we've had, and enjoy the friendship we still have, and say no more about it."

Tom's face was crumpling in grief, but Hilary couldn't believe it was the sort of sadness that would matter for very long. Tom was still so young, and this was surely little more than a temporary disappointment.

"All right, my dear?" Hilary asked. When he received a reluctant nod, Hilary turned away to reach for the box of tissues he kept nearby. They each cleaned up their hands, and their tears, without looking at the other. And when they were done, Hilary said, "Why don't I make you a cup of cocoa to take up to bed with you?"

A mute nod, and Hilary stiffly hauled himself up off the sofa, and headed for the kitchen. Nothing more was said.

Until they parted by the door to Tom's bedroom on the first floor, each with their mug of cocoa in hand. And Tom turned towards Hilary, and murmured, "Please …"

And Hilary stood still while Tom stepped closer, and then bent his head and leaned down to press a quiet gentle kiss to Hilary's mouth. Hilary closed his eyes and pressed back. Surely they might kiss, just once, at the end of the evening on which they had almost become lovers. Surely just this once.

Tom stepped back without needing to be told. "Goodnight, Hilary," he whispered. And then he was gone, and the door had been quietly closed behind him. And Hilary went to climb into his own familiar lonely bed. He fell asleep a long while later, curved around the spare pillow, with his arms encompassing it and his face pressed yearningly close, just as he'd held his love that evening.

Hilary woke early the next morning, and he made a special effort to have breakfast organised and ready for Tom when he got up. It must be as ordinary and pleasant a morning as ever; his own demeanour must be calm and content. They would continue on as before. As friends, as dear friends.

Tom came down not long after his usual time, a wary frown marring that usually candid face. "Hilary," he said a bit uncertainly as he stalled not far from the stairs, taking in the breakfast scene.

"Good morning, Tom," said Hilary oh-so-smoothly despite wondering what Tom apparently found surprising. "I'll make the toast, if you'd like to start on your cereal."

"Thank you," Tom replied, at last coming over to sit down.

Once the young man was safely seated, Hilary reached to pour him his tea, and then got up to get the toast started. "I trust you slept well," Hilary said as he often did – taking a risk with that, perhaps, but honestly wanting to know.

"Yes. Yes, thank you."

Hilary dared a glance back over his shoulder. Tom was looking a bit sad and confused and maybe even defeated, but already he was relaxing. Perhaps the worst was past them as easily as that.

"Did you?" Tom asked politely.

"Yes, thank you, Tom."

They ate their breakfast in silence, and all seemed well enough between them. Rather than immediately start clearing things away afterwards, Hilary stayed in his seat, and they each contemplated their own thoughts over a third cup of tea.

Perhaps that had been a mistake, however, for eventually Tom said, "Hilary."

"Mmm?"

"About last night –"

Hilary tensed up again, and actually maybe he'd been tense all along. "Tom –"

"*Don't* shut me down again. Please."

Of course there was a treacherous part of Hilary that would like nothing more than to listen to Tom pleading whatever case he wanted to make. But there was no future in letting their friendship develop into something more, and it was in Tom's interests to keep things as they were – certainly no more and probably rather less.

"Tom," said Hilary, "I know you only like me for my garden, but it is yours to do with as you will, so there is no need to humour an old man's fancies."

Tom was staring at him in astonishment. After a long moment, he swallowed as if in discomfort, and then offered in raw tones, "You've said that before. I thought you were just teasing me."

It was Hilary's turn to feel discomfort – so much so that he could make no remark.

Tom had sat back in his chair, and was frowning in thought, as if troubling over his memories of their every interaction. Eventually he said, "I would hate it if you thought I was taking advantage … in any way at all."

Hilary couldn't bear not to reassure him. "I don't. Not really. I just –"

"Please. You've said we're friends. You're not denying we're friends, are you? *Real* friends?"

"We are, of course we are." Hilary got himself back onto the front foot, as it were. "I apologise, Tom. You are a very decent young man, and I certainly don't think you would ever take advantage of me."

Tom glanced at him, warily, imploringly; wanting this to be true.

"Perhaps, however," Hilary ploughed on while he could, "it would be better if you spent a little more time with people of your own age."

"But I do, at uni –"

"For classes, yes. But you don't go out on Friday or Saturday nights. Surely *that* hasn't changed since I was your age?"

Tom was scowling now, in hurt and anger, though he seemed to be making an effort to be fair. "You'd rather I wasn't in every night? Is that what you're saying? You'd rather have the place to yourself, like you're used to?"

"No, this is your *home* now, Tom – or at least, I hope so – and you should be here as much as you like. But –"

"But what?" Tom had turned on his chair so that he was facing off to the side, perhaps about to get up and get away from this conversation.

"Surely most young people would like to go out – well, dancing, or to see a film, on a Saturday night. To spend time with their friends."

A moment stretched, and then when Tom spoke it was in an odd kind of stilted tone. "I had a couple of particular friends. Bevan and Mac. Cheryl, too, I guess. We'd go out, like you say. But when we all graduated last year, I was the only one who stayed on. And this year – well, there's been you, and the garden, not to mention the thesis. And being the teaching assistant makes it kind of … well, not *inappropriate*, but I haven't made any new friends this year, other than you. What I've had has been fine, I actually haven't missed all that, and –" Tom suddenly turned to face Hilary very directly. *"And you're telling me to go out and get laid, aren't you?"*

Hilary was made mute by this bald accusation. He stared back at Tom in a kind of terror.

"All right," Tom at last continued, sour and adamant. "I get the message. Though I really did think – Hilary –" He softened a little, though his honesty made him seem pitiless. "Hilary, I really was sure you wanted it, too. I'm sorry I was so wrong about that."

"Tom –" He had to clear his throat to speak it, but Hilary owed the young man a little honesty in return. "Tom, you must know you weren't so very wrong."

The dear fellow simply nodded in acceptance, and was too kind to argue further.

"If I had been born into your generation, Tom, or even your parents' generation, then your other suitors would have some rather determined competition … Some *very* determined competition. But as it is, it's not to be. Don't let us make ourselves miserable over something that can't be helped."

Another nod, and then a bright glance from those candid eyes, from that gaze in which the summer storms had already calmed. "Thank you, Hilary," Tom murmured. And then he stood from the table, and went to fetch his wellies, and a moment later he was out the back door and in the garden.

Hilary was left with the washing-up, but he didn't mind about that. It was rather a relief to face nothing more now than a simple domestic chore. He didn't start on it for a while, though. Hilary sat there at the table for quite some time, until his hands finally stopped shaking.

That evening Tom sat beside Hilary on the sofa reading, apparently quite comfortable. He took great care, however, that they should never touch.

Which was the way things had to be, of course. But that didn't prevent Hilary's old heart from breaking.

# Ten

On the Saturday morning, Hilary left Tom working away on his laptop, and walked into the village to consult with Marjorie Flanagan at the grocery store. He didn't see any point in prevaricating with her, as no doubt she knew everyone's business better than they did, so after they had wished each other a good morning he cut right to the chase.

"Tom needs access to whatever gardening records there might be up at Bedwyn Hall, but I'm afraid he seems to have got off on the wrong foot with the housekeeper. And I myself," he continued, though he saw from Marjorie's suppressed smile that she already knew the story, "have managed to argue with Sir James."

"I heard tell."

"Of course you have," Hilary murmured. After a moment, he ventured, "I'd be sorry to know that the inestimable Mr Reynolds was indiscreet."

"You needn't be sorry, then, for all Sam said was that it didn't pay to be impertinent to you. I do believe you impressed him, Mr Kent."

"Ah. Well, thank you, I suppose."

"The rest we had to piece together from Sir James's complaints."

"I see." Hilary took a moment with this, and then asked, "Is it all beyond remedy, Mrs Flanagan, or can you propose a course of action?"

Marjorie took a moment in turn, no doubt for the purposes of melodrama. "If you'd be willing to smooth your way – and I mean both of you," she added – "then I think you'll find Tom can have what he wants."

"An apology, of course."

"It's a start."

"And perhaps a gift? For the housekeeper – I'm sorry I don't yet know her name – and for Sir James. A token of gratitude."

"Exactly. Wait here." Marjorie headed off through a door just beyond the counter, no doubt into a storeroom, and was back a moment later with a white box imprinted with gold and adorned with red ribbon. "Turkish Delight – the proper kind, imported – for Mrs Carew. The housekeeper," Marjorie added, though Hilary had assumed as much.

"Thank you."

"It's her favourite. I don't put it on the shelves, but she knows I keep some by for her.”

“That’s really excellent.” It occurred to Hilary that Marjorie was in effect adding her seal of approval to his and Tom’s application. He wondered if such useful kindness could ever be repaid.

“And then for the squire …” Marjorie led Hilary over to the shelves of spirits, and the whiskies in particular. She unerringly picked out one of the most expensive bottles for Sir James, but had the grace to blush a little. “A man in his position acquires certain tastes,” she said.

“Quite,” he replied, taking the bottle without any hesitation.

“And then this for Leonard,” she added, selecting a bottle from the lower end of the mid-range.

Again Hilary immediately took the bottle, but he had to ask, “Leonard … ?”

“The head gardener!” Marjorie looked at him a bit impatiently as if Hilary was deliberately not keeping up, but he was almost certain that not even Tom had mentioned a Leonard or a Mr Leonard. “I have it on good authority, Mr Kent,” Marjorie confided as she led the way back to the till, “that all will be well.”

“How so, Mrs Flanagan?”

“You gave Sir James a right shock, but I’m told that before the end of the day he’d given word to receive young Tom a little more graciously next time he turned up.”

“I see. I see … Thank you very much, Mrs Flanagan.”

“Your generosity won’t be wasted,” she concluded a little complacently as she rang up his purchases.

Perhaps it was as well not, for the three items came to almost a hundred pounds. Hilary smiled a little wryly, and swiped his debit card.

When Hilary arrived home, Tom finished whatever he was doing on the laptop with a flourish of hands and a clatter of keystrokes, and then got up to put the kettle on. “Nice walk?” he asked. “I think we’re gonna get more rain this afternoon,” Tom added, with a glance through the windows. Even through the thick glass, it was obvious that the greys of the overcast sky were thickening.

“Yes, thank you, and I don’t doubt it.” Hilary followed Tom to the kitchen and placed his purchases on the work top, then watched for a moment as Tom assembled the tea things in a familiar flurry. Hilary was already finding it difficult to remember that there had ever been a time before Tom, a time in which he'd loved being alone. He hardly dared think about the time to come when he would have to relearn his contented self-sufficiency.

"What have you got there?" Tom asked conversationally. "Was Marjorie in Hard Sell mode?"

Hilary huffed a laugh. "She was, but all to good purpose." He announced, "If you're prepared to apologise to Mrs Carew, Tom, and I to Sir James, then we now have the means to reacquire their favour."

Tom had stalled in mid-flight, box of Earl Grey in one hand and the other hovering over the pot with a spoonful of tea. Those bright clear eyes gazed upon him as if Hilary were all the answers Tom could ever need.

Hilary had to turn away, gesturing towards the satchel as if its contents weren't already the topic of conversation. "Mrs Flanagan was kind enough to suggest the right gifts, including one for a – uh, a Mr Leonard? The head gardener, anyway. And –"

At which point the young man suddenly stepped up behind him and Hilary was surrounded by Tom in the full flow of enthusiasm. "Oh, Hilary, Hilary," Tom was murmuring in the midst of this all-encompassing hug. "What a friend you are!"

"Oh well," Hilary demurred, trying not to be overcome by Tom's warmth pressed all down his back. "It's only what anyone might do."

"It so is *not*."

"Tom …" Hilary began, lifting a hand to where Tom's arms encircled his chest and shoulders.

"I've never had a friend like you before," Tom said, his breath warm where his face was tucked in against Hilary's throat. "There's no one quite like you in all the world, I reckon!"

"I could say exactly the same thing," Hilary responded, though he used his brusque no-nonsense voice. "Come on, my dear. Let me go now. The kettle's boiled," he added, as if that was of any consequence at all.

"All right," Tom said, pulling away at last. He seemed to feel no resentment at being turned away again, though he took the liberty of brushing his lips against Hilary's hair in what was apparently supposed to be a surreptitious kiss, and he sniffed a little, having been genuinely overcome.

Hilary really needed to nip this in the bud. Before it was too late and the bud had unfurled even further. What a beautiful and unusual flower this would have made! But a flower too exotic and too delicate for this world and its uses.

He went to sit down at the table, and waited quietly for Tom to bring the tray of tea things over. Tom sat opposite him, and after casting Hilary a wary glance, dropped his gaze and remained quiet, as if he knew all too well what Hilary needed to say.

Which was more than Hilary did. Eventually he decided that it might be just as effective to talk about someone other than himself. "How is Justin?" Hilary asked in a voice so steady as to be almost normal. "I trust he's well."

Tom was startled, to say the least. His brow flew up, and he sat back in the chair, his hands grasping the table edge for a moment. "He's fine. He's – Well, he's busy with the end of term coming up, but he's fine." A pointed look darted Hilary's way before Tom leant in again to pour the tea. "Why do you ask?"

"Envy, I suppose," Hilary smoothly replied. "Teachers were never thus when *I* was a young man … and perhaps it's just as well!"

Tom snorted with laughter. "Yeah, maybe."

"He seems a very decent man," Hilary continued. "He's mature … handsome … intelligent … enjoyable company. He shares your interests."

Tom had sat back again, and was looking at Hilary a bit sourly now. He could hardly misread where this was going.

"Justin is very fond of you, you know." Hilary said it gently, though he couldn't deny it cost him dear.

Tom's mouth twisted in a moment's disgruntlement, but then he answered honestly enough. "We get along, that's true. We make a great team." His enthusiasm was rekindled. "You should see us work a classroom! I have no idea why so many people sign up for these classes when they expect history to be dull."

"I'm sure you make a magnificent team as teachers," Hilary agreed. "But I suspect Justin would like rather more than that. Once you're no longer teacher and student, of course. Once it's appropriate. And I have to say … I think you'd make great partners. In life, I mean, as well as in work."

"Oh, Hilary," Tom chided with a wry smile, "you *are* a romantic, aren't you? But me and Justin, it's not like that."

Hilary sighed with fellow feeling, and said in a very small voice, "It is for him." Though perhaps, now he thought about it, he wasn't doing Justin any favours in pushing the issue, if Tom was really so oblivious. No doubt it was better to let Tom's feelings develop naturally, once they were free to do so.

"Anyway," said Tom, with his arms folded across his chest, and a strangely distant tone, "I like being with you." Then without waiting for a response, Tom took his cup of tea and got up to resettle at his laptop. Soon he was tapping away again, lost in concentration.

After a while, Hilary quietly got up, too, and took his tea into the front room. He sat on the sofa with a book, and started to read. He couldn't remember afterwards even what book it was, let alone the story.

# Eleven

One of the most delightful things about Tom was his resilient cheerfulness. No matter what the day brought, he was like spring sunshine – occasionally obscured by a light shower or two, but ready to shine in beneficence again just as soon as the rain passed. Hilary couldn't even imagine him holding a grudge.

Tom called Bedwyn Hall to make his apologies, and they were invited to visit on the Monday afternoon once Tom had returned from his classes. The two of them walked up, as it was only a mile or so, and the weather was windy rather than wet. The Hall stood atop a gently swelling hill, with another steeper hill behind it, in the midst of delightful parkland. Hilary was glad to make it up the final slope without getting too out of breath, though the inclement weather had curtailed his afternoon walks lately, and he was feeling the lack.

Hilary and Tom headed around to the service entrance, as they'd been asked to do, and rang the bell. Mrs Carew promptly answered. She was a sharp-looking woman, with long steel-grey hair worn up in a tight bun – but her severity was mostly for show once faced with an honestly humble Tom proffering the box of Turkish Delight.

"Come in, then," she said in a long-suffering manner, beckoning them inside.

"Thank you, Mrs Carew," Tom said, leading the way.

"Thank you very much," Hilary added. He was carrying the whisky. "This is for Sir James. Would I be able to pay my respects to him?"

"Sir James is out for the afternoon, but I'll make sure he receives that, and knows who it's from."

"Thank you," he repeated. "If you would pass on my apologies … Well, I'm sure you know all the right things to say."

"Indeed I will, Mr Kent." The housekeeper put the gifts on a side table in the hallway, and then led them in past the kitchens. "I'll show you to the front parlour. Sir James said you can spend as much time there as you wish. There's a display there of all the paintings and drawings of the estate, and other records, too."

Tom looked thrilled. "Thank you, Mrs Carew!"

"Not the gardener's records, however; they're kept separately." She cast Tom a severe look as she ushered them through a service door into the house proper. "Nothing's to be harmed or marked in any way, and nothing's to be taken away. You can make notes, but if you want copies, then you ask first. Do you understand, Mr Laurence?"

"Yes, of course. Of course, I totally respect –"

"Just see that you do." She swept past and led them along a hallway dark with intricately carved wood panelling. Hilary was no expert in architecture – at least, not beyond an abiding love for the Brighton Pavilion – but he suspected that much of what he was looking at dated back to Tudor times.

They emerged into a much larger and lighter hall, which seemed to include the front entrance of the manor house, though it was screened off, perhaps for warmth.

"Look!" cried Tom, beckoning Hilary over to where a large painted coat of arms was hung on the wall. "Hilary, this is what Sir James was talking about. See the Silverseal leaf? It's really unusual."

"It is, isn't it?" he murmured, peering at it closely. A long narrow leaf with jagged edges forked towards the tip into three such leaves; it resembled a prickly kind of trident.

"Purity and courage," said Mrs Carew. "That's what the Archard family arms and the motto are all about."

"Very commendable," Hilary replied. "I'm sure it's been quite inspirational over the years!"

"I'm sure," she agreed. After another moment, Mrs Carew led them through into a side room. "Here we are, then."

Tom was looking around eagerly at the walls, which were covered in pictures along with another two representations of the coat of arms in the styles of different ages. Tom was barely restraining himself from running amuck. "Awesome …" he whispered.

Mrs Carew caught Hilary's eye, and indicated a bell pull by the fireplace. "Ring if you need anything. I'll have tea sent up at three."

"That's very good of you," he responded.

"There's a powder room directly across the hall. For anything else, please ring."

"Thank you again, so much."

She nodded in rather more friendly acknowledgement, and then she swept out, closing the door behind her.

Hilary turned to watch Tom, smiling to see him gazing about here and there, as if the young man hardly knew where to start. "What are we looking for?" Hilary asked, more for the sake of saying something than not.

"There!" Tom cried, starting forward, and indicating a framed sketch. "See? There's the tower!"

Hilary joined him to peer at the drawing. It was rather small and faded, and perhaps had been worked in blue pencil for some unknowable reason, but it was a general scene that definitely included the tower and the garden walls, and the long curve of the river beyond.

"I see," said Hilary. "But you really want something that shows the garden itself, don't you?"

"Yes. Yes, if we can."

Hilary started browsing the walls to the left, while Tom headed right. Unfortunately they met on the other side of the room, neither of them having found anything. There were drawings and paintings of the Hall itself, the parklands, a gatehouse, and a large fountain Hilary hadn't seen the original of yet, but nothing more that included the tower. "What a shame!" Hilary said. "I'm sorry, Tom."

"Well, we're not done yet," the young man said in his determined tones. He indicated two waist-high bookcases, each full and piled about with books and bound journals. "Do you mind?" Tom asked. "This is where it starts getting really tedious."

"Of course I don't mind." Hilary took the bookcase on the left, and Tom the one on the right; they each took an armful of the first four or five books, and carried them over to the small table and chairs placed by the front window. And they started browsing.

Tom was much quicker at it than Hilary, perhaps used to skimming through material searching for his particular interests, or perhaps feeling more certain that he would recognise anything important when it appeared. Or perhaps Hilary was simply paranoid about missing something that Tom would find important. In any event, by the time the tea tray was delivered by a silent young woman, Tom had been through almost a whole shelf, while Hilary was barely halfway along.

They took the opportunity to stretch out, and then slump back in their chairs. Paying constant attention was in itself tiring, and Hilary was only glad that the younger man seemed to feel that as much as he himself did.

"It's quite the local history collection," Tom commented. "They've obviously been very thorough over the years, to get copies of everything – well, pretty much everything published that relates to the Hall or the village, from what I can see."

"Yes. I wish it were more relevant to your field, though."

Tom smiled at him fondly, sorrowfully. "You must be finding this really tedious. I'm sure if you wanted to head home again once you've finished your tea, they won't mind about me staying on alone."

"I'm happy to stay," Hilary stoutly replied. Of course he wasn't going to be chased away from spending the afternoon helping Tom! "I was just concerned that we find something, for your sake."

Tom did find one reference to 'the well-known vegetable and herb garden at Riverside' in the memoir of a local magistrate, but this was shrugged off with a roll of Tom's eyes, and even Hilary had to admit it wasn't exactly useful. Nevertheless, Tom copied down the full paragraph and the bibliographical details.

They'd had no further luck an hour later, when the chronically impatient tones of Sir James announced his imminent arrival. Hilary and Tom had a moment in which to exchange a grimace, before the squire burst into the parlour.

"Well, well," the man said, his hand remaining on the doorknob as if to indicate this was a flying visit. "It's good to see you two have made yourselves at home."

Hilary belatedly got to his feet, and Tom did likewise. "It's good of you to have us here," Hilary offered.

"Yes, thank you," Tom chipped in.

"Nonsense, nonsense, it's fine. Sit down, won't you? Thank you for the whisky, Mr Kent, that was damned decent of you."

"A token gesture. I really must apologise –"

"Now, there's no need for any of that." Sir James looked back out into the hall, as if wondering whether he could make his escape yet. Instead he came in further, and lowered his voice somewhat as if to speak confidentially, though he also lowered his gaze to somewhere on the carpet. "Here's the thing. When I said the fellow was probably queer, I meant no harm by it. No doubt that's the wrong word to use. Don't be too quick to take offence that isn't meant."

Tom was gaping at the man, and even Hilary was too taken aback to come up with a polite response.

"What's the word to use nowadays, eh? Gay, is it? Old Thaddeus was probably gay – and he was living in less enlightened times, there's no denying that."

"No," Hilary managed to say. "Quite."

Tom drew breath, but subsided readily enough when Hilary glanced at him. Instead he half-turned back to the books spread across the table.

"No, quite, quite. Well, I'll leave you to it, shall I?"

"Thank you, Sir James," said Hilary.

"If you need to come back to get through all this, just organise it with Mrs Carew."

"Oh! Thank you very much."

The squire was out the door – but came back in before Tom and Hilary could do more than exchange looks both appalled and astonished. "No hurry, but ask for the car when you're ready to leave," Sir James added. "It'll be dark soon. I've asked Leonard to run you home."

"*Thank* you, Sir James, that's really very good of you."

"Quite, quite," the man was absently muttering as he left, closing the door behind him.

Hilary and Tom each sank down to their chairs, shared their astonishment for a moment – and then settled on being appalled.

"Why the *fuck* is he so fixated on Thaddeus being gay … ?" Tom asked in a disbelieving whisper.

"Do we know that he was?"

"No! Well, not that we know for sure he wasn't, either. We hardly know anything about him, really, and that sort of thing is notoriously difficult to pin down, historically speaking. The different cultural contexts, the different perspectives …" Tom mimed a one-handed zigzag that flew off into the unknown. "We're talking centuries ago."

"He would have been very discreet," Hilary ventured. "The act carried the death penalty in those days."

"Exactly!" Tom nodded at him significantly. "And you know how things have changed just within your lifetime, let alone since Thaddeus was sowing his wild oats." Tom sketched a grin. "I just don't get why his lordship is so fussed about whether the old priest's seed fell on barren ground or not."

"Well," said Hilary. "Perhaps we'd better look through a few more books before we outstay our welcome."

"Of course." Tom winked at him. "We can gossip tonight during the ad breaks."

Leonard seemed to be known only as Leonard because his Polish surname had about ten too many consecutive consonants for the English tongue to cope with.

"But I would like to try," Hilary offered, quite genuinely. After all, he'd successfully worked for decades with colleagues, and served borough residents, from a vast and occasionally bewildering range of cultures.

"Oh no, Mr Kent. It's not necessary."

"Then you had better call me Hilary instead."

"Yes, sir, Mr Kent. Thank you."

They were at the tower within moments; despite the fact that it was a particularly dark night, Leonard seemed to know every stretch and curve of the roads by heart. He drove daringly fast. But Hilary felt safe enough, so it was actually rather thrilling.

"Thank you very much, Leonard," Hilary said, clambering out of the passenger seat. The vehicle was a four-wheel drive, so there was a long drop down to the ground. Tom was suddenly there, however, offering a steadying hand and a strong embrace in which to fall … Hilary shook himself, and directed a few stern words towards his imagination.

"Ah, Mr Laurence?" said Leonard.

"Yes? Thank you for driving us."

"It's all right. Mr Laurence, Sir James told me to look at the old gardening records for you. I don't think they go back far, but I will let you know, yes?"

"Yes! Oh thank you, Leonard!"

"It's all right," the man repeated.

Hilary belatedly remembered the gift of whisky, and scrambled towards the front door. "Would you wait a moment, Leonard? Tom, don't let him leave."

When Hilary handed over the bottle, Leonard seemed rather stunned. When he found his voice, he said, "I can't accept that."

"Nonsense," Hilary said briskly. "Sir James accepted his."

Another moment passed. "Then I thank you very kindly, Mr Kent. Mr Laurence, I will call you."

"Thank you, Leonard!" And with that they said goodnight, and swung the vehicle's door closed, then watched as Leonard headed back up towards the Hall.

"That sounded promising," Hilary commented as he led Tom back into the tower. "I wonder what he'll find!"

Tom seemed rather discouraged, though. "I'm beginning to think we won't find anything. Or nothing significant. After Thaddeus left, it seems like the garden became nothing more than a hobby for successive gardeners and their families, or at best a vegetable garden for their own use."

"But it was kept going for centuries. Surely there'll be something … There has to be!"

Tom offered him a smile, but it was a rather pale one, and didn't reach his eyes. "Oh well, let's not worry about it for now. Shall we just have something easy for dinner? I could make an omelette, or something."

Hilary felt a happy smile suffuse his whole self. "Only if you can be bothered, Tom – but I love your omelettes!"

Tom's smile turned a bit wistful. "As long as there's *something* you love me for," he said as he headed up the stairs to his bedroom.

"There's something," Hilary murmured to himself. "There's everything …"

"What was that?" Tom called down. "Back down in a mo, all right?"

"All right, my dear!" And Hilary went to make himself useful, gathering the omelette makings from the fridge.


Tom was in a quiet and thoughtful mood that week. On the Thursday evening they ate their cod and chips and pineapple fritters in silence, waiting for the next *Midsomer* episode, 'Dead Man's Eleven'. Tom barely even sniffed in disdain when Barnaby remarked on the 'sexual deviancy' to be found in every Midsomer village.

The episode was set in Badger's Drift, and reintroduced a couple of the previous characters – including Charles, a young fellow dismissed by Troy as 'a bum boy'. It seemed that Charles was no longer 'on the game', as Troy put it, but performing honest work at the Hall, and helping out at the pub where he had a room. Tom seemed to be watching these developments with wary interest. However, it turned out that young Charles was an amateur blackmailer, and soon enough he was found dead with an old Nazi knife protruding from his back … Tom sighed, and metaphorically turned away. But he didn't even grumble about it, let alone launch into a tirade.

Instead, once the episode was over and Hilary had muted the sound, Tom asked as if from out of nowhere, "Why wouldn't you let me touch you as well?"

"Oh!" Hilary exclaimed in surprise. Had it really only been a week ago? It seemed an era had passed since then. For a moment Hilary was tempted to reach out and seek to touch Tom again. He wanted it so very much, and he knew the young man would welcome it … It belatedly occurred to Hilary that the laws enforcing an age of consent and the ethical codes governing the relationship between students and teachers, existed in part because *the younger person would want it, too* – and indeed want it with all the fierce passion of which their newly unfurling souls were capable. The laws were protecting the young not only from the inappropriate advances of their elders, but from what the young people themselves might want.

Not that Tom was underage. Far from it, in fact. Though still a student, he was an adult – and more than that, he was remarkably mature for someone only twenty-three years of age who had yet to make his way independently in the world. One received the impression that Tom Laurence knew who he was and where he stood, and there was little that might truly rock him.

"Hilary?" Tom prompted after a long silent while had passed. "Why wouldn't you let me?"

"Can you honestly question that?"

"I know you were feeling the same way, Hilary."

"Perhaps …" Hilary took a breath, and girded himself to combine an admission with an untruth. "Perhaps I didn't *want* to feel that way, though."

Tom just looked at him askance, knowing full well that was a lie. But he didn't call Hilary on it. He simply sighed, and pushed himself up to his feet. "I'm heading for bed," he announced, already on his way.

"All right," said Hilary, watching him go. He couldn't deny that his heart yearned for all the things that could never be.

A short while later, Hilary knocked gently at Tom's door, and when invited he went in bearing a steaming cup of Assam. "I thought you might like a cup of tea," he said, carefully looking only at the bedside table towards which he was walking.

"Thank you," said Tom.

The young man was still fully dressed, but for his shoes which were askew on the floor. Tom was still fully dressed, but he lay back on the bed in long-limbed abandon. And as he watched Hilary come closer, he put aside his book as if he cared nothing for it. And he simply waited. Lying there. Hilary knew that if he climbed onto the bed beside Tom, he'd be welcomed, he'd be warmed, he'd be held and touched and loved. He *knew* that.

"Goodnight, then," Hilary said, having managed to put down the tea without spilling any. He turned around and headed back towards the door.

Tom sighed. But he said, kindly enough, "Goodnight, Hilary."

And that was that.

## Twelve

Tom's thoughtful mood turned pensive over the following days. As he spent most of his time working away on his laptop, surrounded by books, Hilary pretended to himself that Tom's concerns revolved around his thesis. Of course he was soon proved wrong.

"Why are you okay with me living here?" Tom asked one afternoon.

The question fell into their shared silence and sent ripples lapping against Hilary's sense of comfort. He was sitting down the other end of the kitchen table from Tom, head bent over a book and a cup of tea. It was easy enough for Hilary to pretend for long moments that he was too caught up in the novel to have heard.

Tom wasn't fooled, of course. "You were so much the loner. You'd been living alone for so long. Yet within a couple of weeks of meeting me –"

"I know," said Hilary, gently cutting him off. "I know."

"Why, then?"

And of course Tom already knew the answer. He was pushing, for whatever reason, to have the truth spoken and acknowledged. Which was hardly surprising, Hilary ruefully reflected. What else could he have possibly expected from this young man when it was Tom's candour that had first attracted Hilary?

The answer was, of course, that Hilary had fallen in love, he was deeply in love, and that had changed everything.

"Hilary … ?"

"Tom, please don't insist on me answering. The only thing that really matters is that I am content to – I am *happy* to share my home with you. I could never have anticipated how easy it is to have your company here, day in and day out. Not just easy: rewarding." Hilary lifted a hand, finding another possibility as if plucking it from the air. "Perhaps I have simply been wrong all my life, and it took the rarest of things – a thoroughly *decent* young man – to make me realise."

Tom was quiet for a long moment, before saying in a subdued voice, "Thank you."

"Thank *you* for being such a good companion."

Another sigh was the only direct response. But then Tom said, "Would it be too much to ask to have Justin over for a day? I'm thinking Friday or Saturday. It's just that we'll have all the term papers to mark – and our office is tiny, and his flat isn't much better, and –"

"Of course that's all right."

"– this would be so much more comfortable. Really?" Tom asked as he caught up with Hilary's answer. "Are you sure you won't mind?"

Hilary huffed a laugh, and tried to tell himself it wasn't jealousy at the thought of Tom and Justin being alone in the other man's apartment all day – when really Hilary should be encouraging the two of them to spend time together. To grow together. Instead they'd be sitting here at Hilary's table, drinking Hilary's tea, and behaving themselves.

"That's perfectly fine," said Hilary.

"That's great! Thank you."

"My pleasure."

"And we haven't talked about Christmas yet."

"Ah." Hilary sat back, feeling a bit winded. After all of Tom's recent silences, now it was one thing after another! "Well," he said carefully, "I had assumed you would go home to your parents for Christmas. If you're worried about leaving me alone," Hilary continued, "there's no need. To worry, I mean." He didn't want Tom's pity, but Hilary was well used to spending Christmas on his own.

"No, it's more complicated than that."

"I see."

"Term ends on the tenth of December, right? And I've always spent a few days or a week with my mate Bevan once term ends. I think I've mentioned him? Anyway, he's asked me to go there, at least for a long weekend, and I thought I would …" Tom grimaced an apology to Hilary. "I was kind of assuming you'd appreciate some time to yourself. But if you'd rather I stayed –"

"No, of course that's fine," Hilary smoothly responded. "You mustn't let me interfere with your plans."

"And then Mum and Dad –"

"Of course you'll go on to them from your friend's place." Hilary nodded calmly, knowing he wouldn't see Tom for two or three weeks. It would be bleakest midwinter in all kinds of ways, but what else could he possibly expect?

"No, you see, they want a break this year. So they're coming here for Christmas on their way down to Cornwall."

Hilary stared at Tom in something like dread.

"I mean, not *here* here. They're staying at a hotel in town. This was all organised – well, back when they assumed I'd still be living in town, too. The hotel does a Christmas dinner we're booked in for, and all that. Mum's having a holiday from the cooking."

"I see," Hilary said rather faintly.

"D'you want to …" Tom had to gather himself and try again. "I was kind of hoping you'd want to meet them."

"Well –" Hilary started. And then stalled.

"I just mean –"

"As your landlord," Hilary supplied.

"And my friend," Tom stoutly asserted. "They don't need to know about … anything else."

"There *is* no anything else!"

"As far as they're concerned: absolutely."

Hilary just looked at Tom, and thought about all the drama they could cause with one little slip, one little hint. "Though I don't suppose," Hilary thought out loud, "that anyone is likely to assume that anything is going on."

"No," said Tom in clipped tones. "I don't suppose they will."

"It's hardly the sort of conclusion that anyone at all is going to jump to."

"No. Exactly. Not when even *you* can't seem to imagine it."

Hilary was gobsmacked. "There's forty-two years between us!"

Tom seemed infinitely cheered for some reason. "Forty-two, eh?" He added with a wink, "The meaning of life!"

"What?"

"Never mind. Obscure cultural reference."

Which was almost exactly Hilary's point. "You mean it's something only another young person would understand."

Tom had the grace to wince a little. "Not necessarily."

"I could be your grandfather!" Hilary protested.

"Well, fine! But I'm glad you're not."

Hilary was silenced again. He couldn't quite believe that Tom was actually talking as if a relationship between them were perfectly possible. He'd known they were both tempted to act on the affection that Hilary couldn't deny was mutual. He hadn't even considered the notion that Tom would see the whole thing as unproblematic. Unless the young man was all talk, of course. But that wasn't something Hilary could possibly test or even challenge.

There seemed to be nothing left to say after that. Nowhere they could go. After a while they each grudgingly returned to their occupations, though Hilary could hardly make out the words in his book, and Tom's typing was rather desultory and seemed quite random.

Eventually Tom said in very subdued tones, "Would you like to meet them, then? My parents."

"If you would like that, yes." Hilary looked up and met Tom's rather woebegone expression. "Yes, I would. I'd be honoured."

"Thank you."

"Perhaps they could come here – I mean, I couldn't offer a proper Christmas dinner, I've never even cooked one before – but if they would rather be in a home than a hotel for Christmas morning, or for the evening – Well, we can at least host a meal, you and I," Hilary offered. "Can't we?"

And his reward was a beautiful grin from this young man who owned Hilary's heart and soul. "That would be grand. I was hoping I could show them the garden. Thank you, Hilary."

"It will be my pleasure." And then he didn't even pretend to be reading, but simply sat there pondering the possibilities. It would be his first Christmas shared, other than with strangers in a Brighton boarding house, since Hilary's own parents had died.

Over the following days, though, Hilary became pensive, too. The more he thought about Tom's parents, the greater grew his misgivings. Not on his own behalf, nor in relation to him being introduced to them. But in relation to Tom.

If Hilary had first fallen in love with Tom for his candour, then what did it mean that Tom was now obliged to lie to his mother and father – by omission at least – about the true nature of his relationship with Hilary? It was no use quibbling over the fact that nothing very much had happened – because something *had* happened, something that could be seen in a very bad light. And even if Hilary was determined there would be no repeat of the encounter, he couldn't deny there were romantic and sexual elements to his friendship with Tom that went beyond anything the Laurences could possibly wish for their son.

Naturally, there could be no question of confessing all. The Laurences' peace of mind would be destroyed, and no purpose would be served. But what did that mean for Tom? If he was happiest living as an honest and open sort of fellow, then wasn't Hilary placing him in a truly invidious position? *Could* Tom lie to his parents? And did Hilary even *want* him to?

What with all this headache-inducing thinking happening, some things became rather clearer.

Hilary called a local solicitor's firm to make an appointment, and took the bus into town. Luckily it was on a day when Tom wouldn't know because he was already in town with his classes – though Hilary planned to plead the rather vague case of 'Christmas shopping' if caught.

It was time for Hilary to make a new will. Unlike Evelyn, Hilary had never thought of the distant remnants of his family in this regard, but had left all his possessions to charity. Now he wanted to leave everything to Tom.

The solicitor – a Ms Eliot – didn't even blink at being told this, but she did take a moment to consider. Eventually she asked Hilary in suitably neutral tones, "Is it possible, Mr Kent, that … this young man is taking advantage of you?"

"No. Oh, no, not at all."

"Or perhaps you feel … guilty about taking advantage of him, and you want to atone?"

Hilary stared at her, wondering whether everyone would see through him so quickly – and whether it was even going to be possible to keep anything at all secret from Tom's parents. But then, maybe this was the one situation in which Hilary could and indeed should be completely honest.

"I am in love with Tom," Hilary announced, startled to hear it said out loud even though he was the one speaking – "as you've surmised. Though of course nothing will ever come of it. And he is not the sort to take advantage. Tom is the most decent young man I've ever met, and knowing that came before the love. Do you see? It was a reason that I fell in love. His decency isn't something that I only saw or imagined I saw after I loved him."

"And what will Mr Laurence think of you doing this?"

"He'll be surprised, and wary, and he'll protest. But I'm an old man now, and there's no one else left in my life. That will no doubt seem very sad to you, but Tom isn't taking anything away from anyone in nearer relation to me. No one will challenge this."

She smiled, with a professional kind of warmth. "Forgive my questions, Mr Kent. You're my client, and so I take your interests to heart."

"I do understand, and I thank you for it. But he has been my friend, Ms Eliot. A quite unlooked-for friend, but a true one. In any case, if you want it in practical terms, Tom has an abiding interest in the garden, which has quite a history, and he can make the best use of it – and if he has the garden, then he should have the tower as well – and if he has both, then he will need the money to help him maintain it. I can't put it any plainer."

"There's no need to," she assured him with a rather more genuine smile. "Mr Laurence is very lucky to have found such a good friend."

She promised to have the new will drawn up within a few days, and she took some more details. When she asked who the executor should be, Hilary thought for a moment. The executor of his previous will had been a colleague who had also since retired, and moved to Bournemouth. Hilary wasn't sure that he even had the man's new address. In any case, no doubt it was time to choose someone else, and someone closer to Tom's age.

Ms Eliot offered, "You could appoint your bank, or even myself, Mr Kent. That might be the most straightforward option. Though," she added with a grin, "we do know how to charge for our services."

"And I'm sure you'd work very diligently to earn your fee," he replied in kind. But Hilary had had a better idea. It seemed obvious who the one person was who'd put Tom's interests ahead of his own. "I'd like to appoint Tom's tutor at the university, Dr Justin Ware. They are friends, as well as teacher and student, and Tom is also his teaching assistant. Is that appropriate? I would have to ask Dr Ware, of course, but I don't anticipate any problems."

"Perfect. Let me know when you've confirmed that, and then if you'd like to come back at the same time next week to sign this?"

"Perfect," Hilary concluded. He caught the bus home again that afternoon with a sense of a mission happily accomplished.

Just as happened the previous week, Tom was quiet and still while they watched *Midsomer Murders*, effortlessly keeping to his own side of the sofa.

The episode was called 'Blood Will Out'. It passed in a blur, as far as Hilary was concerned. After some huffing from Tom when Troy got offended at being called 'kinky', the young man was mostly silent. The story this time had to do with gypsies – "Travellers," Tom corrected, which Hilary knew but the term had lost all its romance. Gypsies, and Barnaby on a strict diet, was all Hilary could make out.

Just as last week, Tom challenged Hilary once the credits were rolling. He asked, in strangely peaceable tones, "Why won't you let me love you?"

"Oh Tom …" he chided, as if Tom were foolish to even mention the matter.

"I'll be going away in a week, and then my parents will be here not long after. I want you to answer me, and we're running out of chances."

"I've already answered you," Hilary said, "but you didn't like what I had to say. You don't really want answers. You want me to change my mind."

Tom guffawed at that, though without humour, and he rolled a glance at Hilary to acknowledge the point. "Tell me again, then, and I'll try to listen better."

Hilary let out a sigh. But of course it was a topic of endless fascination to Hilary himself, so who was he to argue? "Some things …" he ventured, "are even less forgivable than others."

Tom scowled a frown. "It's not a matter of what's forgivable or not."

"Isn't it?"

"Who is it that needs to forgive us, anyway?" Tom continued, a sullen kind of anger sparking in his tones. "We're not answerable to anyone, Hilary. This is between you and me!"

"The world wouldn't see it that way," he gently replied.

"Oh, *fuck* the world."

Hilary waited, but it seemed that Tom had no reasonable arguments to make. The young man sat there slumped and defeated, but his hands were tightly knotted fists resting on his thighs. Eventually Hilary said, "Justin will be here tomorrow, and –"

"Oh God! Will you stop going on about me and Justin!"

A beat passed before Hilary found his voice again, and mildly replied, "I only meant to wish you a good night's sleep. It sounds as if you'll have a very full day of marking."

Tom turned to him, full of chagrin. "Of course you did. I'm sorry. Look,

I'll go make the tea, all right? And then we can settle. You're right, we shouldn't have a late night."

And so the discussion was placed on hold yet again. Hilary was beginning to wonder how on earth he could finally end it.

# Thirteen

Justin knocked on the front door promptly at nine on the Friday morning. Tom helped him carry in two plastic storage boxes full of papers, and they got themselves set up down Tom's end of the kitchen table, while Hilary made tea. The two academics were already focussed on their task, quietly chatting back and forth in what seemed to be a familiar kind of shorthand, sharing a couple of amused predictions about what they would find in the papers.

When Hilary brought the tray of tea things over, though, Justin made the effort to politely ask after Hilary's health and his plans for Christmas. Hilary reassured him on the former, but wasn't quite sure what to say about the latter. He started to say something vague about having always been one for a quiet festive season – but then Tom rather succinctly explained that his parents coming to town, adding that he hoped they'd spend at least part of Christmas Day here at Riverside with Tom and Hilary.

"Oh, that's marvellous," Justin said with exactly the right amount of enthusiasm – though the glance he couldn't help but throw Hilary betrayed a moment's confusion, a pang of jealousy. Hilary nodded gently in response to what was said and in acknowledgement of what wasn't said. Justin ran a hand back through his hair, and made an effort to slip back into his previous focus. "Shall we get started then?"

"Sure," said Tom.

They soon fell into a rhythm. Hilary didn't inquire or interrupt them, but it seemed that they each read through the papers, pencilled notes, and then swapped to reread the paper and notes, and write out feedback for the student. Once Justin had signed off on this, Tom logged the results against a class list. Hilary meanwhile read a book, or pretended to read while actually watching the two younger men – or he pottered about, and made tea, until Justin finally broke ranks and asked if it was possible to have coffee instead.

Tom laughed. "I wondered how long you'd last!" He got up, and joined Hilary in the little kitchen, stretching tall beside him to reach the top shelf of one of the overhead cupboards; Hilary was too short to ever use those shelves. "Hilary, I got his favourite when I popped down the store the other day. I knew he'd crack eventually!" And Tom handed over a jar of instant coffee, with a luxurious label of black, red and gold.

Hilary contemplated the coffee for a moment, turning the jar around in his hands, and then he looked up into Tom's mischievous eyes. "How wicked you are!" he chided gently. "Letting our poor guest suffer, and making us appear to be the most heartless of hosts."

"Aw …" Tom seemed honestly chagrined. "Aw but, Hilary, I thought maybe you'd find wicked … rather appealing."

How wonderful and how awful all at once, that Tom should flirt with him so! Hilary huffed in mock disapproval, which he hoped masked his real discomfort. Justin didn't deserve to have the insult of Tom flirting with Hilary added to the injury of coffee withheld.

"*Some* kinds of wicked, perhaps," Hilary said in severe tones. "Now, show me how Justin likes his coffee made, and then you'd better get back to work!"

The two younger men took a break for lunch, and wandered together around the cleared area of the garden for a short while after eating their sandwiches. Otherwise, they worked diligently through the day.

When it got to seven o'clock, however, and Justin weighed up the last small pile of papers left to mark, his weariness abruptly became apparent. Even Tom seemed unnaturally subdued.

"It would be a pity to leave these for another day," Justin observed. "It's hardly enough to reconvene for, really. And they'd probably only take us another hour, if we kept on with it."

"Sure," said Tom, managing a smile but only just. "We can keep going."

"Sorry. I'm sure this isn't your idea of a fun Friday evening."

Tom huffed a laugh. "It's not so far off, actually."

"Why don't we have a break for dinner?" Hilary smoothly put in. "You can come back to these last papers a little fresher afterwards, and get them finished."

Justin looked keen but wary. "I really don't want to impose …"

"Nonsense," Hilary replied. While he had the makings of dinner in the fridge, he'd since had a far better idea. "Tom, perhaps you can quickly ride down to the village, and fetch us three rounds of cod and chips. They do them very well here," he reassured Justin.

"So I've heard!" Justin said, glancing in amusement at Tom.

"Sure," Tom agreed rather more enthusiastically. He got up and stretched. "Anyone need anything else while I'm down there?"

No one wanted anything else. Justin insisted on giving Tom enough cash to cover the meal, despite Hilary's protestations. And then Tom was gone, and the night quietly settled around them.

Justin was sitting there, staring at the next paper on the table before him, though Hilary thought that he wasn't really seeing it. After a moment, Justin said, "Am I wrong, Mr Kent? I get the impression that Tom's absence is a matter of convenience."

"It is, you're right. And I suppose we'll only have a few minutes." Hilary sighed, and sat down again at the table. "I won't beat about the bush. Dr Ware, I'm having a new will drawn up, and I was wondering if I could name you as the executor."

Justin was looking at him a little guardedly – which was fair enough, as it was a lot to ask when they weren't really more than acquaintances. "I should think you can take it that the answer is yes. But may I ask why?"

Hilary spread his hands flat on the table. "I'm leaving everything to Tom, you see. You mustn't leap to any untoward conclusions about anything going on. It is simply that he should have the garden, and therefore the tower, and therefore anything else that will help him maintain it all."

"I see."

"I know I can rely on you to take care of Tom's interests, and so I thought you would be the ideal choice."

Justin remained mute, watching Hilary as if uncertain of what should and shouldn't be said at this juncture.

Hilary ventured, very gently, "I know you feel a great deal of affection for him." He added, "As do I."

A nod acknowledged the former and accepted the latter with no compunction. "Are you sure, Hilary?" Justin finally asked. "About the will, I mean. Are you sure that's what you want to do? I wonder if it's in *your* interests to be so generous, when you've only known Tom for a few months."

Hilary smiled wryly. "How long was it before you fell in love with him?"

"Oh … Weeks. Days. Hours. Moments." Justin's smile echoed Hilary's. "You know how it is: love grows gradually from one thing to another over time. It changes and deepens. But I imagine the seeds of it were sown the first time I ever talked with him."

"Yes," said Hilary. "That's how it was with me."

"It is so unusual to find someone *that* intelligent, and *that* mature – who is also so honest and uncomplicated – at any age, let alone in someone who's still quite young. Well, I don't need to tell you … it was exhilarating to recognise something of who he is!"

"Yes. Exactly so."

Justin cast a shy frown at Hilary that displayed all his vulnerability. "There's no one else in the world I can talk to about this."

"I respect your position. Your reticence. I very much appreciate your honesty."

"Thank you. And … likewise."

"It won't be long now," Hilary reassured him, "and he won't be your student any more. You'll be able to … court him."

Justin smiled at what was no doubt a very old-fashioned notion. "Thank you for the thought, Hilary."

They heard the slight crunch of gravel from outside which meant that Tom had returned. The sounds of him leaning the bike against the wall, and locking it.

"Then you will?" Hilary quickly asked.

"It would be my honour," Justin averred. "I'm glad we can be friends, Hilary."

"Thank you, Justin. I'm very glad, too."

The remaining days flew by. Tom was madly busy – and so was Hilary, though even at the time he could hardly have explained with what. There was always the sense of important things to be said or done, with time running out, and never a chance to say or do them. Hilary couldn't have really said what those important things were, either, but the accompanying anxiety made him fretful. Maybe this was why he'd lived alone for so very long. To avoid days like these.

On the Thursday night, once they'd eaten their desultory way through their cod and chips and pineapple fritter, Tom snuggled back against Hilary for the evening, and Hilary turned towards Tom to make his embrace more encompassing. They hadn't allowed themselves this for what seemed too long a while now, but perhaps Tom needed it almost as much as Hilary did.

The next day, Tom would be leaving to visit his friend. And after that, he was indeed going to stay with his parents in Colchester. When his mother had asked, Tom later explained to Hilary with a woebegone face, he hadn't been able to come up with a good reason why not. He could work on his thesis at home as well as he could here, while his mum fed him and he caught up with his dad who'd be on leave. He could help them with the garden that he'd always loved. And she didn't seem to realise that he might actually want to refuse.

"Never mind," Hilary had replied. "I wasn't expecting to see you at all for weeks."

"We'll be here for Christmas, I promise. They're driving here on Christmas Eve, and I'll be coming with them. I'll get back here just as soon as I can."

"I know you will, my dear. I know you will."

Now they held each other pressed close, as if no longer able to dissemble. The *Midsomer Murders* episode played out. 'Death of a Stranger', it was called. There were fox hunts. Hilary couldn't have cared less about the story, but he wanted it to last forever, if that meant he could encircle Tom in his arms.

"I'll miss you, Hilary," Tom whispered fiercely a long while later.

"You'll have your friends, and your family …"

"I'll miss you *so much*."

"I know." Hilary pressed a gentle kiss to the precious head tucked in against his shoulder. "I'll miss you, too. Just as much, I assure you. But I want you to have fun, my dear. You have certainly earned a break, with how hard you've been working, and you must enjoy yourself."

"*Will* you miss me?"

"You know I will," he chided. "You know I'm not the loner I used to be."

"Oh, Hilary … *Hilary* …" There was an edgy silence then, until Tom finally burst out, "I wish you'd let me love you in all the ways I want to! I would never leave then. Never! Or … only if you came, too." The young man twisted around to look up at Hilary with a woeful humour patchy on his face. "You'd come, too, wouldn't you? Hilary?"

"Oh, Tom," he murmured helplessly. "Oh, my dear, *don't*."

"Why not?"

"You know we can't."

"Because of what the world would say?"

"Yes!"

"But the world doesn't even have to know!"

It seemed that Hilary's heart would break and break again over this young man. "You don't want to live with such a secret, Tom, and I don't want you to, either. For your sake."

Tom scowled, and turned around further within Hilary's arms. "I thought you'd understand! You've told me about how secretive you had to be when you were younger and it was illegal."

"But no one should have to live that way – certainly not any more. And most especially *you* shouldn't have to live that way, Tom. You should enjoy the freedoms you were born to."

Tom, always so transparent, thought for a moment, and then turned obdurate. "If I'm so free to live the way I want to, Hilary, then why can't I choose you?"

Hilary actually let out a moan of protest at that. It wasn't fair, it really wasn't, for him to have to argue so hard against the one thing he wanted more than air or food or water. After a moment, he ventured, "Maybe there's a reason why the world wouldn't understand. It's – it's perverse to choose me, when there's a man far closer to your own age who loves you probably every bit as much as I do, if not more –"

"Oh God! How can you even *say* that!" Tom had pulled away a little, and was staring at him wild-eyed. "Am I so utterly wrong about us, then? If you really loved me, you wouldn't be so keen to pass me off onto Justin, would you!"

Never mind that it had almost killed Hilary to speak those words. After a moment, he managed to say in wobbly yet reasonable tones, "If I felt a shallow, selfish kind of love then, no, I would take any opportunity I could to keep you for myself. But I love you more deeply than that, Tom, and so my interests are nothing compared to yours. I am thinking only of you."

And Tom, to Hilary's surprise and relief and only the tiniest hint of disappointment – Tom seemed to finally take this to heart. He drew away, and sat up by himself on the edge of the sofa, staring back at Hilary with wet eyes and a slightly snotty nose. Hilary had never seen anything more beautiful.

"My dear –"

"Well, maybe I'm the shallow, selfish sort," Tom forced out thickly, overriding him, "but I want to keep you for myself, Hilary. How you can say all that to me, and then expect me to walk away, I have no idea. Why wouldn't I want that kind of love in my life … ?"

"Tom …"

"I'm sorry. I'm going up to bed now." Tom stood, painfully dignified as if barely holding himself together. "I'm sorry. I'll be all right once I get back at Christmas. I promise. I won't keep hassling you."

"Oh, my dear," Hilary murmured, as confused and torn and maddened as he'd ever been. If Tom had argued any further, Hilary would have been his. Hilary suspected he already was Tom's, if Tom had but realised it. However, Hilary seemed to have argued so well that Tom felt he had to withdraw from the field.

"Goodnight, Hilary," Tom managed.

And he sounded so unhappy, and in such desperate need of escaping and regrouping, that Hilary had to let him go. "Goodnight, Tom."

Tom nodded, and headed towards the stairs.

"No doubt," offered Hilary, "things will seem clearer in the morning."

Tom had paused to listen to this tawdry pearl of wisdom. "I hope so," he said, muffled. And then he turned away.

# Fourteen

They were both subdued over breakfast the next morning, and Tom seemed rather morose. They didn't meet each other's eyes, and Tom didn't eat more than a slice of toast, or drink more than a cup of tea. As soon as he was done, he slung on his backpack and picked up his holdall, and Hilary walked him to the front door.

They paused there. Despite the fact that Tom was so much taller than Hilary, the young man's head was down and shadowed, so Hilary couldn't make out very much of his expression. Eventually Hilary reassured him – or no doubt more to the point, reminded himself – "It's only for a couple of weeks."

"Two weeks and a day," Tom corrected him, "until Christmas Eve. It'll be better then."

"Yes," said Hilary, though he hardly knew to what he was agreeing. "Of course it will."

Tom let the holdall fall to the floor, and stepped forward to encompass Hilary in a great hard hug. "I'm sorry," the young man mumbled. His face was tucked in against Hilary's head, so that it seemed his voice was conveyed directly to Hilary's ear via the husky vibrations. "I'm not handling this very well, am I?"

"No worse than I am," Hilary assured him. "In fact, probably far better."

"All right." Tom pressed a rough kiss to Hilary's hair, and then pulled away. A moment later he was outside and pulling the door shut behind him, and then he was gone, walking into the village to catch the bus into town and then the train station. And he'd be gone for two weeks and one day.

Hilary sighed, and turned away. Made himself another cup of tea and took it out the back door to stand on the terrace and contemplate the garden. After a while he went back in, sat at the table, and contemplated Tom's books and other gear all neatly arranged at the far end of the living area.

Tom would be back. This wasn't goodbye yet.

As Hilary had promised Tom – though he'd hardly believed it himself at the time – things did indeed begin to seem clearer that day, and became clearer still in the quiet empty days that followed. Perhaps it was Hilary who'd needed the sharper perspective brought by time spent alone. Perhaps Tom was the one who'd been in the right all along.

Hilary had plenty of time for thinking as he pottered about cleaning the ground floor rooms, tidying and rearranging them with the thought of receiving a pair of real visitors for Christmas. And the more he thought about it, the more Hilary asked himself who he was to deny this mutual affection that had grown between himself and Tom, quite unbidden.

Of course it had taken Tom's absence to make Hilary realise all that he was now missing. Not only Tom's presence and his cheerful companionship, but his fondness for Hilary, even his – Well, Hilary thought, forcing himself to be realistic. It wasn't so much Tom's *desire*, for how could Tom desire Hilary? It was more Tom's willingness for Hilary to play a part in fulfilling Tom's desires.

Once the ground floor was as neat and fresh as he could make it, Hilary started on the first floor, which of course contained their bedrooms. It would have been impossible not to think about Tom and love and sex while cleaning the young man's bedroom, even if Hilary didn't have all too clear a memory of that night, a week after Hilary had touched him, when Tom had lain here on the bed in loose-limbed abandon, waiting for Hilary to join him. And all Hilary had done was leave a cup of tea on the bedside table, and walk out.

Hilary didn't entirely understand why Tom would have welcomed him then and would welcome him still, but perhaps a mutual sense of trust and comfort might explain it. An instinctive sense of relaxation each in the company of the other. And, on Tom's side at least, a willingness to turn a blind eye to all the personal defects and blemishes in his lover. Perhaps such generosity did exist.

Hilary spent a day packing up some of the old junk that still cluttered Tom's bedroom, and then made the effort to haul one box each day up the stairs to store on the second floor. In turn, he brought down an attractive green glass vase that he'd found hidden away in his own bedroom. Once properly washed, it looked rather lovely on the wide windowsill near the kitchen table. Hilary also picked out what he thought was the best of the framed pictures stacked against the wall in Tom's room, and brought it down to clean and then hang on one of the empty hooks in the front room. Hilary had always felt at home here, even in the bare-boned early days, but now the place was beginning to look the part as well.

For that matter, Hilary reflected, Tom had always seemed quite at home here, too. Hilary wondered if Tom would live here once he'd inherited the place, or if by then Tom and Justin would have a home of their own in which they felt settled. The Riverside tower could then become Tom's retreat, or their holiday home, perhaps, or Tom could rent it out for some extra income. Hilary pondered the possibilities, and wondered if he would at some stage in the future dare to ask what Tom's intentions were. It would be comforting for Hilary to spin himself a tale or two about Tom's future happiness, and he didn't doubt that once Tom had got over the shock of the intended inheritance, he'd instinctively know what he wanted to do with it all.

Actually, Hilary thought it undeniable that Tom knew his own mind in so many areas of life; Tom was perfectly competent both intellectually and emotionally. And while he was still a young man, he had come of age in legal terms. He was certainly well past the age of consent. So, Hilary pondered throughout one long quiet afternoon, if Tom had decided for whatever reasons that he could enjoy a relationship with Hilary for this little while, then really what was the point in Hilary being so restrained?

Hilary himself loved Tom in ways he'd never loved before in his life. It wasn't that he'd never felt attracted to anyone else or that he hadn't cared for them. But the feelings had never before gone so deep, nor indeed been founded in such a satisfying friendship.

When the phone rang at ten the next morning, Hilary's heart started pounding, and while he answered in quite a sane and rational manner, the words 'I'm such an old fool, Tom, I love you' were waiting to spill off his tongue at the slightest provocation.

It wasn't Tom, however, but Sam Reynolds offering to deliver a Christmas tree himself, if Hilary wasn't already sorted and wouldn't mind buying one to benefit the local Bedwyn scout group.

"Oh!" Hilary blurted. "Do you know, I'm so used to living alone that I haven't bothered with a tree since I was a child."

"Never mind, then, Mr Kent. I don't mean to impose!" Sam seemed quite ready to say farewell and hang up.

"No, no. I should have one. Tom will like it, I'm sure, and his parents will be visiting."

"Well, only if you're sure."

"I'm sure. Thank you for the offer!"

When Sam and his late-teens son Samuel arrived with the tree that afternoon, they helped Hilary set it up in the front room, and then also handed over a small grocery bag containing some pre-loved tinsel and baubles in reds and golds.

"We thought, if you don't usually have a tree …" Sam offered.

"How marvellous!" said Hilary, feeling quite gobsmacked by this thoughtfulness.

"To be honest, I think Julia – the missus – is glad of the excuse to be rid of them. She's going for a newfangled colour scheme this year. Blue, purple and silver, or some such thing. Not very Christmassy, if you ask me, but she seems to like it."

Hilary smiled in sympathy with Sam's bewildered scepticism, but said, "That sounds rather marvellous, too. Please thank her for me. This is really all very much appreciated."

"Will do, Mr Kent."

Hilary was left to arrange the tinsel and baubles in what he hoped was a vaguely pleasing manner. No doubt Tom would help sort it into something more artistic on his return.

*Tom* … Hilary indulged himself in saying the name out loud. "Tom …" A simple enough name, prompting a constant tide of deeply felt emotion. Surely, Hilary reflected, this kind of love demanded its due.

In a slightly maddened state of euphoria, Hilary consulted with Marjorie about menus, recipes and supplies for Christmas dinner. Hilary would have had to make three or four trips to carry it all back home in his satchel so, for an extra pound, Marjorie organised to have one of the local lads deliver his order later that day, and then the perishables on the twenty-third.

The time without Tom passed slowly but steadily.

Hilary watched the *Midsomer Murders* episode alone, with his spare pillow encompassed in his arms, most of the details of the story lost in daydreams of pressing kisses to Tom's hair. It seemed rather a confusing story, in any case, and wasn't called 'Blue Herrings' for nothing. In a darker moment, Hilary reflected on the fact he would have been uncomfortable watching the episode with Tom, as it was set in a 'nursing home for the elderly', and there was no denying that Hilary was somewhat closer in age to the residents than he was to Tom. The point was made even clearer when

Troy declared one of the residents a 'poofter', and mentioned how nervous he'd seemed around a detective; Barnaby said he wasn't surprised, as being gay had been a crime when the man was young.

For a while, Hilary wondered whether Tom was also watching the episode, on his own or with his parents, and whether he identified Hilary with the 'elderly', whose lives were winding down, and who seemed so unwanted by their young relatives … But such notions were unnecessary. Tom was too kind a man to think so poorly of someone who at least was a friend. Whom Tom himself had declared love for. It was entirely unnecessary, and there were certainly happier thoughts with which Hilary could occupy his mind.

That night in bed Hilary realised too late that he'd left the spare pillow downstairs. He felt even lonelier without it, so got up despite the fact he had worked himself deep under the covers and had already warmed up. As he padded in his slippers past Tom's open door, he had a wickedly better idea, and instead crept in to borrow Tom's pillow. He fell asleep curved longingly in his own bed with the slight scent of Tom pressed against his face.

*I'm such an old fool, Tom, I love you …*

Yes, Hilary concluded, this kind of love demanded its due. So perhaps Hilary should pay it, and then when the time came he would let Tom go as he'd always known he must. It would be harder than he could even imagine, he was certain of it, but at least once he was over the worst of the pain, he would have the sweetest of memories to hold dear.

The time without Tom slowly passed.

# Fifteen

The time passed, and then suddenly it was Christmas Eve, and a car was pulling up outside – Hilary's heart was pounding, and it wasn't wrong, it wasn't wrong. Tom was clambering out of the back seat, looking for Hilary waiting there on the steps, Tom's gaze seeking him out, Tom's brow knotted in an unhappy frown – and then Tom turned disbelieving for a moment when he saw Hilary, and then Tom began *grinning*, Tom was grinning at him fit to burst with happiness. The truth was written all over Hilary's face for those who wanted to read it, and in response Tom seemed to soar. 'Yes,' they seemed to say to each other. 'The answer is *yes*.'

But then of course Tom's parents were also getting out of the car, and Hilary needed to sober up enough to greet them in a more acceptable manner. But that was all right, for he knew that this precious gift of love was such a fragile thing. He must keep it safe for its own sake to allow it to thrive, like an exotic plant in its own little glasshouse – and more importantly than that he must protect Tom. Nothing ignoble must attach itself to this wonderful young man. Nothing must harm him in any way.

And so Hilary stepped forward and instead of hugging his love, he said, "Welcome back, Tom, I trust you had a marvellous holiday."

"Yes, thanks, it was grand," Tom replied – and if the back of his hand happened to caress the back of Hilary's as they passed, then no one was any the wiser.

"How do you do, Mrs Laurence, Mr Laurence? I'm Hilary Kent."

Tom's father shook his hand. "How do you do, Mr Kent?"

"I hope your trip has been uneventful."

"Thank you, yes," replied Tom's mother. "Mr Kent, it's a pleasure to meet you at last. Tom's talked of almost nothing but his new home here, and you, and the garden …"

"Has he indeed?" Hilary smoothly asked as if politely sceptical of such polite nonsense. Except that Tom winked at him behind his parents' backs as he ushered them in, and Hilary knew it was all true, and his heart gambolled along like a spring lamb.

They were all on first-name basis as soon as there was breath for it. Tom showed his parents Dulcie and Eric the garden while Hilary made tea and set it up in the front room with a platter of shortbread and mince pies.

"All shop-bought, I'm afraid," Hilary confessed.

"Thank heavens for that!" Dulcie exclaimed. "I don't know anyone who makes their own these days, though I did use to, years ago when Tom was a boy. And now look at us! Eating our Christmas dinner at a hotel!"

"If there's any chance of you dining here instead … Hilary offered diffidently. "I'm sure it won't be anywhere near as fine, but you'd be very welcome."

There was much said on one side of not wanting to impose, and on the other of it being a pleasure; a counteroffer was made of spending either the morning or the evening at Riverside; but soon enough it was settled that the Laurences would return late in the morning and stay for an early-afternoon dinner. Upon which agreement, Dulcie made their excuses, and said she and Eric would get out of the way, unless there was anything they could do to help; but Hilary protested it was all in hand, and of course Tom said he'd be there to do anything that was needed.

Then there was the fuss of Tom fetching his luggage from the car, and the Laurences making their farewells before driving into town. When Tom came in from seeing them off, Hilary was standing before the Christmas tree contemplating the presents that had suddenly appeared at its foot. Two of them appeared to be addressed to Hilary himself: one from the Laurences, which looked like a book, and one from Tom – which was a box rather larger though perhaps somewhat lighter, and might be anything.

"What have you done?" Hilary murmured as Tom came to stand by him. Everything had been going surprisingly well, but now it felt as if Hilary were back on shaky and unknown ground. He hadn't even thought of presents – at least, not for Christmas – and even if he had he wouldn't have the first clue what to give Dulcie and Eric.

Maybe Tom didn't hear him or realise the significance, for all he did was comment cheekily, "Went with minimalism for the decorations, did you?"

Hilary cast him an imploring look. "I didn't even have any, but Sam Reynolds' wife Julia took pity on me and sent me her discards."

Tom considered Hilary for a long moment, and seemed to add up the whole story. "Oh, that's so cool of her! Never mind. We can make a couple of paper-chains or something, yeah? Or maybe there's some decorations stashed away upstairs that we haven't found yet."

"Tom –" Hilary began in a rather fraught voice.

"I know," Tom softly replied. His hand slipped into Hilary's and their fingers dovetailed while they stood side by side and stared at the tree. "You've changed your mind, haven't you? I saw it in the way you looked at me when I arrived."

"You haven't changed *your* mind, then?" Hilary asked, hardly daring to even glance at the young man, though they both knew it was a rhetorical question.

"No." Tom squeezed his hand in reassurance. "Hilary? Will you let me kiss you now … ?"

He wasn't so proud that he didn't groan a little with sheer wanting. However: "There's something I need to do first."

"Of course," Tom said lightly.

"Here, come through to the kitchen and sit down. We need to talk. Shall I make some more tea?"

"If you like." Tom had already turned away to begin regathering the used tea things from the coffee table. "But there's no use in trying to talk me out of loving you again. It's *way* too late now! You know that, right?"

"I know that, Tom," Hilary agreed. "Thank you." And they exchanged a look in which all the important things were finally settled between them. Hilary knew he had the best six months of his life to live now.


They sat in their usual places at the kitchen table with Tom at the head and Hilary round the corner to his left. Tom seemed too happy to be impatient, but he was a little jittery. It put Hilary in mind of the day they'd first met, when Tom had been so nervous in asking about the garden. Well, Hilary was about to put that subject to rest once and for all.

Hilary took the folded legal paperwork from the tray of tea things, and turned it over in his hands. He'd thought of ten different ways of starting this conversation, but none of them seemed particularly useful or clever now, so he would have to do this in his usual way, which was to blunder blindly ahead.

"Tom, I want to give you this, and talk it through as much as we need to. Before anything – Well, before anything happens, or doesn't happen. Anything further, I mean. Or not," he added lamely, valiantly trying not to presuppose.

Tom was looking at him expectantly, with a kindly interested smile. It seemed he really didn't have a clue what was coming, or even realised how closely it involved him.

"I want everything clear and above board, you see. So that there's never any question. If anything happens between us, then it's only because we want it to. There'll be no complications. Or as few as possible."

"Hilary," said Tom, his smile dampening a little, "I thought we'd finally agreed –"

"Well, yes –"

"– that *we're in love.*"

Even now happiness sank peacefully through him to hear it spoken of with such certainty. "We are," Hilary dared to concur – and he reached for Tom's hand and held it there between them on the table, while Tom's smile brightened again and Hilary's smile matched it. "But whether we are or not, and whether anything comes of it or not, *this stands.*" He proffered the paper, but didn't yet give it to Tom. "This will stand, my dear, no matter what happens today, tomorrow, next summer, or at any time through whatever years remain to me. So we will both know that anything more between us is something freely chosen."

Tom had begun frowning a little during the middle of that, and he now reached for the folded papers as if needing to work out this puzzle. Before he opened them up, however, he met Hilary's gaze and said very levelly, "It always *was* freely chosen."

"Indulge me, then. Humour me. For the sake of me having a relatively clear conscience."

The frown grew a little, and Tom started reading. For the first seven words, he was concentrating so hard that his lips shaped the words – but then after a sharp glance at Hilary, Tom simply scanned the rest, a scowl growing.

'THIS IS THE LAST WILL AND TESTAMENT of me HILARY KENT of Riverside, Bourne Road, Nether Bedwyn, Wiltshire. I REVOKE all earlier Wills and testamentary dispositions made by me. I WISH my body to be cremated and the remains buried in the garden at Riverside or in the countryside nearby. I APPOINT DOCTOR JUSTIN WARE of Flat 10, 23 Blackthorn Lane, Marlborough, Wiltshire to be the sole Executor and

Trustee of this my Will. … I GIVE the residue of my estate … to my dearest friend THOMAS DALE LAURENCE in recognition of his decency, candour, wit and affection …'

"Hilary," said Tom in hard tones, "you can't *really* think I love you for the sake of the garden, can you? This is completely unnecessary!"

"It is what I want to happen when I die," Hilary replied very steadily, "no matter what else happens or doesn't happen between us before then."

"But – No! And Justin … ? You talked about this with *Justin*?"

"Whenever this comes into effect, Justin will know where to find you, and I know he'll take care of your interests as well as I could want him to."

"But –" Tom stared at Hilary rather wildly.

"If people find out about us," Hilary continued, "as they may well do no matter how careful we are, I want to be able to say that all such matters had been agreed beforehand. That there was no question of taking advantage."

"Who, you or me?"

"Either of us."

"Hilary –" Tom stared some more, and finally dropped the will on the table out of their way as if he really didn't care about it – then threw up his hands in exasperation. "Fine. You know what? You do what you want with your property. You're perfectly entitled. You *must* know I'm grateful, Hilary, but I've never had any expectations. I've always known I have to make my own way. So if you change your mind –"

"I won't."

"– I'd understand."

"I won't. The garden will be yours, and therefore the tower, and therefore the rest. And there's no one else. No one with any claim whatsoever, let alone a better one. But even if there were –"

"Fine," Tom repeated shortly. Then he took a breath, and looked at Hilary askance. "And you? Are you mine as well?"

"Yes," said Hilary, suddenly breathless.

"Because that's *really* all I care about," Tom grumbled. "Can I kiss you now? If you've finally acquitted your conscience?"

"Yes."

"Good!" And at last Tom leaned in across the table, and proceeded to do just that.

It wasn't the most spectacular kiss. Even Hilary knew that. It was clumsy.

They had yet to really take each other's measure, get a feel for each other's rhythm. But the kiss was too determined to allow room for any doubt, too passionate for either of them to feel daunted by what was ahead.

When Tom finally broke away, he said, "Can I take you to bed now? Is that too weird, in the middle of the afternoon? I don't want to wait any longer!"

"I don't want to wait, either," said Hilary.

"Oh thank God for that," Tom replied in fervent tones.

"In fact," said Hilary, standing, and letting Tom take his hand to lead him to the stairs, "if it weren't for the turkey I need to put in the oven in the morning, I'd be perfectly happy to stay in bed from now right through to tomorrow afternoon – as long as you were there, too!"

"Amen," Tom said, and paused to take Hilary's face in both hands and kiss him again. "I'm *so* in love with you," he declared. "Come to bed!"

Hilary went with his heart tripping giddily.

Tom led him to Hilary's room. Not that Hilary minded either way, but he raised an eyebrow to ask the question, and Tom shrugged. "You've got the bigger bed," he explained – before adding with a wink, "not to mention plenty of elbow room."

They seemed to naturally drift apart as they entered the room. Tom heeled off his shoes while Hilary sat on the side of the bed to undo his and put them aside. Then he sat up again, and confessed, "I'm very nervous about this part."

"Are you?" Tom hauled off his own sweater, and then clambered onto the bed beside Hilary, kneeling there tall and towering over him. "What exactly … ?"

Despite asking the question, Tom wrapped an arm around Hilary's chest from behind, and was now encouraging him back further onto the bed. They were still fully clothed and on top of the covers. Hilary didn't question any of that, but instead went with it.

"What are you nervous about, Hilary? If there's something we shouldn't do – or should do – you can tell me."

"No, I'm nervous about you seeing me undressed, of course. You are so very beautiful, Tom, and even if I was when I was your age – which I wasn't – I'm long past it now."

"None of that matters," Tom whispered huskily. He hauled Hilary closer still, and then Hilary was lying back on the bed cradled in Tom's arms, and they were warmly spooning. It was the most delightful thing, even though Hilary had expected them to be face to face at this point, and kissing. "You think I care about any of that?"

"You'd be a very unusual person if you didn't." Hilary sighed in surrender as Tom encompassed him further still. "But then, I was forgetting for a moment that you *are* an unusual person, Tom."

"If I'm nervous about anything, it's how very ordinary I am, and you thinking I'm beautiful and unusual. But I like you, just the way you are, and you seem to like me …"

"I do like you, I *do*, so very much – but how can you – ?"

"Hush …" Tom tucked his head in close, and murmured in Hilary's ear. "Don't worry about that. First, I owe you one. I'm going to do to you what you did to me not so long ago. Just like this, all right? I'm going to touch you, and make you come. I hope it feels as good for you as it did for me …"

Tom's hand had already found its way down into Hilary's trousers, and now took his hungrily solid flesh in a firm grasp, began a steadily devastating rhythm. Hilary couldn't help himself; he moaned wantonly, and reached an arm back over his head to run over Tom's hair, to press Tom closer still. His entire body twisted and turned in place, stretching and arching as if he were still a limber twenty-something.

"That's it, that's it," Tom was whispering fiercely. "Man, I *knew* you'd be something. As soon as I saw those great strong virile hands of yours, I *knew* how it would be."

Hilary let out something that was close to a whimper, and thrust up to meet Tom's hard caress. It was all going to be over in an embarrassingly short time, but no doubt it was better to be done too quickly than not at all. "Tom," he muttered gutturally. "Tom …"

"I'm here. I'm here with you, Hilary. *Fuck*, you're something. God, *God*, I've been wanting this …"

And Hilary, who'd been wanting this, too, cried the young man's name once more, and suddenly it was upon him – rather shocking in some ways but not devastating after all, and his cry became a happy sob – it was sweet, so very sweet these crashing waves of pleasure that ran through him – and sweeter still was his love's embrace, and his love's echoing moans.

Not to mention his love's fervent promise: "Hilary … Hilary … Oh man, that was awesome. But let me know when you're good to go again, and I'll make it more awesome still."

They lay there together for a lovely warm while, simply enjoying the embrace and the fact that they *could* embrace. Sharing their smiles. But then Tom started pulling away.

"Don't go," said Hilary, clutching at Tom's arm. "Please don't go."

"I'm not going anywhere," Tom said with a chuckle. "Haven't you realised that by now?" He swung up to kneel beside Hilary, and began unbuttoning his own shirt. Soon his chest was bared, and Hilary enjoyed looking now that he was allowed to. Tom was slim, but he had nicely proportioned shoulders, and he looked fit in the way an active young man might. Dark hair embellished his breastbone.

"I must be a very shallow man compared to you," Hilary observed. "I can't say that I don't like your body."

Tom just laughed, and started unbuttoning Hilary's shirt. "You're allowed to!" he said as if this were all very amusing. "It's not the only thing you like about me, right?"

"Not the only thing, no."

"And you'd probably still like me even if I looked different."

"Yes, Tom," Hilary assured him with a smile. "I'd still like you very much indeed."

"Well, there you go! Enjoy it while you can. Some attractions are all too transitory."

"I am rather aware of that just now," Hilary said with heavy irony. Nevertheless, he sat up to allow Tom to help him off with his shirt – and then he was bare-chested, too. Hilary lay back, and looked up at Tom with some trepidation.

Oddly, Tom was looking down at him with an interest just as eager as Hilary's in Tom. "You're a handsome man, Hilary, and you look how you *should* look after six-and-a-half well-lived decades. There's no shame in any of that."

"You are very kind," said Hilary, watching while Tom began unbuttoning and unzipping his jeans. "And no doubt very wise."

"And … ?"

"And … I *do* like your body," Hilary confessed, as even more of it was revealed.

Finally they were both naked, and Tom was still kneeling there beside Hilary as they each drank in the sight of the other. Unlike Hilary, Tom seemed completely unselfconscious. He knelt with his thighs wide and his cock hanging heavily engorged and the weight of his balls just behind – while Hilary lay there anxious, and only just managing not to cover himself up again with hands or clothes or bedcovers. But Hilary's tension gradually eased as he watched Tom watching him; as Hilary realised that the younger man truly did have a wisdom beyond his years. For Tom didn't once flinch as he looked with clear eyes at Hilary's old body, gazing upon it hungrily as if it were just as desirable as his own supple strength and smooth skin. Hilary's pent-up breaths slowed and deepened.

After a while, Tom's cock stirred impatiently, and at last the young man leant in to kiss Hilary again, then press mouthy kisses down Hilary's breastbone, swathe a path down Hilary's belly with his tongue, nudge a trail through rough grey curls with the tip of his nose – until finally Tom was nuzzling his face, his whole beautiful face, against the sensitivities of Hilary's genitals and the tender skin of his thighs. Tom explored there quite happily, already becoming more familiar and more intimate with Hilary than anyone else had ever troubled themselves to be, while Hilary wallowed in the pleasure, moaning his appreciation, abandoning at last any wish for propriety. He reached a hand to encourage Tom closer and return the favour in kind – but the young man shifted his nethers away so that Hilary must content himself with tracing the graceful line from his shoulder down his ribs to his waist, the sharp curve of his hip, and the lean strength of his thigh.

Despite Tom receiving his pleasure so indirectly, after a lovely while they were each of them as hard as the other. Tom lifted up a little to look at Hilary, his eyes summer-bright. "What d'you want me to do?" he asked, his tone entrancingly, promisingly rough. "What would you most like?"

"What would *you* like to do?" Hilary countered. "You must take your turn, my dear."

"Just your hand. Just your wonderful hands on me would be – so fuckin' awesome."

Hilary chuckled, and looked again at these hands – surely no better than serviceable – of which Tom seemed to be so fond. "Come up here, then," Hilary said. "I want to hold you in my arms while I touch you. I want to feel you against me – *all* of you."

Tom obligingly stretched out beside him and pressed up close, kissing him, holding him, those arms and hands and legs blessing him, the arch of Tom's foot running down Hilary's shin … All of that long limber body caressing him, just as he'd asked. And then a wicked promise in his ear: *"I'll do anything you want, Hilary."*

"Oh …" he groaned, wondering what on earth he could have done in this life to have ever earned an offer of such bounties. But now was not the time. Even if there would never be another chance, this was the time for the sweet directness of simplicity. Hilary caressed Tom's hair, and held him tight before releasing him far enough to return his hot gaze. "I'm enjoying just being with you so very much, my dear. Let's leave the complexities for now."

And so he made love to Tom, and Tom couldn't seem to resist but must make love to Hilary as well, each with a hand on the other, kissing ardently, with Tom shifting beautifully beside him. When the end came again, Hilary lost himself in Tom's sky-blue gaze, and the intense pleasure ebbed through them both, bringing the profoundest sense of peace.

They each got up to go to the bathroom, and then met again under the covers this time. Snuggled up warm, they both dozed for a while, with Tom wrapped up around Hilary, who'd never felt so treasured. He'd forgotten how magical the simple feel of skin against skin could be. As they woke again, Tom was already pressing against Hilary, his hips already rocking in a gentle rhythm, as if he were listening only to his physical instincts.

"Hilary, *God* …" Tom was murmuring. "Please – Please, I want to …"

The younger man arranged them both so that Hilary was on his back, and Tom was lying half over him, his cock hard against Hilary's hip. Hilary happily cooperated, his body stretching and shifting to fit snugly against Tom's, even while Hilary murmured in reply, "Of course, my dear … But you'll forgive an old man, if I don't –"

Tom tensed into stillness, then dropped a kiss to Hilary's cheek more affectionate than impassioned. "Oh. Sorry. Of course I won't, then."

"I want you to."

"I'm not that selfish!"

Hilary looked at him impatiently. "You *can* be, you know, and I'll be *just* as selfish. Do you think I won't take great pleasure in you taking your pleasure? Tom, you must do whatever you want with me."

And so he did.


Later, Tom went down to make tea and sandwiches, and brought them up a tray. Hilary sat up in the bed, leaning back against the piled pillows and the headboard with the sheet discreetly pulled up past his waist, while Tom sat cross-legged facing him, quite unashamed of his exposure. He might have seemed unconscious of it, too, except that he caught Hilary looking, and winked and said, "That's for pudding."

Hilary laughed, but then sobered and said, "Can we talk about more prosaic matters, however briefly?"

"Of course. Whatever you want."

"Your parents –"

"It's all right," Tom immediately assured him. "I won't tell them what's happened. I've already said enough about, you know, an affectionate friendship to explain how happy we are together. Although …" Tom winced. "I think I kind of outed you in the process. Sorry!"

Hilary blanched and went a bit cold.

"It's all right, though!" Tom scrambled to reassure him. "It's all right. They've always been so cool about me being gay. I never even had to come out to them; we just kind of figured it out together. And they've never so much as hinted that they wished I was any other way. So when I said vague things about you and me clicking together, and having so much in common, I think they just kind of leapt to that conclusion. You know?" he finished rather lamely.

"Actually, I don't know. I can hardly even imagine! I'll have to take your word for it, Tom, that that's how things work these days." Hilary pondered for a moment. "To be honest, I'm glad you didn't tell me that before meeting them, but it *did* go well, didn't it? They didn't seem to mind."

"Of course they don't mind. And they really don't need to hear about anything else that's happened between us."

Hilary took another moment with that. "We might need to revisit this subject in the near future, Tom, when I've had a chance to get used to it all! But for now," he said, "I was actually thinking of a far more prosaic matter than that."

Tom chuckled. "Sorry! Tell me, then."

"I was simply wondering about Christmas presents. I hadn't got that far at all. I had no idea they'd bring me anything."

"Oh, *that's* all right," Tom airily replied. "It's not like they expect anything in return. Especially with you having us all here for dinner."

"Even so –"

"They'll consider it a thank you!"

"Even so, I'd like to give them something," Hilary insisted. "Though it must be too late to shop for it." He had vague thoughts about not spending the rest of Christmas Eve in bed after all, but instead taking the bus into town. Then he looked at Tom again, and couldn't bear the thought of tearing himself away and putting on clothes.

Tom had been thinking. "Well … maybe there's some hidden treasure you can unearth. That green vase downstairs is new, isn't it? Or newly found, anyway."

"Newly found – in this very room."

"If there was anything more like that around here that you wouldn't mind parting with, my mum loves that kind of thing. Any kind of fancy glassware … They organise holidays around places like Murano in Venice, you know? And you should see us at home! Glassware *everywhere*. Once I was old enough not to accidentally break anything, she went kind of mad. And it looks great, it's so colourful, but she spends half her life dusting."

Hilary thought he knew where he could find just the thing, so he thanked Tom and put that problem aside for now. Once they were done with the tea things, Tom got up to put the tray safely on the far bedside table. Then he hesitated for a moment.

"This has all been very decadent, hasn't it!" said Hilary. "Shall we get up now, do you think? No doubt there's things you want to do to settle back in."

Tom favoured him with a lovely smirk. "You're the only thing I want to do, Hilary. But while we're waiting for round three or whatever, I know where to find some nice coloured paper. D'you want to make paper-chains for the tree?"

"I'd love to," said Hilary. And so they did, right there in Hilary's bed.

Late that night in the dark, with the moonlight pouring in through the crazed diamond panes of the window, they made love once more – this time with Hilary sitting up against the pillows and the headboard, and Tom's thighs wide as he straddled Hilary's hips. Tom's lovely neat hand was wrapped around both their cocks, and his hips rocked gently as he thrust against Hilary within his own grip. Such a simple act, and yet creating a slowly intensifying delirium of pleasure. It didn't hurt that Hilary's hands and gaze were free to explore his love's beautiful body with its long curves and narrow planes of fine cool skin. He thought he could touch Tom forever and it would never be enough. Tom gazed down at him with those light eyes a strange enigmatic silver in the moon's glow, setting the deliberate merciless pace as he chose … until eventually Tom began trembling in a need he could barely contain, and then the trembling became a shuddering, Tom's breath panting loud in the quiet night, until at last it was too much and Hilary was shaking, too, his hands firmly grasping Tom's neat rear, holding him near … and the pleasure welled up through him and out of him, then welled up again as Tom cried out and came, too, collapsing heavily into Hilary's crushing embrace, and they clung each to the other for a long precious while.

It was well after midnight before they finally settled. "Happy Christmas, Hilary," Tom murmured with a smile in his voice.

"The very happiest of all," Hilary averred.

They fell asleep, burrowed in together under the blankets for the night. The joys of snuggling were almost entirely new to Hilary, but this perfect luxurious comfort was surely one of the best things he shared with Tom. One of the very many best things.

"I'm so in love with you, my dear," Hilary whispered once when he woke during the night. And Tom smiled in his dreams.

# Sixteen

The cooking, with Tom's advice and assistance, seemed to be going to plan when their guests arrived late on Christmas morning. Tom greeted his parents with resounding hugs, and they all four wished each other 'Merry Christmas'. Hilary shook Dulcie's hand, and then Eric's, beaming happily. He'd had a moment to reflect that any excessive exuberance on his part could be safely attributed to festive cheer when really, of course, it was due to the joy of having been very well shagged by the young man he loved. By Dulcie and Eric's son.

Hilary sobered a little as he looked properly at Tom's parents and realised that despite their old-fashioned names they were so very much younger than him. It brought home to him yet again the fact that there was a two-generation age difference between himself and Tom. He wondered whether the Laurences thought it odd that Tom and Hilary were even friends. And they were indeed so much more than that …

As Hilary made the tea, he listened with half an ear to the three Laurences chatting between themselves as if they hadn't just seen each other the day before. They seemed so comfortable together. They obviously got on well. And meanwhile Hilary was remembering how he'd woken early that morning, but instead of starting the day once he'd got up and relieved himself, he'd climbed back into bed and let Tom warm him up again in the most thorough ways possible. Hilary hadn't come again, but he'd taken endless pleasure from his love's embraces, and Tom had seemed to soar with joyous fulfilment.

Then at last they'd dragged themselves out of bed, giggling like mischievous children, and come down to the kitchen to put the turkey in to roast. The turkey which was smelling rather mouth-watering already.

The kettle boiling brought Hilary out of his sensual reverie. The kettle boiling, and his love's mother asking, "Hilary, could I trouble you for a coffee instead of tea? I do so like a coffee in the mornings."

"Of course," he replied, remembering the jar of coffee that Tom had bought for Justin. "I'm afraid we only have instant, though I believe it's a rather good brand."

"I only ever bother with instant at home," Dulcie assured him. "Thank you."

Judging by his descriptive gestures, Tom was busily talking with his father about the garden; Hilary was sure he recognised the pond and the water channel from the shapes Tom was making with those neat hands of his. Hilary shook himself before he could get too distracted by recent memories of all that those hands could accomplish, and fetched the folding steps from beside the refrigerator so he could reach the coffee on the top shelf himself without bothering Tom. While he was up there he found not only the jar of coffee but what seemed to be a sugar canister that matched the spare set of crockery. Murmuring his surprise, Hilary brought that back down with him, too.

Once he'd prepared Dulcie's coffee, Hilary investigated the sugar canister – and found it full of twenty- and fifty-pound notes, standing randomly curled together on their sides. He let out a surprised "Oh!" and quickly riffled through the notes. There must be a good few hundred pounds there. Dulcie was discreetly not asking, but was obviously curious about his bewilderment.

"This must be a stash of my cousin Evelyn's," Hilary said. He could think of no other explanation, and didn't want her thinking it was his own, and he'd forgotten about it. "The lawyer and his people mustn't have found it, though I know they had cleaners go through this floor in particular rather thoroughly."

Dulcie declared, "May you find many more such stashes!"

"I suppose I shall have to declare it to them," Hilary continued. "What a bother! There might be tax implications for the estate."

"Seems a pity," said Dulcie.

"No, it's better to be sure," put in Eric.

Tom stepped forward, looking a bit self-conscious. "There's no need," he eventually said. When they all looked to him to explain, he shrugged uncomfortably. "It's mine. Well, more to the point, it's *yours*, Hilary."

"What do you mean?"

"That's the difference between what you charge me for board, and what I'd budgeted for. It seemed only fair."

"Oh. I see." Hilary thought for a moment, and then put the money back into the canister, and put the canister out of the way on top of the refrigerator. He feared that Dulcie and Eric would think it inappropriate that he'd offered Tom such a low rate of board – or indeed that Tom wanted to make up the difference. Perhaps it was little clues like this that would start adding up to the realisation there was something untoward going on between their only son and his elderly friend. "Well, never mind that for now," Hilary said briskly. "That's a discussion to be had on another day. Let's take our tea – and coffee – through to the front room. Perhaps now is the time to open our presents?"

"Excellent!" Tom cried, rubbing his hands together in childish glee. He led the way, carrying the tray, while Hilary took up the rear with the platter of mince pies and shortbread.

The presents were a great success. Hilary had found three plates in different places within the tower, of varying patterns and sizes, but all of a beautiful deep-blue glass. He had no wrapping paper, but Tom had located a lightly embroidered white cotton tablecloth that served well, and a red ribbon with which to tie it all up. Tom had headed out along the lane to cut a few branches of holly for a table decoration, and then finished off the present by tucking a holly twig with leaves and berries in the bow. It looked rather superb, Hilary thought – and then he took a moment to hope that Tom's familiarity with what might be found where in the tower indicated that he was still searching for any papers to do with the garden.

Most importantly, though, once Dulcie had unwrapped the folded layers to reveal each plate in turn, she seemed breathless with pleasure. Hilary hadn't managed to concoct a present for Eric, but he was gentleman enough to take pleasure in his wife's happiness, and seemed to feel all the force of the compliment on her behalf. If either of them noticed Hilary hadn't bought a present for Tom either, they didn't remark on the matter.

Dulcie and Eric's present to Hilary was a volume titled *Culpeper's Complete Herbal*, a magnificent reprint of a book dating back to 1653, bound in leather and printed on thick sensual paper.

"Oh, how marvellous!" he declared, leafing through it and taking in the quaint old English language imparting curiosities and wisdom. The carefully inked illustrations of various plants seemed to be original, but each had been gently brought to life with watercolour. "What a wonderful gift."

"We thought," said Eric, "it might help you understand some of Tom's ramblings."

"Yes, that is very considerate of you."

"It was written after Thaddeus's time, of course," put in Tom the pedantic scholar, "but Culpeper was working with the same knowledge, and developing it further."

"I've already glimpsed some of the plants you've talked about for the garden," Hilary said to him – and to Tom's parents he offered his heartfelt thanks.

Then Tom brought his present to where Hilary sat, and handed it over with a look both anxious and affectionate. "I hope you like it …"

"I think I can promise you I will," Hilary said a little wryly. He unwrapped the box with hands that trembled, conscious of three pairs of eyes on him … opened it and discovered, under a layer of silver tissue paper … a knitted waistcoat with a mid-blue back and ribbing, and a front that seemed to be … a homage in pinks, greens and blues to Monet's water lilies. "Tom! How extraordinarily beautiful!"

"A friend of mine back home makes them. Well, she makes all kinds of things, but I thought you'd like this. I know you like to look smart."

Hilary chuckled under his breath. "This is far lovelier than anything I'd have dared buy for myself." Though he already knew which pale-blue shirt would perfectly complement it, and maybe it was time to acquire a pink shirt, as well. "Thank you, Tom. Thank you."

"Oh, that's all right," the fellow said bashfully, for once seeming younger than his years.

Hilary was still marvelling over the detailed work. "How has she achieved the effect? It seems to be a combination of knitting and embroidery, is that right?"

"Yes, I think so. She has a website, you can look it up. She talks a bit about it there."

"Thank you, Tom. This is truly beautiful." Hilary tried to convey all his gratitude in a look, and Tom went rather pink, and wandered off with his hands stuffed into his jeans pockets. After a moment, Hilary looked at the Laurences, and was relieved to find they were regarding their son and his friend fondly rather than with dawning horror. But perhaps it was as well to redirect everyone's focus. Hilary carefully folded the waistcoat away into its box. "I really must finish off our dinner preparations, if you'll excuse me. Tom," he called, "would you find some appropriate music? And fetch our guests another drink, or anything they might like."

"Course," Tom agreed, turning and walking back past Hilary, and letting their hands brush on the way.

Hilary headed for the kitchen, feeling as if he were walking on air.

Dinner went surprisingly well. This was the most challenging meal Hilary had ever made, and for the most people, but it had been well planned and he felt it didn't fail in the execution. Most importantly, the company was convivial and more than willing to be pleased.

After they'd well and truly eaten their fill, the four of them returned to the front room where they watched a DVD of the film *Pride & Prejudice*, with Keira Knightley and Matthew Macfadyen. This was Tom's choice, Hilary was interested to discover. Dulcie and Eric dozed off a couple of times, and excused themselves by explaining that Tom played it all the time. Hilary hadn't seen it before, but found it funny and romantic and rather beautifully filmed.

Once the appropriate happy ending had been achieved, Dulcie insisted that they help with the washing-up. Hilary was rather taken aback by this, and thought it a bit improper to accept, but he was glad enough of the assistance. They cheerfully made short work of the task, and with Tom directing matters managed to not get in each other's way too much.

It was late afternoon by then, or early evening, and the short midwinter days meant that it was already dark. Dulcie and Eric repeated their thanks and said their farewells, but also invited Hilary to join them and Tom in a trip to Avebury stone circle on Boxing Day. Hilary glanced at Tom for his agreement, and was delighted to accept.

Then at last Hilary and Tom were alone again, and indulged in a heartfelt hug as soon as the front door was closed and locked. "What a brilliant day!" Tom declared, face tucked in against Hilary's hair. "Best Christmas ever!"

"I'm so very glad you felt so, my dear. I did my best, though I fear it was actually quite inadequate."

"Hilary, you were great!" Tom pulled away, but only a little, so that he could see Hilary directly. "Thank you so much. They really enjoyed themselves – and I think they really like you!"

"*Do* they? And did they … ?"

"I'm sure of it." Tom leaned in again to squeeze Hilary in a hug, and drop a kiss to the top of his head. "Now, come on, let's have some tea and watch another movie … before it's time to go back to bed." And then without waiting for Hilary's agreement, Tom was heading for the kitchen with a lively wink thrown back over his shoulder.

Tom was soon back with a tray of tea things, and a sandwich each made from the cold roast turkey and cranberry sauce, along with what was left of the shortbread.

Tom's choice of film this time was *Maurice* with James Wilby, Hugh Grant, and a delectable young Rupert Graves. This was a film Hilary had seen before; he had visited the cinema for its sake, a number of times, both dreading and desiring he would be recognised and finally *known*. Despite the all-too-briefly-shown happy ending for Maurice and Alec, it was an almost unbearably poignant story, and even now left Hilary rather damp-eyed. He found that Tom, tucked in against Hilary's side, was weeping.

"All right, my dear?" he asked, with his soft old heart pitter-pattering.

That beautiful tear-stained face was turned up to his, transparent with sorrow. "No one should have to go through all that, just to be with someone they love!"

"That's very true," he agreed.

"How did you bear it, when you were young?"

"I don't know …" Hilary pondered this, wondering if Tom would despise Hilary's younger self for not being more of an activist. "It was just the way it was, I'm afraid. The laws and the … the lack of approval or understanding didn't stop me – though they did make me very careful."

"Poor Hilary!"

"You mustn't make too much of that, however. I've always been a cautious soul."

"Ah, but not too cautious to kiss me!" Tom declared, pushing up to prove that true. "You would have kissed me back then, too, wouldn't you? If you'd known me."

Hilary smiled a little. "Of course! The rest is speculation, though. I was never so much in love back then as I am now, and no doubt that would have changed things a great deal indeed. You might have made me very reckless, if I'd known you then."

"Very *brave*," Tom corrected. Then he added in the most welcome of demands, "Say that again. Say that you're in love!"

Hilary gathered the young man up close and warm in his arms. "I am so *very* much in love with you, Tom Laurence."

"And I with you, Hilary Kent." Tom pulled away from the embrace, but only to say, "Come to bed!"

They had already found this perfect way to make love, with Hilary sitting up against the headboard, and Tom straddling him; Tom cool and a little eldritch in the moonlight, so supple and smooth under Hilary's marvelling hands; Tom's hand holding their cocks together, each so eager for the other's press; Tom's hips rocking and Hilary's own tilting up to meet him. Hilary couldn't imagine anything more enchanting or fulfilling. Soon enough but not too soon they came like that, each spilling over the other and over Tom's fingers, Tom pushing in close so their moans spilled into shared mouthy kisses, Hilary's hands firmly curved around Tom's rear. It was perfection.

"Perfection," Hilary murmured afterwards as they lay there bound up close together under the blankets. "It has been the most perfect two days."

"Me, too," mumbled Tom, already more than half asleep. "Mean perfect, too."

Hilary was physically and emotionally tired to the point of exhaustion, but he felt the overwhelming urge to say, "You've made me so very happy, my dear. If nothing else were ever to happen between us –"

"Hush," said Tom. "Nonsense. Go t' sleep."

"Yes, my darling," Hilary said – and obeyed.

The trip to Avebury was also a success. Hilary began to feel as if he were waiting for the other shoe to drop. In the meantime, though, he endeavoured to relax and enjoy himself.

The day was fine with a high blue sky, and a cool breeze that was rather refreshing once they were all properly bundled up. Hilary had never visited Avebury, despite it only being about ten miles from his new home. He was fascinated by the startlingly large henge – the circular bank and ditch – the great outer stone circle and the two smaller stone circles within it. There was a manor house nearby, and a quaint though lively village that actually ambled through the circle itself.

"They'd never allow this kind of development nowadays," Hilary reflected.

"No …" Tom was rather thoughtful. "It's hard to argue with preserving things as they are, though, as much as we can."

"It is," Hilary allowed. "But this is rather charming in its own right. The place would lose something without the village, don't you think? The accumulation of so many centuries, and different ways of life."

"True." A shrug indicated the impossibly epic nature of this topic. "I suppose there'll always be a tension between preservation and use. I'm sure we'll argue the points a hundred times or more while we're working on the garden."

"Discuss, I hope, rather than argue."

Tom smiled at him. "Discuss, of course." And as the two of them passed behind one of the larger megaliths that faced out across wide bare fields, Tom gently pushed Hilary back against the sarsen stone, and leaned in close to kiss him for long lovely moments under the high arch of pale sky. Then he wandered off with an innocent air, and Hilary happily followed after, with his heart tripping out a wicked beat.

The four of them ate a late lunch at the pub that was located almost in the centre of the henge. Dulcie and Eric were full of talk about Cornwall, where they were travelling the next day, with the intention of staying a week. If that were the only thing on their minds, as it seemed was the case, then Hilary assumed he had kept his and Tom's secret well enough. He still felt some misgivings about that, but there was no point in upsetting the apple cart for the sake of a relationship that would last barely six months.

The drive back to Riverside, with Tom sitting beside him in the back seat, brought home to Hilary how beautiful this county was, in a chalky, green, windswept kind of way. It certainly seemed worth exploring.

"Is Stonehenge nearby as well?" he had to ask, his geographical knowledge being rather vague.

"Not too far," Eric replied. "About twenty miles south of Marlborough. But I don't think we'd get there before the evening draws in."

"No, no, of course. I was thinking of other outings …" He turned to Tom. "Can you drive?"

"Yes," Tom replied with his eyes sparking bright.

"Perhaps I should buy a car. Nothing fancy. Just something in which we might go exploring. I never needed one in London, you see, and I haven't driven since I was about your age, Tom, when I needed to for work for a few years. No doubt things have changed rather since then!"

"If you want to, Hilary," Tom said. "That would be fantastic! You know, there's a physic garden in Hampshire we could visit."

"Now, don't get too excited, Tom," Eric chided. "You mustn't take advantage of Hilary's generosity."

Tom abruptly looked so woebegone that Hilary almost laughed. "Thank you for defending my interests, Eric, but it would suit me very well to have a car available. And it is I who'd be taking advantage of Tom, I'm afraid, as my chauffeur."

"Oh, that's all right, then," said Tom's father, apparently perfectly content with such an arrangement. And Tom, while watching the scenery go by his window, surreptitiously slid his hand over to hold Hilary's where it lay on the seat between them.

# Seventeen

"This is my first day for a while now without any plans," Hilary said the next morning as he and Tom lazed together warmly bundled up in Hilary's bed. The Laurences had phoned to say goodbye, and were safely on their way to Cornwall, and the rest of the Christmas and New Year break stretched before Hilary and Tom, with a promising lack of commitments. While Tom would no doubt need to work on his thesis, the spring term didn't start until the ninth of January. Hilary asked, "What would you like to do today?"

Tom snorted.

"Other than exhaust an old man sexually, of course," Hilary smoothly supplied. When Tom shifted to look up at him with a worried brow, Hilary added, "Which isn't a complaint, by any means."

"Good," said Tom. "Well, other than that, of course, I was wondering if … if we could possibly start exploring the attic?"

"Of course we can!" Hilary replied, wondering why Tom still seemed so wary about even asking. "Haven't you been up there already? I had the impression that you've been busy exploring under your own steam."

"Oh. Do you mind? I've only gone back over places we've already been, and I've been dusting as I go. I don't want you to think I'm prying, or anything."

"You are perfectly welcome to pry all you want to, my dear – and it's hardly prying when it will all be yours one day. In any case, it's proved very useful, when you've known just where to find things when we need them."

Tom shifted up further in Hilary's embrace, in order to kiss him in slow gratitude. "You're awesome, Hilary," he said once he was done. "I love the way you think!"

"Do you?" Hilary asked in gentle amusement. "You mean my conclusions suit you very well."

"I suppose … But what's wrong with that? Isn't that one of the reasons why we get along so well together?"

"I suppose." Hilary sighed, but in contentment. "It's all right, Tom. I don't think you're taking advantage, and I never have. It is very convenient how our needs dovetail so neatly, though. I don't mean anything more than that."

Tom was frowning over this. He hauled himself up a bit so he could prop himself on his elbows – as if he could think better when his head was upright. "I'm not … trying to be anything I'm not. You know, for the sake of the garden or whatever."

"I know that, my dear. The first thing I liked about you was your candour, and that hasn't changed in all these months. You are who you are, Tom, and I love you dearly."

"Then what are we disagreeing about?"

"I don't think we are, really! It's as you say: we get along very well. If it wasn't for such a ghastly difference in our ages, I dare say we'd be a rather good match."

"We *are* a good match," Tom fervently agreed. "We just *click* together, you know? I think I felt it almost right away, you know …"

"Did you, my darling?"

"It was so much fun to flirt with you, right from that first day … and then later I realised the flirting was just the tip of the iceberg." He lay back down, and snuggled in close to Hilary to kiss him and stroke at his shoulders and chest and belly with his lovely neat hands. Hilary caught him up in a warm embrace, and they revelled in each other for a while. A short while – until Tom pulled away again and asked, "So, the attic … ?"

"Of course."

Tom eyed him askance, apparently sensing that Hilary was reluctant. "We can pick this up later, you know. Just try to stop me!"

"Never that," said Hilary, shifting himself to sit up and then swing his legs out of the lovely warm comfortable bed. "Shall I make a thermos of tea?"

"Please. And I'll get the torches!"

As it happened, there was a light up in the attic, but only one and with a very weak old bulb, so they were glad of the torches. It seemed from the undisturbed dust and general fustiness that no one had been up there in a very long time, and the feeling of disarray indicated that no one had felt the contents worth their while either. Hilary looked around the room, which extended the full diameter of the tower, wondering where to start. The place wasn't jammed full of discarded gear, but there was certainly plenty to be getting on with – and some of it rather unexpected even at first glance. Hilary frowned at what appeared to be an old bicycle, wondering why anyone would have bothered even bringing it up here, especially if it was then to be left forgotten.

Tom was obviously feeling far less daunted by the challenge than Hilary. "Why don't you begin looking around – just start on the left there, if you like – and I'll see if I can get through to the windows on the back wall. Get a bit of light and air in here."

"All right." Hilary started with the first pile of oddments, which seemed to involve various carpet offcuts on top of an old trunk. He peered in confusion at the carpet pieces – many of which had curved edges, which indicated they had been fitted within the circular tower – but none of the patterns were at all familiar. So they must predate any of the current carpets, which themselves were worn well past their natural life.

Hilary shrugged, and worked his way down to the trunk – which seemed to contain nothing but children's books. As he was looking through, a welcome gust of chilly air swept past him and down the stairwell into the tower, and the room brightened a little. "That's better!" cried Tom. "I'll try for the other one."

The effect was mixed, Hilary thought wryly, though he didn't dampen Tom's mood by saying so. There was more light, but it only made the place look dirtier and drearier. Perhaps once they had had a look through what was here, it might be worth hiring some professional cleaners to help them get this and the second floor shipshape.

"Do you know if there's a way up to the roof?" Tom was asking.

"I think there is," Hilary replied, trying to remember the old plans he'd fleetingly seen when he'd inherited the place. He might even have a copy of them amidst the legal paperwork, now he thought about it. In any case, it was a flat roof beyond low battlements, so there must be a way of gaining access.

"Probably a great view from up there! Well, maybe we'll unearth a staircase or ladder or something if we get into all this …" Once he had the second window open, Tom came over to see what Hilary was looking at. "Anything interesting?"

"Not for your purposes. Children's books. They might be of great interest to someone out there, now I think about it. But nothing about the tower or the garden."

"Right, well, I'll start over here, then."

They worked through to lunchtime, diligently sorting through what was there, and keeping aside the few things they found intriguing or thought might be useful. Finally Hilary had to call it quits, at least for the morning.

"I'm going to head downstairs and make up some sandwiches, Tom. Will you manage to drag yourself away soon?"

Tom cast him a smile that sparkled in his summer-sky eyes. "I'll come down, don't worry. Thank you, Hilary!"

"Don't be too long, then," Hilary said, not as an admonishment but only because he knew what Tom was like when he got caught up in something.

"I won't be."

Then, before he went down, Hilary stepped closer to where Tom was kneeling, and pressed a kiss to the top of his beloved head. For no better reason than that he could.

The words "Love you, too, Hilary!" sang in his ears all the way down to the ground floor.


Hilary had been sitting at the kitchen table, waiting along with their lunch, for perhaps ten or fifteen minutes before he heard Tom coming downstairs. When Tom finally appeared, he seemed shocked and pale – and he was carefully carrying something in both hands, a bundle wrapped in what might have been a shawl or throw.

"What is it?" Hilary asked, quickly getting up to clear Tom's place so the young man could sit down and put his discovery on the table before him. "Tom, are you all right?"

"Yes," was the faint reply.

"What have you found?"

"Letters." Tom cleared his throat, and stirred himself to look up at Hilary. "More letters, like the one we found already from Lady Bryony to Thaddeus."

"Oh, my dear!" Hilary slowly sat down again in his seat, and considered Tom, who looked back at him steadily but as wide-eyed as if the earth had shifted under his feet. Hilary wasn't quite sure how to read Tom's reaction, nor what exactly to do about it. "Is there … something about the garden?" he asked, for want of any better ideas.

"I don't know. I doubt it. I think – maybe this was her shawl the letters are wrapped up in. I think – maybe Thaddeus and Bryony were – friends."

"Friends? Wouldn't that have been somewhat … unusual at that time?

Inappropriate, even?"

"Yes. What does that matter? That only makes it more – exciting." Tom took a shuddery breath. "Interesting, I mean. That makes it of particular interest."

Hilary smiled at the fellow. For whatever reason, Tom had become more *involved* with Thaddeus than his academic self was comfortable with, but Hilary was hardly surprised by that. It was surely to be expected that Tom identified with the man who'd created the garden he cared so much for.

"Will you eat something?" Hilary asked gently. "Before you read the letters?"

"I don't think I could."

"Well, then. I'll pour the tea, and perhaps you'll indulge me by drinking half a cup before we proceed."

"Of course," Tom agreed, apparently willing to be guided through his state of shock. And in fact he drank the whole cup, before at last setting it down, and drawing aside the layers of shawl in a manner reverential. "The first one," he said, "is from Bryony to Thaddeus.

'My dear friend T – I have read the pamphlets you were so good as to send, and now you must come yourself and debate the matter with me. As soon as you can contrive to visit us, please do so, and I will insist on taking the time to enjoy your company. All else here is bustle – but very dull bustle indeed. – Lady B'."

"It was a friendship of the mind," Hilary supposed.

"Perhaps," said Tom. With his hands each draped in loose corners of the old shawl, he carefully shifted the first letter aside, and started reading the second one.

"'My dearest friend T – You bring my soul much comfort, and you quiet my timorous mind. You gift me the sweetest rest. I would wish you to remember that, when I rudely interrupt your own peace. Please visit when you can, and assure me all is well. – B'."

The next one was more formal, beginning with 'My esteemed pastor Thaddeus' and being signed 'Lady Bryony'. Hilary frowned. "It sounds as if they became estranged."

Tom shrugged a quibble. "The letters aren't dated, and they're probably in no sensible order. Thaddeus must have decided they were worth keeping. If he reread them during the years he was here, they could be all over the place in terms of the original sequence.”

“I see what you mean. It’s as if we have a number of paragraphs, but we need to assemble them in the right order to tell the story.”

“Exactly. The more formal language might indicate it was from earlier in their relationship, before they became real friends.” Tom scanned the fourth letter, and said, “Listen to this!

‘Thaddeus, my dear Thaddeus – What I have both feared and longed for has come to pass. I am by turns humbled and joyous. No, I must be honest with you, if no one else – I am overflowing with joy, and only humble on occasion. Remember me in your thoughts and your prayers. You are my dearest friend, and will always remain so. – Your faithful B’.”

The two of them looked at each other with a wild surmise.

Tom said, “Perhaps they fell in love.”

Hilary chuckled at the scholar throwing caution to the winds. “And you accused *me* of being a romantic!”

“You are,” Tom insisted with a grin.

“Perhaps … there was a child.”

“D’you think?” Tom turned back to frown down at the letter before him. “You think that’s what she ‘both feared and longed for’?”

“Of course it could be any one of so many other things … but a child was my first thought.”

“With Thaddeus as the father?”

“Would she write to him in such terms, if the child belonged to another man?”

“I don’t know.” It seemed Tom was being wary again. “I don’t know much about young women and babies. And it’s best not to leap to conclusions about different times, different cultures. All the things that *aren’t* said, all the assumptions they made, the unspoken understandings and meanings. Whatever we conclude might say more about us than them.”

“I know I’m only interpreting this as a layman –”

“Well,” said Tom, “it’s hard to imagine what else she might be referring to, but perhaps there are more clues in the other letters.”

Tom was just about to shift the letter onto the pile of ones they’d already read, when there came a knock at the front door. He slid a resentful glance in that direction, and then carefully covered up the letters with the shawl again.

"All right?" asked Hilary. When Tom nodded, Hilary went to answer the door – and he found the squire there. "Oh! Good afternoon, Sir James."

"Mr Kent. I hope you're enjoying the festive season, as I suppose we must call it these days, though why we can't call Christmas 'Christmas' I have no idea."

"Thank you, yes," Hilary smoothly replied. "Is there something I can help you with?"

"Just paying my respects! And I must thank you again for the whisky. It provides a great support in times of need."

"I'm very glad you appreciated it." Hilary was just standing there *not* inviting the man in, thinking that Tom would prefer it that way – but Tom himself suddenly appeared by Hilary's shoulder.

"Ah, so the young fellow's with you for the holidays, then," the squire observed, rocking forward and back on his feet, and looking around elsewhere as if searching for an excuse to leave.

Tom demanded, "Have you come to tell us all over again about Thaddeus being queer?"

"Tom!" Hilary protested.

"Now, don't be like that, young Laurence."

"Because we found a letter," Tom ploughed on, "that suggests he was in love with Lady Bryony. You know, the squire's wife back then."

Sir James's face fell. "No, that can't be right," he protested, but weakly.

"And she was in love with him, too!"

"Young man," Sir James said, rather more forcefully, "I hope you're not suggesting anything untoward –"

"Why not? Love is love! You were happy enough suggesting Thaddeus 'felt up the wrong fellow' and got himself killed for it."

"Tom," said Hilary, "I think we might save any discussion of the – the letter for another day, don't you?"

"Maybe *the squire* had him killed in a fit of jealousy!"

Sir James was furious. "*Now, look –*"

"*Both* of you," said Hilary. "This is neither the time nor the place." And when Tom opened his mouth, Hilary took Tom's wrist in a firm grasp. "That's enough, Tom."

Tom obediently subsided.

The squire cast a suspicious glare at their joined hands, and then began backing away. "Well, no doubt in the new year … I'd be very happy to hear more … though of course Lady Bryony isn't my direct ancestor, so really there's no bearing …" He was almost at his car already. "I'm sure it won't come to anything."

"Goodbye, Sir James," said Hilary. "We'll be in touch in the new year, as you say, and share what we've found with you. Thank you for stopping by!"

"Goodbye, Mr Kent!"

"Bye," said Tom, with only a hint of sullenness – but it was too late, and Sir James was in his car and driving off.

Hilary closed and locked the door, and followed Tom back through to the kitchen. "Are you all right, Tom?"

"Yeah. Sorry." He had the grace to look sheepish. "I'm not like that very often, but that guy really gets on my wick."

"I noticed!" They settled at the table again, and Tom began to desultorily pick at his sandwiches, leaving the letters aside for now. Hilary asked, "What did he mean about Bryony not being his ancestor?"

"There was no child. Well," Tom amended with a humourless smile, "there was no direct legitimate heir, and the title and lands ended up passing to the squire's youngest brother. I don't know that Sir James is directly descended even from *him*; I haven't looked into the more recent lineage. But I know a fair bit about that era."

"Food for thought," said Hilary, pondering the possibilities, "if there *was* a child …"

"Certainly is!" Tom agreed in something more like his usual bright self. "Shall I make a fresh pot of tea?"

"Thank you," said Hilary, smiling at him. "Thank you very much indeed."


"What do you think Barnaby would make of the mystery?" Hilary asked as they settled in to watch the *Midsomer* episode on the last Thursday of December.

"What, do you mean the baby?" Tom asked, tucking his head against Hilary's shoulder as if it belonged there.

"Yes. Would he have solved the puzzle already?"

"Probably. But he's got the advantage of being in a fictional world where he ends up being proved right within two hours, no matter how many wrong conclusions he leaps to in the meantime."

Hilary laughed. "Very true." The *Midsomer* episode was called 'Beyond the Grave'. It could not be said they were paying much attention to it. Hilary asked, "Did you find an order you like for Bryony's letters?"

"No," said Tom with a sigh. "I'm prepared to cautiously posit a pregnancy, but what the exact circumstances were is anyone's guess." There had been another letter anticipating a 'happy event', and Bryony's tone and manner seemed both joyous and scared, so it seemed a fair assumption to Hilary. Even though, like Tom, he had to admit to little knowledge of young women and babies.

"There are other possibilities," Tom continued. "I mean, other than Thaddeus being the father. What if Bryony and James had been childless for a long time, and Bryony had asked Thaddeus to pray for them? That could explain why she was so excited about telling him the good news."

Hilary pondered that for a moment. "I'm not sure … It felt a little more personal than that. And why would she have *feared* the pregnancy if it was a legitimate one? Surely she would have *hoped* for it."

"I would have thought any woman back then would fear pregnancy."

"True."

"And what eventually happened," Tom slowly continued, "is a complete mystery. No matter what order I put them in, I can't make the letters provide any information about the 'event' itself. At some point they just stop, with no reason given."

"There might be another stash of letters somewhere up in the attic, that continue on from these."

"Maybe," said Tom – though Hilary suspected Tom would have been up there searching until he found them, if he really thought they existed. "I suppose the obvious explanation is that Thaddeus left, probably to return to Kent, and any later letters followed him there." He sighed again, and tilted his head up to look at Hilary. "Sorry, I shouldn't be talking through the programme."

"I don't mind. Do you think there's anything I prefer to talking with you, Tom?"

The young man chuckled. "Yes!"

"There's nothing I prefer to doing *anything* with you," Hilary amended.

"I knew it. Watching the show is just an excuse for a snuggle, isn't it?" And the chuckle turned wicked. "Or a snuggle and a tug, maybe …"

Hilary crushed his beloved in his arms for a moment, and pressed a kiss to Tom's hair. "Tom –"

"Hang on!" Tom exclaimed, lifting a hand to ask for quiet. One of the characters in 'Beyond the Grave' was apparently coming out as gay by declaring his allegiance to the Civil War-era Cavaliers … Gavin Troy, of course, immediately responded by retroactively signing up for the Roundheads. "How cool is that?" Tom asked. "We bat for the Cavaliers!"

"That is very, um, cool indeed," Hilary agreed. It was the first time he'd ever used the word in relation to anything other than temperature.

Tom grinned at him. "Sorry, what were you going to say?"

Hilary knew it was a rather silly question, but he asked anyway. "Did you watch *Midsomer Murders* while you were away?"

"Of course!"

"*Both* episodes?"

Tom twisted around within Hilary's embrace to snuggle in closer, and push his arms around Hilary's waist. "Of *course* I watched them both. D'you think I wasn't thinking of you? Last week's – you know, the one with the Perfect Village competition, I thought it was rather good, actually – I spent the first half wondering if you were fancying Orlando Bloom!"

"Who?" said Hilary.

That earned him a chuckle. "The pretty guy who got done with a pitchfork! We really have to do something about broadening your horizons, Hilary. Anyway, I even insisted on buying Mum and Dad cod and chips for dinner when we were watching *Midsomer*!" Tom's laughter turned wry. "Though I have to admit something about that felt a bit weird. Inappropriate."

Hilary held on close, his hands stroking, stroking at Tom's hair and shoulders and back.

"You know …" Tom added in a low voice, "I ripped your Bach CD, the *Contented Rest* one, so I had it on my laptop."

"Ripped it?" Hilary asked.

"Yeah, copied it. Because, you know … that was playing when you first touched me."

"I remember."

"So I'd play it in bed at night with my earbuds in … you know … when I tossed off."

"Oh, *Tom* …" he said rather brokenly, images burgeoning in his mind which he wanted to save for later, because for now he had the real thing, warm and limber and so very lovely in his arms.

Tom twisted around further still in Hilary's embrace, pressing in close for a kiss … and wrapped up in each other as they were, Tom's hand slid down to tease and tug Hilary into such profound delight, while Hilary's hand sought out Tom's lovely cock and echoed his young lover's every move. Though they were still fully clothed, their completion was so very intimate, with their faces nuzzled in close together, caressing each other, sharing panting breaths and muffled groans and inarticulate endearments.

They cuddled peacefully together for a long while afterwards, as the television quietly burbled on to itself, and their intense joy gradually transformed into a superb contentment.

Hilary woke, as he often did, at around three in the morning. He discovered that Tom was lying there awake, and turned on the bedside lamp to find that Tom was troubling over something, chewing on his lower lip. The scowl might have been in response to the sudden light, but there was definitely something wrong.

"Tom –" he began, though Hilary was torn between two rather different priorities.

"Go on," said Tom, knowing why Hilary woke. "I'll be here when you get back."

So Hilary went to use the bathroom, and then hurried back to lie on his side by Tom, not touching but within easy reach. "What's the matter?"

"I was just thinking … about Thaddeus."

"Yes?"

"Well, what if his idiotic lordship is right, and someone killed him?"

Hilary belatedly put two and two together. "Because of the love affair with Lady Bryony, you mean?"

"Yeah. I mean, all we know is that at some point Thaddeus disappeared while under a shadow of some kind, and no one seemed to know what happened. What if the squire at the time – his name was James as well – What if *that* Sir James realised what was going on, and had Thaddeus done away with?"

"I suppose it's possible …"

"And then, if there *was* a baby, what happened to it?"

Hilary reached a comforting hand to grasp Tom's shoulder. "I don't think you need to assume violence. The infant mortality rate was horribly high back then, wasn't it? And if the child survived, surely it would have been fostered out if there was any question of its paternity."

"I guess. But – Thaddeus –" Tom looked utterly woeful.

"Hush, my dear, hush …" Hilary moved in closer to gather Tom into his arms, and gently rock him. "You used to think that Thaddeus had simply returned home to his family in Kent, remember?"

"Yes …"

"Maybe he took the child with him," Hilary suggested, feeling inspired. "Maybe he raised his son or daughter himself."

Tom sighed happily at this new version of the story, and relaxed in against his lover. "I like that," he said in a small voice.

"So do I," said Hilary, before reaching to turn off the bedside lamp, and then soothing Tom back to sleep.

# Eighteen

It was Tom's birthday on Saturday the thirty-first of December. He turned twenty-four. "See?" said Tom over breakfast, grinning cheekily. "I don't know what you're worried about. There's only forty-one years between us now!"

"Ha ha ha," said Hilary, and tried not to let such a reflection ruin his enjoyment of the day. He ran a glance over Tom in his pyjama bottoms and scruffy old t-shirt. "You look utterly delectable, of course, my dear, but we're receiving a delivery at ten. Will you mind getting dressed by then?"

"On my birthday?" the fellow mock-grumbled. "What's the world coming to? Should be allowed to run around naked, shouldn't I?"

"After the delivery," Hilary smoothly responded, "that would be fine."

At ten on the dot there was a knock on the front door, and Sam Reynolds and his son delivered Tom's main birthday present, which consisted of a large bookcase, crafted in wood by Sam, with a subtle carving of plants down one side. The three younger men moved it into position along the interior wall of the living area by the kitchen, so the books would be in easy reach of where Tom worked on his laptop.

"It's very beautiful, Sam," Hilary said.

Tom appeared gobsmacked, but managed to make a noise that indicated his agreement. The bookcase certainly made Tom's current arrangement of bricks and boards look rather ramshackle.

"Thank you, Hilary," Sam replied. "The matching one will be done within the week, as I promised." He indicated the carvings, and said to Tom, "I chose rosemary, peppermint and basil for the pattern, because they're supposed to stimulate the mental energies or some such thing. You should say if you want something different on the other case."

"No!" said Tom in a kind of squeak. He cleared his throat and managed, "No, that's kind of perfect, Sam. Thank you!" He ran a hand over the smooth wood of a shelf. "God! How long has this taken you? Hilary, when did you think of this? You must have ordered it before —" Tom thought twice about finishing that sentence.

Hilary smoothly replied, "Yes, the morning you first went away after term had finished. I was sitting here with a cup of tea looking at your bookshelves, and I thought we could probably manage something more fitting."

"It's so beautiful! And there's a second one on the way? God! Thank you so much, Hilary. Sam, thank you *so much*."

"It's been good to do some real carpentry work," Sam said. He was obviously pleased, though his demeanour remained calm as usual.

Sam looked across at Hilary with a gently observant gaze, and Hilary had cause yet again to reflect that probably everyone would know sooner or later that he loved Tom. This was a fairly extravagant gift, after all, from a landlord to a lodger. Tom would remain safe, however, as Hilary knew no one would imagine that Tom could possibly return the favour.

After a moment, Sam said, "We'll be on our way, then. Thank you again, Hilary. Happy birthday, Tom!"

They all shook hands, and said thank you and farewell, and then Tom and Hilary were alone again. Tom flung himself at Hilary and hugged him fiercely. "God, what a present! It's my books, and our home – and even our garden! – all combined in one beautiful thing. Hilary, you're brilliant. I'll never be able to think of something that brilliant for your birthday!"

"I wanted to make it clear," mumbled Hilary, feeling a little overcome. He hadn't expected Tom to be quite so enthusiastic about such a practical gift.

"What?" Tom asked gently. "What did you want clear?"

"That I shall be very happy to think of this being *your* home, in the future."

"Hilary, you are way too generous to me. And all I care about right now is that it's *our* home, and I love it so much." Tom smacked a kiss to Hilary's hair, and headed back towards the bookcase. "I'm going to re-shelve my books now, and put these bricks and things back outside where they belong. I don't know why I ever thought this was a good idea …"

"It *was* a good idea." Hilary followed him, bearing an envelope. "This is to help towards filling up any empty shelves," he said, diffidently handing over the envelope. It was rather a large amount in vouchers that could be spent at a range of different bookshops – including academic bookshops, he'd made very sure of that.

Tom was damp-eyed by now, and a little flushed with emotion. "D'you want to make some tea?" he suggested. "Have some biscuits, if you want.

You need to keep your energy levels up," Tom went on to advise, "because once I'm done here, Hilary, I'm taking you back to bed."

"Oh," said Hilary lightly, while his heart tripped. "If you must."

Tom seemed completely impassioned. Hilary wasn't entirely sure what to attribute it to, unless Tom always celebrated his birthdays thus, but Tom was *alight* – and there was a *purity* to it, that Hilary had never before associated with sex.

Hilary was already lying in bed – modestly dressed in his pyjamas again and under the covers with his head and shoulders propped up against a couple of pillows – when Tom finally came into Hilary's bedroom, naked and padding along silently on his bare feet, as if they mustn't risk disturbing the growing mood.

"Are you all right?" Hilary asked quietly.

"I've never been better!" Tom declared in a husky whisper, as he eased onto the other side of the bed. He settled to lie beside Hilary, but on top of the covers and not touching him. Yet Tom's cock was as hard as Hilary had ever seen it, and the curve of it seemed to yearn towards Hilary as if no one else would do.

Hilary huffed a laugh at the thought, and turned towards the younger man, reaching a hand to caress his shoulder – but even before he quite touched Tom, Hilary felt a wave of warmth through the air, which was utterly shocking when Hilary was so used to Tom feeling slightly cool. Too concerned to feel foolish, Hilary burst out, "You're so hot!"

Tom laughed. "I am!"

"Oh *Tom*, are you ill?" Hilary lifted himself up on an elbow to consider the man. After a long moment he had to conclude that Tom didn't really appear feverish – but only *infinitely* excited. And now Hilary thought about it, he remembered that the very first time he'd touched Tom, the younger man had *radiated* warmth.

"I'm well enough," Tom said. "I'm needing a bit o' lovin', though. Oh Hilary!"

"Tom, do you –"

Tom was usually far too polite to interrupt Hilary, but he did so now. "*God*, Hilary, I need you so bad. I need you to have me. I need to be had." He lifted a hand towards Hilary, which contained an ambitious number of loose condom packets and a tube of lubricant. "*Please.*"

"Ah." They hadn't yet done such a thing, of course, nor anything like it – and Hilary wasn't sure whether his fear outweighed his hunger or if it was the other way round.

"I know we haven't had the Safe Sex Talk, and we don't ever have to talk about that stuff if you don't want to. I'm pretty sure I'm negative, but I don't expect you to take my word for it, and anyway we can keep using rubbers whenever we need to, I don't mind, it's what I'm used to – and actually I've never done it without."

"Tom –"

"I don't do this often, I *don't*, but I really need it right now."

Hilary left a pause, and then asked rather diffidently, "Why is that, do you think?"

Tom's expression grew wild for a moment, and then bewildered. "I don't know. Some things – can't really be explained. Can they?"

"No doubt you're right." Hilary let out a breath, and then nodded his agreement – though he still had to ask, "What exactly do you propose?"

"Just like – you know when you sit up against the pillows, and I'm riding you, and bringing us both off together … ?"

A delicious shudder went through Hilary to hear that Tom thought of it as 'riding'. "Yes."

"Well, like that. Except I'll be –" Tom groaned, and looked for a moment – if it were even possible for a modern young man – as if he might swoon. "I'll be riding your cock this time. And you don't have to do anything, Hilary, except sit still for it."

Despite everything, this rather hurt his vanity. "It is possible that I might be able to contribute something more than just sitting still, you know."

Tom spared him a brief apologetic smile. "Even better, then." And Tom was kneeling up, and gathering the pillows from his side of the bed to add to those already behind Hilary's back, and helping him sit up. Tom was now growing implacable, and the lust in him glowed bright. Hilary couldn't help but get caught up in his urgency.

Tom hauled the bedclothes down and cast them to the foot of the bed, and between them they wrestled Hilary's pyjamas off. Then Tom was straddling his hips before Hilary was even half-hard, and they found the familiar configuration – though this time Tom's hands reached down to tug expertly at Hilary's cock and balls alone – and this time, once Hilary's hands had shaped themselves around Tom's rear, he let his fingers dig into the hot damp skin. Tom shifted sinuously, and moaned into their kiss. He had been such a delightful lover this past week, but today he was *alight*, he was *afire* …

Hilary groaned, and tightened his hold. "Tom …" he murmured, wondering even now how he could trust this – but then wondering how could he not, when Tom seemed so utterly stripped to his essential truths.

"Are you ready, Hilary … ?" Tom asked. And when Hilary met his gaze, Tom's eyes were so clear as well as so wild.

"My darling, you must have whatever you need."

Tom kissed him for that – and then reached for a condom. Hilary was so intent on Tom that he hardly noticed the condom being rolled onto his cock, but he certainly noticed when Tom, still straddled there, began preparing himself with his own lubricated fingers … Hilary gasped, and feared for a moment that he himself might swoon – but then he took the opportunity to push his fingers further down until he was touching Tom's fingers as they thrust in and out, and he was stroking the skin there, feeling the slight tension ease as Tom readied himself, both of them so sensitive that it was as if Tom might feel even the whorls on Hilary's fingertips …

Tom's breath was rasping in urgency, and on another day they might do no more than this and count themselves well satisfied. But today Tom needed more. At last Tom groaned, withdrew his fingers – and then swayed rather as he pushed closer into position.

"Don't force it, Tom, if you're not ready."

"Oh Hilary *God damn* Hilary I am *so* ready …" And then Tom was impaling himself, and sinking down as if finding his natural home, and for Hilary it was the depths of the dark earth and the heights of rarefied air all at once. He sat up further so that he could loosely enfold his beloved wanton, who swayed again and moaned gut-deep, and they were so closely joined now that every move and every sound vibrated through them both.

Tom finally settled heavily down against Hilary, and he arched back with a low cry within Hilary's steadying embrace, his torso a long rapturous curve.

"You're *beautiful*," Hilary was instinctively telling him. "You're as beautiful and righteous and *dangerous* as an angel."

"Oh God," Tom muttered again, before at last moving, lifting and twisting his sinuous hips in a pattern so divinely wicked that Hilary thought it might destroy him. "Oh God Oh God *Oh God!*"

Hilary hung on, wanting only that Tom should have what he needed, knowing that Hilary himself would be devastated by pleasure soon enough and for now his role was to let Tom give himself over. 'I need you to have me,' he'd said. 'I need to be had.' Hilary groaned a wordless prayer that he'd be up to the task.

But Tom seemed to be in much the same state as Hilary, for soon he imploringly cried out Hilary's name.

"Yes, my darling," Hilary replied. And he already knew just what to do. With one arm remaining firm around Tom's waist, Hilary freed a hand to wrap around Tom's rampantly hot cock, and tug once, twice, thrice –

The seed poured out of him, and Tom arched back further, his hold on Hilary's cock suddenly clenching in a pleasure so tight it was almost unbearable – and as Tom's weight shifted, Hilary followed him back down, rediscovered a young man's limberness, and thrust into him while Tom still shook with his own pleasure, thrust and thrust again until the promised destruction fell through him and took him away.

They dozed for a while after, dazed with satiation, curled up together with both heads on the same pillow. When Hilary drifted back to wakefulness he found that the afternoon was already well advanced.

Tom was watching him, lazily, lovingly. He asked, "Are you all right?"

Hilary smiled. "I am so very all right that I don't have the words for it. Some things can't really be explained, can they?"

That provoked a breathless laugh. "No doubt!"

Hilary lifted a gentle hand to caress that beautiful face so close by his. "Are *you* all right, my darling?"

"This really is the best birthday *ever*."

And Hilary could hardly believe such a thing, but he simply said with all his heart, "I'm so very glad."

"And it isn't even over yet!" Tom added with a grin.

# Nineteen

The new year began, but winter continued – and Hilary was perfectly happy that it do so, because winter meant that he could hibernate with Tom. The spring term began on the ninth of January, and Tom began cycling into town on three or four days a week for his classes and his work with Justin. Otherwise, Hilary and Tom spent almost all their time together. Tom would accompany Hilary on his walks, and on his shopping trips to Marjorie's store. Tom would curl up with Hilary while reading and making notes for his thesis, or he'd work away on his laptop down one end of the kitchen table while Hilary would sit nearby reading a novel or potter around in the kitchen cooking them a meal.

With Justin's advice and assistance, Hilary bought a car, an ex-rental Ford Focus. Tom got into the habit of suggesting an excursion each Sunday, despite the cold weather. They started with Stonehenge, and the physic garden in Petersfield, Hampshire, and then they both fell in love with all the wonders in Winchester which became their destination on alternate Sundays. They visited Chawton and Salisbury. It was delightful.

Hilary didn't want spring to come, because spring arriving meant summer would follow, and the end of the summer term on the thirtieth of June meant the end of his affair with Tom. Hilary would be happy if this winter lasted forever.

But too soon, leaves were pushing up through nature's detritus to hint at the snowdrops and primroses and bluebells to come, and the tips of tree branches began swelling and showing light green. Hilary watched it all, warily noting the new growth each afternoon as they walked up along the river and back.

Tom was happy for the changing seasons, as he was able to spend more useful time out in the garden. Hilary helped him as much as he could – and even Hilary couldn't help but feel keen anticipation as he watched the cleared areas of the garden starting to stir with new plant life.

"Well, don't get too excited," said Tom. "A lot of this will likely be weeds. We'll need to try and identity things as early as possible, and get rid of what we don't want; keep the beds clear for what we do."

In mid-February, Tom and Hilary decided that they should at last take up Justin's offer of having his students help work on the garden, for the sake of clearing the oaks of ivy. Tom organised it carefully, making sure that people knew where they could and couldn't step, what they could and couldn't touch. Justin got in there and worked as hard as anyone, while helping guide the students and enforce Tom's rules.

While Tom remained polite and reasonable, he was in such a state of anxiety about the students accidentally destroying anything precious that Hilary was forced to come out of his shell and play the genial host. Luckily this didn't prove such a chore, as the students – who'd all volunteered – seemed rather a pleasant and friendly bunch. They obviously liked Tom a great deal, and Justin, and apparently were prepared to take it on faith that Hilary was likeable as well.

Hilary and Tom had set up a trestle table in the garden, on which Hilary provided sustenance: a range of home-delivered pizzas for lunch, and then three homemade cakes for afternoon tea; along with urns available all day for tea and coffee, a bowl of apples, and a water dispenser, and homemade lemonade to have with the cakes.

At one point as he was setting out the afternoon tea, Hilary thought he saw Sir James standing just outside the wide-open gate, watching proceedings with wary curiosity. Hilary took a moment to free himself of what he was carrying and cover it up, and then turned to at least greet the man and perhaps invite him in – but the squire had already gone. Hilary was left wondering if he'd imagined the whole thing.

The students worked hard, and the transformation of the garden was extraordinary. They lost the 'magical glade' effect created by the canopy of ivy across the rows of trees, but gained a stately avenue of oaks that ran down towards the river. Hilary gazed at the sturdy thick trunks, and the branches that spread their crooked arms to the sky. He felt as if the trees were rolling their stiff shoulders and standing taller now they were no longer shackled.

"Grand, aren't they?" Tom said, standing beside Hilary with his arms folded and looking as smug as if he'd created the oaks himself.

"They are," Hilary happily agreed.

"Not sure how much foliage we'll have this year, but they don't look as if they've taken much harm. They're not old enough to have been planted by Thaddeus of course, but –"

"But we'll keep them anyway?" Hilary supplied.

Tom grinned at him. "But we'll keep them anyway, of course." Tom cast a friendly arm around Hilary's shoulders for a moment, and hugged him – before his attention shifted to the trestle table, and the depleted supplies it bore. "You didn't happen to keep a slice of the ginger cake aside for me, did you?"

"Of course I did," Hilary assured him; "and a rather generous one, too." He went to fetch it along with a cup of tea.

Everyone seemed to have enjoyed themselves well enough. Hilary made a particular point of thanking each and every one of them as they left, and they all grinned at him quite happily. One of the girls even pressed an affectionate kiss to his cheek. No one seemed to expect anything more than they'd had in return for all their hard work. It was a very successful day.

That evening, Tom curled up beside Hilary on the sofa looking well satisfied. "Mmm, time for snuggles and snoozles now," he murmured – before fitting his head into the hollow under Hilary's shoulder, and falling asleep. Hilary sat there quite happily embracing the young man, and basking in the comfortable warmth, until at last it was time for bed.

He woke Tom gently, and they headed upstairs together, helping each other along, until with minimal fuss they were snuggled up again under the covers, and they could both fall into a well-earned sleep.

Tom seemed so oddly content, despite sharing the home of a much older man and therefore living what must be a comparatively quiet life. He'd told a tale or two about the house he'd shared in town with other students or ex-students, that made it seem so very different, with parties and practical jokes; the thin walls failing to shield him from hearing and almost feeling other people's arguments and banal conversations and uninteresting sex lives, not to mention the sheer impossibility of working out a laundry schedule that suited them all.

"You don't miss the excitement of living in town?" Hilary tentatively asked one evening as they were – yet again – settling down to snuggle on the sofa, each with a book, and a pot of Assam steeping before them.

"Not in the slightest."

"Or the, uh … the *variety* of living with people more your own age?"

"I *love* being here with you," Tom said, wriggling in closer and then relaxing into place. "I feel so very … *satisfied*."

"Satisfied?" Hilary repeated. He thought about that for a moment, but he had to say, "I'm glad – in a way – of course! But that makes it sound as if you're becoming old before your time."

"I'm happy, Hilary. It feels good!"

"You should be out there having fun, and getting up to mischief with other young people."

Tom looked up at him, and grimaced his disagreement. "I can always head into town if I feel like it –"

"Of course you can!"

"– or stay on after classes one day. I know you'd be okay with that."

"I'm glad," Hilary said again. He loved that they could talk about things like this without creating any unnecessary drama, although he had to admit that he still fretted over a number of these issues despite Tom's calm assurance that all was well.

"But I've never been majorly into all that, you know? Not even while Bevan was still here – and Bevan *does* love to party."

"But –"

"Hilary, I'm really loving this. I feel *satisfied*. You understand that, don't you? I think it's a rare feeling, but you have it, I know – and it's rubbing off on me!"

Hilary pondered him very earnestly, ignoring the wink with which Tom made that last remark. Oh, he loved this young man, he loved him so much, and Hilary was afraid that he was a rather poor influence on him. "I suppose I do know what you mean. I think of it as contentment, and it means the world to me."

"Exactly!"

"But at your age you should be *happy*, not satisfied. Not content. It should still be the middle of the day for you – it should still be late morning and time for elevenses! You make it sound as if it's the evening already."

"But it *is* the middle of the day! Hilary, loving you is the midday sun, and I am soaking it up … like a lizard on a rock!"

Hilary sighed. "Tom –"

"Actually," Tom said slowly, as if only now thinking of it. "Sometimes people have said that I have an old soul. Does that explain it? I don't know … What I *do* know is that I want you in my life. As my friend and my lover."

Hilary lifted his head, and gazed sightlessly at the far wall as he tried to think about all this. Tom snuggled closer, curling up on the sofa seat and sliding his arms around Hilary's waist. Hilary let himself stroke Tom's hair. And Hilary sighed in defeat, though he said a little wistfully, "If only I wasn't such a selfish old man."

"I'm happy," Tom said once more. "I promise you, I've never been happier." And they stayed like that for a long while, acknowledging that sense of satisfaction and contentment, until at last they poured the tea and each picked up his book.

On another evening, Hilary finally said, "I don't want to pry –"

Tom tilted his head to smile at him. "I don't have any secrets from you, Hilary, and I don't mean to have, either."

"I am just trying to understand, my dear. Have you – Have you loved an older man before?"

"Not like you!" Tom said. But then he frowned in thought for long moments before finally saying, "The few times it's really mattered to me … it's been older men. I was so in love with one of my teachers, all through secondary school. Everyone just dismissed it as a crush – including him. The sort of crush that even straight guys feel in their teens. You know? It was only afterwards I realised actually it was the real thing. Or that's what it had become, anyway. For me, at least. And maybe even for him, as well. He was gay, too, you see."

"What did you do?"

Tom shrugged. "Nothing. If ever there'd been a moment in which it might have become something more, that time had long gone."

"Was he – very much older than you?"

"Not really. Seemed like it then, though! The last time I saw him, I was eighteen and he was thirty-seven. And then –" Tom sighed, and twisted around so he could talk more directly to Hilary while still resting his head on Hilary's thigh. Tom's book lay against his heart, with one neat finger keeping his place. "This is a secret, all right? I've never told anyone this. I had rather a thing for Bevan's father for a while … My friend Bevan, who I stayed with at the end of term? His dad. And he was pretty tempted, I think – and I *did* try for something more that time. I ambushed him with mistletoe one New Year's Eve. God, it was such a bittersweet kiss, I just *ached* forever after. But then he avoided me after that, which was probably just as well, because a couple of weird things happened later, and I realised he was a bit fucked up, really. Like, it wouldn't have been good, or even wicked, but just horribly sordid. You know? So I managed to give up on that, thank God. He's since run off with some bint, and left Bevan's mum with the younger kids and a whole heap of debt. That's why Bevan didn't stay on here once he graduated."

"Surely there have been some young men more your own age who cared for you …"

"Yeah." Another shrug from those supple shoulders. "When it's just been hooking up, having sex, or a friends with benefits thing – then it's been guys my sort of age. Sometimes it's meant a bit more than that. But like I said, I always knew that when it mattered, when it was love, it would be an older man. I just – That's just what I want. Someone who's mature, and grounded, and experienced. Someone who has … a different perspective on the world."

Hilary considered this for a while, and then pointed out one of the many flaws in their current arrangement. "I am sure that when you met me I actually had rather *less* experience than any of the young men you might have … hooked up with."

Tom grinned up at him. "I'm not talking sex. What a one-track mind you have!" he added with a delighted laugh.

"You can hardly blame me when I have such a beautiful young man in my bed each night."

"Flatterer! What I *mean* is: you've lived an examined life, haven't you? You've worked – and I know you dismiss your work as not being very important, but it *was*, and what a way of engaging with life, helping all those different people over the years! And you've read – you're always reading – and you've made a home for yourself. You have a sense of priorities. You know what's important, and what isn't. You know how to get along with people, whether they're idiots like his lordship or busybodies like Marjorie Flanagan, or they're like Sam Reynolds and have a quiet noble soul that no one else can see. I love all that in a man."

Hilary was carefully stroking Tom's arm, and paying great attention to it, as if he could deflect attention from what he must ultimately ask. He began with something a little easier. "You could love Sam, could you?"

"Yes … Yes, actually, I think I could. He's entirely loveable! Not that it would do me any good. He'll be faithful to his wife until his dying day. That's one of the most loveable things about him! But anyway, I bet he's not half as wild in bed as you are, though he's got twenty years or more on you."

Hilary flushed a little, with pleasure and pride and vulnerability. "Why won't you –" he said, refusing to get distracted by the compliment or the invitation in Tom's bright clear eyes. "Why won't you –" Hilary said, before clearing his throat. "Why won't you love Justin, then?"

Tom groaned, and pushed away to sit up so that he was no longer touching Hilary. And Hilary was left feeling cold where Tom had been, and yearning, and shaking with nerves. He could hardly tell whether it was courage or stupidity that made him constantly force the issue, but Hilary did know that Tom's future belonged with Justin or perhaps someone very like him, and not with Hilary.

"Would you *please* just leave that be?" Tom eventually said. "I have to *work* with Justin. All right? I *want* to work with him – and I don't need any more complications than there already are."

"All right," Hilary agreed in a small voice, wondering how Tom could possibly see any wisdom in Hilary, because surely Tom wasn't fooled by Hilary's age and his wrinkles and his white hair. *I'm such an old fool, Tom …*

"And anyway, I love *you*, Hilary. I *love* you."

Hilary took Tom's hand when he reached back towards him, and bent his head to press a humbled kiss to the palm. "And I you, my dearest friend," he whispered to the sensitive skin there. *I love you.*

# Twenty

The spring term ended, and a five-week break stretched ahead of them until the summer term began in late April. Tom obviously didn't consider the time as a holiday, however, as he was working more intently than ever on his thesis, and less happily as well. Hilary left him to it, of course, and tried to quietly support him as much as possible. One evening when Tom finally stood up after spending hours scowling over a mess of open books, Hilary dared to ask, "Has something gone awry with your research?"

"No. No, that's not it," Tom said, stretching tall, then walking over to where Hilary sat, and bending over him to enfold him in a hug. "It's just … getting serious, you know? It's crunch time."

"Already? You still have another term to go."

Tom stood again, and stretched, before heading over to the kitchen to fetch himself a glass of water. "I should try to get a decent first draft finished before the end of the break. There'll still be so much work to do on it after that, let alone everything else with the teaching and all."

Hilary had only the vaguest ideas of academic life. "I wish there was something I could do to help," he said rather piteously.

"You do! You keep me fed and make me cups o' tea."

"Ah, yes."

"And between you and the garden, I get plenty of fresh air and exercise," Tom added with a wink. "Not to mention entertainment."

The young man was perfectly genuine, though Hilary couldn't really say that he felt comforted. "I'm glad."

"I'll tell you what," Tom continued, coming back to sit by Hilary at the table. "If we have a spare day or two at some stage, you can help me pull my bibliography together. It's the sort of thing I always have good intentions about updating as I go, but of course it always gets forgotten along the way."

"Oh, I'd like that," said Hilary, rather more cheerfully.

"We can go through all the books here – in their beautiful bookcases – and sort through my Kindle. You could come into the uni library with me one day, too, if you like. I'll tell them you're my research assistant! You could have lunch with me and Justin. I don't know why we haven't done that before! It'll be great, if you really want to be more involved."

"I'm sure Justin is pleased with how your thesis is coming along."

Tom shot him a wry glance. "He is. But he's not going easy on me, if that's what you think."

"No, of course not –"

"He's as critical as he needs to be … As we both need him to be!" Tom glanced at Hilary again, warily this time, and then seemed to find his own clasped hands of great interest. "If I want to stay on there in the long term – and I do. Well, there's nowhere else nearby, unless I commute to Winchester or Swindon, so really we have to make this work. It's in his interests, and in mine, if I can demonstrate that I've earned the place. If it's clearly not just favouritism."

Hilary stared at Tom aghast. "Oh, Tom, surely –"

"Justice has to be *seen* to be done, and all that."

"But surely anyone who knows either of you must realise – that he cares so much for you *because* you've earned his good opinion. Not the other way around."

Tom smiled wanly. "I like the way you think, Hilary. You're always so fair-minded!"

If Hilary had had any small complacencies about their shared situation before then, this conversation rather shattered them. When left to his own devices, Hilary found his thoughts tending towards gloomy.


Tom's attention was wholly taken up by his studies, the garden, and their love. He seemed perfectly fulfilled in the latter two, at least. Despite April turning cold and wet after a warm, dry March, Tom managed to work in the garden for a while every day. New growth was pushing through the newly cleared soil, and turning straggly plants plump, despite the poor weather. It seemed that every time Tom came in to shed his damp clothes and be warmed with tea and kisses, he had some exciting news to report.

One day after Easter, he came inside with a particular gleam in his eye. "I've made a discovery!" he announced once he was in dry clothes again, and they were sitting at the kitchen table each with his hands wrapped around a steaming cup of tea. "Or I hope I have. And then I had a thought – which I'm trying not to get too worked up about."

"Oh yes?" Hilary asked with a smile quirking his lips.

"There's a plant out there … I'm pretty sure it's Silverseal. You know, from the Archard family arms?"

"How marvellous!" said Hilary.

"Well, we won't know for sure until it flowers, but the leaves are so distinctive …"

"Very distinctive, from what I've seen."

"Yes, and it's not just the shape but the silver-green colour of the foliage …" Tom sighed. "The problem being that it's supposed to have died out *ages* ago. So this would be … well, almost too good to be true."

Hilary grasped Tom's hand. "I hope it's true, my dear," he said lightly. "You deserve miracles."

Tom smiled at him with a kind of warmly lopsided affection. "Then what I thought was … what if some of the other older herbs have survived out there? Or any of the older plants, not just herbs! Maybe not since Thaddeus's time, but still … There's all kinds of possibilities, really, for plants that could have survived the neglect. And the ivy." Tom took a breath. "If that really is Silverseal, or if there are even a few of the rarer plants out there … we could cultivate them. You know, grow them, and sell the seeds or young plants. Supply the public or the specialist nurseries. I should think we could develop it into a business, in a small kind of way."

"Oh."

"Wouldn't that be good? At least it will be a bit of a return for the money you've already spent out there."

"That's not why I'm spending the money, though. It isn't an investment in that sense."

"I know that."

Hilary considered the young man, with his mussed hair still rain-dark, and his clear-sky eyes now losing their glint as he faced this unexpected resistance. "If that's really something you'd enjoy, Tom –"

"I thought it would be cool! We could call the business Hilary's Rare Seeds. Though we should try for a bit of innuendo, if we can," Tom added with a wink.

"I thought you'd want to concentrate on an academic career."

"Hilary's Precious Seed."

"Wicked boy," chided Hilary rather lovingly. "Of course it should be Tom's Rare Seeds, though."

"Hilary and Tom's," he countered. "Well, I guess it would have to be a part-time concern anyway. It's not going to earn us a proper income! But I'm already working out there part-time, so why not just continue, once we have it cleared and replanted?"

*Why not indeed?* Hilary asked himself. And actually he knew why, but he wasn't brave enough or thinking clearly enough to say it out loud. The problem was – The problem was that Tom was somehow envisaging a shared future that Hilary knew was impossible. Added to which, he knew that arguing Tom out of his lovely fancies and back into cold clear sense was going to prove more impossible still.

Leonard, the head gardener from the Hall, showed up early one morning a few days later. Tom and Hilary were still in their pyjamas, and Hilary was wearing a new dressing gown he'd treated himself to. They were still sitting dozily over cups of tea at the kitchen table, and Leonard didn't need much persuasion to join them. He had what looked like an old bound journal in his hand, which Tom eyed with politely restrained interest.

"Yes, I have found a little something for you, Mr Laurence. Not very much, I think, though."

"Anything at all would be great," said Tom.

Leonard opened up the journal to a particular page, and pushed it across to lie on the table between Hilary and Tom, who bent their heads over it. "A sketch done in a quiet moment," said Leonard. "It's not even finished."

"No, that's wonderful," Tom insisted.

"Thank you so much, Leonard," Hilary offered. The sketch was indeed quick and simple, showing the outlines of plants rather than the details, though done with a clear eye and a deft hand. No doubt Tom would be able to broadly identify some of the plants in any case. The artist seemed to have been standing on the terrace just outside the back door of the tower; Hilary knew the view very well by now. Perhaps the artist had been waiting for someone, and was filling in the time. The paper was brown and its edges brittle, and the ink was faded; it seemed very old. None of them was touching it, out of respect for its obvious age.

"Those are apple trees, aren't they?" Tom asked Leonard, his fingertip hovering gently over the page. "A row running down either side of the oaks. I wish *they'd* survived!"

Leonard pondered the sketch for no doubt the twentieth time. "It's not clear which varieties these are, but we grow Bedwyn Beauty and Corsley Pippin up at the Hall, both native to Wiltshire. If there's something here to graft onto, I'll give you cuttings. Or seeds, if you decide to replant, though I'm sure you know there's no guarantees with seeds."

"Oh, that would be marvellous!" Tom cried.

"We'd be very grateful," Hilary said. "When does this sketch date to? Do we know?"

Tom glanced at him, apparently amused that the scholarly question had come from someone other than Tom himself.

Leonard carefully turned a page or two to show them. "The rest of this is accounts relating to the gardens and parklands at the Hall, from the early seventeen-hundreds. I guess it's from around the same time." He added, "I'll have to take this book back with me, I'm sorry, but I've made copies of these pages for you to keep."

"Marvellous …" Tom murmured happily, sitting back with a joyous little wriggle that sent frissons through Hilary. Tom laughed, perhaps realising the effect he'd had, but instead turned to Leonard. "Come out to the garden and see what I've found. I'm actually hoping it's Silverseal – *Hydrastis argentum*, you know? A nice robust specimen, too."

"Ah! Well done, Mr Laurence."

"Well, wait until you see it. And I know it's all too good to be true, so don't be afraid of telling me I'm dreaming."

"I've never seen another plant with leaves shaped like that. It's unmistakeable, I would have thought, Mr Laurence."

Tom took a long shuddery breath, but all he said was, "Wait until you see it."

A moment later, Tom had thrown his coat on over his pyjamas, pulled on his wellies, and the two younger men headed outside. After a short consultation with their heads bent together over the plant in question, Leonard stood and folded his arms with a slow but firm nod – and Tom grinned up at Hilary, and did a little jig. Hilary's heart sang for him. Then Leonard and Tom rambled off, examining the garden – perhaps looking for other specimens of Silverseal – and chatting quite happily together. Hilary left them to it, and readied the kettle and the tea things to make another pot as soon as it might be required.

Next time Hilary looked out to spy on them, Leonard was obligingly helping Tom dig up the roots of a bramble Tom had been battling on his own. It appeared that the war was at last being won through their joint efforts. Hilary settled at the table with the novel he was currently reading.

"Hilary –"

He looked up, startled – and then icy shock poured through him when he saw Tom's extraordinarily pale face. Hilary stood up, and reached for him. "What is it? Tom?"

"I think – I think – we need to call Inspector Barnaby."

"Sorry – ?"

"The police. We need to call the police."

Hilary glanced to find Leonard there in the doorway, also somewhat pale but obviously whole and unhurt. Hilary strode the two steps necessary to take Tom's cold hands into his own warmer ones. "Why, what is it? What's wrong? Are you all right, Tom?"

"Nothing that a cup o' tea won't cure," Tom said, obviously trying to sound brave.

Leonard said, "Why don't you both sit down for a minute?"

Hilary obediently drew Tom over to the table, and sat him down in his usual seat, then slid into his own seat, never once letting Tom's hands go. "Please, Leonard. Tell me what's happened."

"We've found some old bones out there, that look human. Once we were sure, we didn't dig any further, just in case. The police will want to see if there's anything there for them."

"Yes," said Hilary. "Yes, of course. I should call." But he couldn't tear himself away from poor Tom, who looked thoroughly shaken. "Tom … Tom, are you all right, my dear? Such a horrid thing for you to find."

After a moment Tom lifted his head to gaze back at him with wide maddened eyes. "What if it's Thaddeus?" he whispered hoarsely. *"What if it's the baby?"*

"Oh, my dear …"

"It's no baby," Leonard stoutly asserted. "I saw enough of a foot and a leg to think it a full-grown man or woman."

"I see," said Hilary.

Tom whispered hoarsely, "What if the baby's there with him?"

"Let's not imagine the worst, my dear. Not yet, anyway." Hilary clasped

Tom's hands closer for a moment. "Let me go, and I'll call the police. Maybe they'll have some way of identifying this poor soul. All right, Tom? Let me go, just for a few minutes, my dear – then we'd better go up and get dressed properly, and we'll have that cup of tea you wanted."

"Yes," he said distractedly, clutching at Hilary as if never wanting to let him go. "Yes. Oh, but what if it's poor Thaddeus … ?"

The morning became moments of chaos interspersed with waiting for so long they almost became bored. A local constable turned up, and had a brief conversation with the three of them. Hilary made tea. To save Tom or Hilary the trouble, Leonard obligingly took the constable out to the garden to show her the skeleton.

Tom still wasn't looking any happier, so Hilary went to fetch a throw from the sofa, and wrapped it about Tom's shoulders, taking the opportunity during the wait to hug him for long lovely heart-wrenching moments.

When Leonard and the constable came back in, she announced rather heartily, as if this was reassuring, "It's certainly not a *recent* death."

*"Oh …"* groaned Tom, his head sinking to the table.

She blinked, but didn't question him; Leonard had probably already mentioned the possibilities of Thaddeus to her. "I'll give you the number of Wessex Archaeology, and they'll send someone to lift it, and take it away for examination. When they're done, there'll need to be some form of interment, though you needn't concern yourselves about that."

"Well," said Hilary. "But if we want to be involved … ?"

"Of course; that's your decision to make. Now, Leonard and I have already covered up that garden bed with a tarpaulin, and weighted it down. I expect you not to interfere with it further in the meantime."

"I think we can promise you we won't," said Hilary. He didn't even find himself curious to go out and see the bones – although he felt concerned that the right thing be done, and that the poor person be identified, and avenged if necessary, and then properly laid to rest as soon as possible.

Tom was quiet now, his attention sunk within himself. Hilary had been indulging his own need to maintain contact with the younger man, and either held his hand or stroked his hair or clasped his shoulder. No one seemed to make anything of it beyond an avuncular concern – and the fact they could hide in plain sight like this brought it home yet again how unlikely his and Tom's love was.

Hilary dragged himself off to the phone once more, this time to call the archaeologists, and was rather surprised to be told that someone would come around early that afternoon. "They seem rather keen," he observed a little doubtfully.

"That they are!" the constable agreed with a wry smile. "I put it down to them liking field work more than desk work." She reviewed her notes and jotted down a few more items while drinking a cup of tea, and then headed off, saying she'd come back again herself that afternoon to find out what had happened.

Meanwhile, Leonard had called Sir James to explain where he was and what had happened; Sir James apparently insisted on him staying on, if he could be of any use whatsoever. Hilary made more tea, while Leonard distracted Tom by sitting beside him with the sketch of the garden between them and discussing with him what the various plants might be. This worked rather well, and soon Tom was also examining the pages of accounts before and after the sketch, to see if there were any useful details to be found.

The three of them managed to eat two sandwiches between them for lunch, mostly thanks to Leonard. And then at last not one but two archaeologists arrived, were shown through to the garden – and almost immediately relayed a message via Leonard that the skeleton was centuries old rather than years or even decades. Tom shuddered, and sank away within himself again. "It's Thaddeus," Tom muttered to Hilary. "I know it is. He never went home after all."

Hilary made tea, and then went to find the key for the gate, and asked Leonard to open it for their visitors. And then they waited, unable to settle to anything, while the skeleton was dug up and the surrounding earth was searched for anything related. The welcome news, such as it was, was that the garden bed appeared to contain only one adult skeleton.

"Not the child, then," Hilary reassured Tom, who nodded glumly. "That's something to be grateful for."

Leonard was about to say something, but then seemed to think better of it. Hilary wondered if he'd been going to remark that Tom might be grateful for the bramble being sorted as well.

At last the skeleton was safely ensconced in a serious-looking cardboard storage box, and the constable returned just in time for them all to head out the front to pay their respects as the box was carried to the Wessex Archaeology van and placed inside. Then, as the van drew away and headed off down the road, but before the constable had left, Sir James finally arrived.

"How are you all?" the squire was amiably asking as he walked over to them. "A terrible thing, this. A terrible thing."

*"You!"* Tom cried in fury, the throw swirling around him dramatically. "You had him killed!"

Sir James stalled. The constable gaped.

"You had him killed because Lady Bryony loved him!"

"Now, look here, young fellow –"

"Tom," said Hilary, taking his love into his arms. "Tom, please."

*"What happened to the baby?"* Tom roared.

"Perhaps we'd better take this inside," said the constable, "and someone can explain this to me."

"Someone might explain it to me as well," Sir James blustered.

They didn't get further than the front room, and regrouped in the same configuration.

Leonard was wise enough to immediately point out why the accusation needn't be taken literally. "The body had been there for centuries, Sir James; that much was clear. We know it had nothing to do with you personally. Mr Laurence has been upset."

Hilary added, "The squire back then was also a Sir James. You understand. Tom has taken Thaddeus's story very much to heart."

"There was a baby," Tom insisted, his voice low and intense now. Hilary could feel him shaking. "Thaddeus and Bryony had a baby. That's why Thaddeus was killed. I want you to tell me what happened to it!"

"Well, I'm sure *I* don't know," Sir James replied huffily yet honestly. "First I've heard of such a thing! There was no direct heir in that generation; James and Bryony had no children." He nodded to acknowledge the point, and corrected himself: "No legitimate children."

"Hilary had such a nice idea," Tom said, at last a bit calmer, "about Thaddeus taking the child back home to his family in Kent, and raising it himself. But if that was Thaddeus buried in the garden …"

"The child must have been fostered out, then," Hilary supplied. "It would have been raised well, and lived a happy life. There's no need to assume the worst."

But something more had occurred to Tom, and he was again staring darkly at Sir James, and pointing an accusing finger even as he thought whatever it was through. "Wait a minute … Now I know why you were so keen on insisting that Thaddeus was gay …"

"What?" Sir James huffed. His colour heightened.

"Thaddeus – *of Kent*," Tom said significantly. "You were worried there was a family connection with old Mr Kent and Hilary here. You were worried about a challenge to the inheritance!"

"Don't be ridiculous!"

"Tom, I really don't see how that's possible," Hilary murmured – even as he tried to get his mind around how Tom might have added A to B to find a rather unexpected C.

Sir James said, "The title is only passed down the male line, in any case. A child of Bryony's couldn't have inherited that."

"No, but the hall and the land here came from her family, didn't it? That's worth a legal challenge! With the whole estate going to James's brother, rather than to Bryony's child."

Sir James shook his head in bewilderment. "You're far cleverer than me, young man, to come up with such a convoluted thing. It never even occurred to me –"

"Nor me," Hilary agreed. "Tom, we don't even know for sure there *was* a baby, let alone what happened to it, or what surname the child or its descendants might have taken. And I have almost no idea of my own family history beyond my grandparents. This is … very imaginative, but perhaps we can save the speculation for a quieter day?"

Tom at last turned from Sir James, and considered Hilary for a long moment. Then he took a breath, and visibly sagged. "You're right, of course. It *is* speculation. I shouldn't – I shouldn't have –"

"That's all right," Hilary said, rubbing at Tom's arms as if to warm him. He asked the constable, "Is there anything more we need do today, do you think? Or can we leave all this for now?"

"We can leave it," she said. "Wessex Archaeology will investigate the bones, and they'll get in touch. It might be a while! I know you want the mystery solved, but there's no real urgency, I'm afraid, given the age of the skeleton."

"No, we understand," said Hilary. "Should we leave the garden bed undisturbed in the meantime?"

She tilted her head in consideration. "If that's convenient, yes – though I doubt it will be necessary for anyone to return. All right, Mr Laurence?" she added.

"Yes," Tom whispered.

"Thank you, constable," Hilary said.

"Sir James?" the constable continued. "Was there anything else?"

"No, no. Leonard, no doubt it's time we left these people to what's left of their day."

"Of course, sir."

Hilary took the opportunity to say, "Sir James, if I may reassure you … Even if all that were true, I have no interest in your estate. Whatever happened has happened, and such a long time ago. Even so, I am perfectly content with what I have."

"Then you're a wise man, Mr Kent, and this young fellow is lucky to have your friendship." Sir James came to shake Hilary's hand, and then clapped a friendly hand to Tom's shoulder.

And they all said their farewells, some of them chastened and some of them wary, but all with goodwill. The constable lingered until Leonard and the squire had left, and then drove away as well.

And at last Hilary and Tom were alone.

"Are you all right?" Hilary asked, his hands on Tom's upper arms. He could feel that Tom was still trembling in the aftermath of shock and high emotion. "My dear, let me take care of you."

"I'm all right," Tom replied, though not very convincingly. "I'm cold," he added a bit woefully. "I just feel so cold."

"Of course. I'm going to take you back up to bed, and tuck you in, then I'll bring us up a tray of tea and toast."

"Yeah … ?" The faintest hint of a smile started to curve Tom's lips.

"And then once we've eaten, we're going to get some serious snuggling done. For as long as it takes."

"As long as what takes?"

"Until you're smiling again."

"Oh …" And the corners of Tom's mouth abruptly turned down as if he were making an effort not to smile right then and there. "Come on, then," Tom said, taking Hilary's hand and leading him towards the stairs. "Come on up and tuck me in."

"You like my plan?"

"Hilary, I *love* it."

"Then that's what we'll do."

# Twenty-One

Of course they never did manage to identify the skeleton they'd discovered in the garden at Riverside. There was nothing ever found there but bones – no clues such as old leather shoes or a belt, no ring or chain, no scraps of clothes nor even a shroud. The body was that of a full-grown man, who seemed otherwise in good health, bearing the marks of having done mild labour in his time. There were no signs to indicate how he'd died, but as he seemed to have been buried naked in a garden, there was plenty to suggest secrets and foul play.

The age of the skeleton certainly made it possible that this was Thaddeus, and that's what Tom chose to believe. Hilary thought it probable as well, but remembered that they would never know for certain. Just as they would never know the fate of Thaddeus and Bryony's baby, if ever there was one. It was at least easier to imagine a story with a happier ending for the child.

With the vicar's cooperation they had the bones interred in the churchyard at Nether Bedwyn. Hilary paid for a modest grey stone, elegant in its simplicity, and Tom chose the words to be carved upon it, from a verse in the Song of Solomon: 'My beloved is gone down into his garden'.

On a dry windy day in June, Hilary and Tom stood there together in the churchyard to pay their respects to the man who'd created their garden, and who'd been the means of bringing them together. They were silent for a while, until Hilary at last ventured, "If we have read his story correctly, then he had two great passionate loves in his life."

"Which was over too soon," Tom countered.

"For a man to have such a purpose as he had with his garden, strikes me as a very fine thing. You'd know more about that than me, Tom. But to have had Lady Bryony's love as well … We don't really know how long they were together, do we? But such a thing can still be perfect even if it doesn't last forever. Am I saying that right? A loving relationship doesn't have to last forever to be perfect. I'm sure you know what I mean."

"D'you really believe that?" Tom asked, sounding as if he desperately wanted to believe it as well.

"Of course! Tom, I've known you for almost nine months now. It's been the very happiest time of my life. The other sixty-five years of my life count for nothing when weighed against it. And when it's over, my dear –" Hilary's breath caught as Tom's hand reached to clasp his, there in the open beneath the high dome of sky. "When it's over, any sadness I feel will be nothing compared to my gratitude for the great happiness you've brought me."

"Hilary …" Tom said brokenly.

"Let me thank you now for all your kindnesses to an old man."

"Hush …" said Tom. And then another silence stretched, before Tom gathered himself and spoke the whole verse: "'My beloved is gone down into his garden, to the beds of spices, to feed in the gardens, and to gather lilies.'"

As the end of June approached, there never seemed any time to talk properly. Tom grew more and more anxious and was more and more involved in his studies and his teaching responsibilities. As far as Hilary could tell, Tom's thesis and his and Justin's classes were all going well, but they were both frantically busy, and they both cared enough to worry themselves ragged. Hilary let Tom be, and quietly supported him in ways he knew wouldn't intrude. He was anxious himself, though he tried to hide it – anxious that it would all be over too suddenly, and there would be no real chance to take stock, to give the relationship its due. The great love of his life might well end not with a bang but a whimper.

Tom's parents, of course, expected Tom to go to them the day after his university work was complete. As far as they were concerned, he was a single man, a student, whose real home was still with his family. Tom had agreed, with some reluctance, though was adamant he would only stay with them for two weeks, and not for the full break. He pleaded the cause of Thaddeus's garden in general, and the Silverseal in particular, which he hoped would bear berries during the summer – and they agreed, with some reluctance, that he might return to Riverside sooner than they wished. Such were the results, Hilary reflected, of being in an unconventional relationship.

Over dinner one evening, Tom ventured, "I wonder if you'd come, too … To Colchester, I mean, for those two weeks."

"Oh, my darling …" said Hilary, moved beyond measure. "What a lovely thought! But, no. It's impossible. You must realise how impossible this is." He sighed. The whole thing had been so very beautiful, and so very fragile, and so utterly impossible a dream. Perhaps they were lucky it had survived this long.

"They *do* like you, you know," Tom said wistfully.

"They wouldn't if they knew." Hilary sighed, and stared down wretchedly at the dinner he couldn't possibly finish now. "You won't tell them, will you. You won't tell your parents about us."

"No, of course not," Tom said, thinking that Hilary wanted to be reassured.

"That's why this is impossible, do you see? It would always have to be a secret. I'm afraid that my feelings for you are rather … well, alarmingly transparent. But we could never be open about being together."

Tom shrugged a little impatiently. "Does that even matter?"

Hilary gazed at him imploringly. "For someone of your age in my generation, there could be nothing ahead but lies and sadness – and occasionally tragedy. You don't have to live like that now, Tom. You can live honestly. You can *marry*."

"Just because society accepts a broader range of relationships than it used to – Well, I'm sure there's still plenty of people out there who have to keep their love secret, even if everyone involved is a consenting adult! If that's us, then *I* don't mind."

"Oh, Tom, but to have your love accepted and acknowledged – even *validated* by those around you –"

Tom shook his head, refusing to agree even though he seemed to have lost his sense of righteousness. "Hilary – if I can live the life I want – that life is with *you*. Secret or not."

"You are your parents' only son, their only child. You should be free to confide in them – to celebrate with them! But you couldn't tell them about me, could you? It's impossible!"

"If the reality is that you don't want to ever meet my parents again, then that's fine! God, *I* don't care."

Hilary's head was aching, and his heart as well. "That's not what I want for you. Or for Dulcie and Eric."

Tom shrugged, and pushed his plate away. Apparently he'd lost his appetite, too. "You know what? I don't tell them everything, and they don't share everything with me. There's a line to be drawn, yeah? Maybe you want to draw it in a different place than I do, but still – even if I was with … Justin or whoever, there's only so much I'd ever actually *say*. Isn't there?" he demanded. "Doesn't mean I don't love them, or them me."

"Oh, Tom ..." Hilary said, fretful and unconvinced.

"It's like you've said yourself, I've got to start making my own life. We have so much talking to do, Hilary. I mean, not right now," Tom offered with a wry grin. "I think we're pretty much all talked out for now!"

"But –"

Tom overrode him. "It's not that things aren't complicated, but I know what I want, Hilary. I wish you'd trust me when I tell you that *you're* what I want."

"I wish I could, too, my dear friend."

"Then find your courage, Hilary. Trust me. I know you want me, too. And the rest of the world can just go mind its own fucking business for once."

For which Hilary had no answer. He took one of Tom's hands in his, and they sat there for a while contemplating their linked fingers and caressing palms, until eventually it was time to get up and clear the table. They washed up the dinner things together, neither speaking, but each rediscovering a sense of peace. Then they took a pot of tea up to bed with them, and read their books, until they felt like making love. And then they slept.

# Twenty-Two

Early on the morning of Saturday the thirtieth of June, Hilary rose from dreams to linger just below the sun-dappled surface. He was *alive* in all ways and in all senses. His skin tingled with awareness of Tom's presence wrapped in Hilary's arms, and his ears gentled with the sound of Tom's breath, and his cock prodded boldly at Tom's slim buttocks. Hilary chuckled softly, and sent up silent thanks for all he'd been blessed with.

Tom stirred, and stretched luxuriously, and then pushed back further into Hilary's embrace, his hips wriggling as if to incite them both. He murmured, "Well, and good morning to *you*, Hilary Kent."

Hilary laughed contentedly. "I was dreaming about you, Tom Laurence. Such wicked dreams …"

"I'm sorry to wake you, then!"

"Ah, but the reality is even better …" And he snuggled in closer still for a warm sleepy kiss.

Cool reality intruded briefly as they each got up for the bathroom, but that was all right, too. That was part of how their bodies worked, and Hilary did love their bodies so very much.

Without anything needing to be said, they each came back to bed. Simply and sweetly, warmly and wickedly, they made love with hands and skin and mouths and cocks. And then they slept again, so perfectly rested.

Of course cold reality disturbed the idyll eventually. Tom was driving to his parents that day to stay for two weeks now that the academic year was done. And Hilary knew, though Tom did not, that this absence must mark the end of their relationship. He hoped they could be friends. He knew they mustn't be lovers.

Still, Hilary had this one last morning on which to make Tom breakfast, and fuss over him, and press an occasional kiss to his dark-toffee hair. He remained light-hearted and loving, so Tom would have nothing but good memories of their last hours together. He hugged Tom wholeheartedly in farewell. And then he waved as the Ford Focus smoothly powered through the road's curves, and the silhouette of the dear driver disappeared from view.

Hilary stayed there for a few moments, letting the peace of the countryside sink back within him. And then he wrapped his dressing gown closer around him, and went back inside, and started cleaning.

It wasn't ever a conscious decision, though Hilary found himself approving once he realised what was happening. It was perhaps a true instinct, or perhaps an accident that slowly became fact.

He didn't eat much that first day, not having the appetite for it, and not having his dear Tom to cook for. He drank tea, and water, and managed half a sandwich at dinner time. On the second day he woke with rather a sharp headache, which only became more intense, so he kept to tea and water, and idled in bed or on the sofa. He liked being in the bed, and resting his head on Tom's pillow, for he could breathe in Tom's lovely warm scent; his apple shampoo, and under that the indescribable salty poignancy that was Tom himself.

On the third day, Hilary woke clear and refreshed, and in fact felt so pure for the previous day's fast that he could hardly bear the thought of food. He drank water, and when he made tea he chose the black tea with ginseng, for he couldn't even face the thought of milk. A few hunger grumbles were ignorable, and even welcome for they made him feel healthy, as if everything was perfectly right.

He wasn't in the mood to do very much, so he read for a while, until even that became a little too much effort. So then he put the book away into its assigned place in the bookcases that Sam had made, and nothing else needed doing, everything was clean and orderly, so he simply made himself comfortable on the sofa and dozed, and then later he went up to bed.

The night merged into day and into night again. He drank water. He liked how the water made him feel, so pure and fine. He slept curved around a pillow, dreaming of Tom, remembering how blessed Hilary had been by their love, and daydreaming of how happy Justin would be when his own dreams of love came true. Justin was Tom's future, and it would be a happy future, and Hilary thought he could watch their story unfurl with nary a pang. He imagined how it would be: the shared smiles, the joyous sex, the insightful conversations. They might even marry. It was a wonder to Hilary that two men might marry these days. Perhaps they would hold the ceremony in Thaddeus's garden, by the renewed pond starred with water lilies, their handfasted reflections stretching long and sure on the water's surface as they gazed soul-deep into each other under the high arch of sky.

Hilary sighed wistfully. He was too tired to want to get up any more, so he quit drinking the water, and soon all he needed to do was lie there in the bed he'd shared with his love, and dream … The beams of daylight falling through the distorted diamonds of glass in the window shifted and then faded; the night passed in quiet comfort; and then another day dawned, and Hilary thought how very happy he'd been for these past nine months, and he'd been so right when he'd said to Tom that nothing else could possibly matter when balanced against the fact that for this little while his love had been fulfilled. It was time …

It was time now to move on, and to neatly remove the complication from Tom's life. Tom would have his beloved garden, and a home of his own, and there was plenty of money still. *Plenty.* In his own time and when at last it was right, Tom would be free to return Justin's faithful love, and all would be as it should be. Tom's delightful candour would shine again, and when he married Justin he could declare his love to all the world. Tom would be wholly himself. That was how it should be.

The slow rhythm of day and night and day continued.

It was time for his own rhythms to come to an end.

"Take care of him for me," Hilary whispered to Justin. "Fare well, my friend, and take care of this man we both love so dearly."

*"Hilary? Hilary! Come on, wake up. Wake up! For God's sake. … Sam, call for an ambulance. Tell them to hurry! … Hilary! God damn it, Hilary, he loves you, Tom loves you, and I won't have you break his heart like this. Do you hear me, Hilary? Come on, wake up, wake up, stay with me here."*

# Twenty-Three

He was aware of the ambulance and the siren, and of Justin's hand holding his own, Justin's expression so sorrowful, so empathetic, so fierce. There was an ambulance officer, and there was an oxygen mask on Hilary's face, and a drip in the back of his other hand. But mostly there was Justin sitting beside him.

They didn't speak at first, but just looked at each other. An endless moment dragged oddly … but then Hilary surfaced again, and Justin said, "Tom's on his way. He's driving, it'll take two-and-a-half, three hours. I told him to be careful," he added, as if reading Hilary's instinctive concern, "but he'll be here as soon as he can."

"Thank you," Hilary whispered hoarsely through the mask.

"Don't try to talk," said the ambulance officer, even as Justin said, "Don't speak."

A wry smile, and then Justin continued, "Don't worry about the house. We had to break in, I'm afraid. Well, Sam Reynolds did, so it was all done in a very civilised manner. He stayed behind with Samuel to fit a new lock, and make sure everything's secure. Tom can pick up the new keys from him, at any time this evening – Sam said it didn't matter how late."

Hilary nodded his understanding and his gratitude. He suspected he was going to feel rather silly later, but for now he just felt very cared for.

"So you don't need to worry about anything now, other than getting well again." Justin sighed. "Though how you're going to explain this to Tom, I have no idea. You can't expect him to like the notion of you leaving him, let alone in so final a manner. So untimely, too! You'll have to promise – not just Tom, but *all* of us – you'll have to promise us that you won't try this sort of thing again."

Hilary almost grinned at this rather unexpected lack of reticence from Justin. It was a wobbly grin, and Hilary felt that a storm of tears or laughter was trembling within him just waiting to spring forth – but it was a grin nevertheless. "How long?" he managed to ask.

And he might have meant so many different things, but Justin knew what he was asking, and answered him truthfully. "Oh, a while now. Since the beginning of spring term, when he showed up with a little extra verve in his hips. The answer didn't quite occur to me right away, but there was never anyone else I could attribute it to."

Hilary glanced at the ambulance officer, who remained studiously oblivious to whatever they were talking about. Despite which, Hilary felt all the delicious scary giddiness of coming out and being known. He looked up at Justin with the trust that Justin deserved, with something of Tom's candour, and with a large portion of his own courage.

Justin nodded, and gripped his hand tighter, and said, "So you'll promise us … ?"

"I promise," said Hilary. And he honestly did.


When Tom finally tracked Hilary and Justin to a cubicle in the Emergency Department of the hospital, he stalled for a moment, his gaze greedily gulping in the sight of Hilary alive and not quite so badly off as he probably should have been. Then it seemed there was nothing else to do but for Tom to take those last two strides to stand close by the bed, and throw himself into Hilary's arms. They clung to each other, and babbled in idiotic relief.

"What were you even *thinking*?"

"I don't know that I was!"

"Oh God, Hilary, I *can't* lose you, I *can't* lose you."

"But one day you'll have to let me go, my dear."

"Not yet. Not yet!" Tom pulled away enough to stare hard at Hilary, and he emphasised his point with a jab of his finger at the innocent air. "I want at least twenty years with you, d'you hear me? Twenty years! *At least.*"

"Yes, Tom."

"A lot of people don't even get that much, you know, so don't you go thinking this is just a short-term concern."

"No, Tom," he said, very contritely.

Tom finally paused, and he smiled, and then he stood tall again – but only so as he could heft himself up to sit on the edge of the bed by Hilary's hips. Hilary curved around him quite happily, while Tom took one of Hilary's hands in his, the one without the drip, and he stroked at it gently. After a time, Tom said in a low tone, "Justin went to Riverside to get you for me."

"Yes. Justin and Sam, I understand. Thank you."

"Where *is* Justin?" Tom asked, looking around with a frown. "He was here, wasn't he? When I got here?"

"I suspect he went to find a discreet cup of tea."

"Oh." Tom nodded. "Anyway, it's not me you have to thank. You called Justin, d'you remember?"

"Not really. I suppose I must have, but all I remember is wanting to tell him to take care of you." It would have been his last thoughts.

"Well, whatever you said, he realised something was wrong. He was already on the way when he called me from the car. I thought of calling Sam. I couldn't think how else Justin would get in the front door, unless he ram-raided it, or something."

A quiet moment welled between them, and then Hilary quietly said once more, "Thank you," and added, "I'm sorry."

"Well, don't scare me like that ever again, and we'll call it quits."

"I won't, I promise."

Which was when Justin returned, wearing his familiar old genial smile and bearing three polystyrene cups of tea.

"*Black* tea?" Tom asked as he peeled back the lid.

"Some things within me have changed," Hilary offered in what was probably a fairly useless explanation.

"Only for the better," Justin equably suggested.

"Oh, well, that's all right, then," said Tom.


Hilary was kept in overnight for observation of his physical, mental and emotional state. Some of this was very humbling, of course, but then his acceptance of the fact he must bear being humbled seemed to help convince the hospital staff that he would be all right. He couldn't decide whether he'd feel more foolish if the episode had been intentional or if it had been accidental. He supposed it had been a mix of both, and his honesty about that stood him in good stead, as did his brief and tactful explanations of why the circumstances wouldn't reoccur.

Late the following afternoon Hilary was released, clutching detailed dictary instructions and a long list of appointments for health checks and psychiatric evaluations. Justin drove Hilary and Tom home to Riverside, and then once he'd seen them settled, he discreetly headed off again. Tom sat Hilary down on the sofa, and made the perfect amount of fuss over looking after him. Sam soon dropped by with two bags of groceries courtesy of

Marjorie – on account, of course. Sam also bore a worried look that didn't finally ease until he'd sat and considered Hilary for the length of time it took to drink a pot of tea between them.

Eventually Hilary and Tom were alone again, and for a moment Hilary feared awkwardness. But then Tom announced he'd bought Hilary a gift. "Even before this melodramatic turn of yours, I wanted to show you that I mean to hang around. So …" He produced a carton full and overflowing with DVD box sets. "It's the entire run of *Midsomer Murders*! Well, as far as they've released it, anyway. All right?"

"Yes, Tom. That's perfect."

Tom put the carton down on the floor, and then folded to sit sideways beside Hilary on the sofa so they could look at each other while they talked. "I made a spreadsheet of the correct running order, though," he said, brandishing a printout. "These box sets, the episodes are all over the place! I don't know how they get away with it, actually."

Hilary chuckled. "That's even more perfect than I can say." After a moment, he ventured, "What did Dulcie and Eric think of you dropping everything to come to the hospital?"

"They understood! They were worried about you, too, you know. Dad made us a cup of tea while Mum helped me pack quickly – otherwise I'd have been out the door and in the car before Justin had even hung up!"

A slight silence lengthened, before Hilary prompted, "I wondered if they're beginning to guess …"

"Well, I suppose they might be. It's going to add up sooner or later, isn't it? I've been thinking, after my little outburst yesterday – if two gay guys end up living together for twenty years or more, without either of them ever seeing anyone else, then everyone's going to guess eventually, aren't they? Probably starting with my parents. Not that they're the sort to make a great big drama out of it, even if they don't approve right away. So," Tom continued, "what do you think? I mean, we don't have to deal with this *now*, but are you all right with the idea? That one day, at some stage, we're going to be 'out' as a couple?"

"I'm feeling rather braver about it than I was."

Tom grinned in relief and took his hand. "*That's* my man. That's my love …"

"Justin has been perfectly wonderful about it all," Hilary continued.

"I have to admit I hope there's not *too* much drama – but even if there is, I'll pay the price, Tom. Oh *Tom*, I've never asked for anything more from life than contentment, and for most of my years I've had exactly that. I suppose it seemed too much and too late to start asking for happiness."

"But that's what you have, isn't it?"

"Yes, my dear. That's what I have."

Tom mulled this over for a minute, and then said, "The way I see it is: you've got a heart that loves … and bits that give you pleasure … and dignity to be respected. And so do I. We *all* do."

"Oh, Tom!"

"What else does any of us need? And what do white hair and wrinkles matter, compared to that?"

"That is a truly beautiful thought," said Hilary, meaning it. Such unconditional acceptance, unconditional *like* was nigh on miraculous, he thought.

"I'll get it embroidered on a cushion," Tom said a bit dryly. He added with a cheeky grin, "Then I can hit you over the head with it when I need to!"

Hilary laughed, and he drew his dearest love into his arms, and they snuggled. "That's all right," Hilary murmured. "I think I've got the idea now."

And they lived happily together for the rest of Hilary's long years, and when he had gone, Tom eventually took other lovers, but he mourned Hilary to the end of his days. And if their best selves met and loved hereafter, who is to say?

**The End**

# About Julie Bozza

Ordinary people are extraordinary. We can all aspire to decency, generosity, respect, honesty – and the power of love (all kinds of love!) can help us grow into our best selves.

I write stories about 'ordinary' people finding their answers in themselves and each other. I write about friends and lovers, and the families we create for ourselves. I explore the depth and the meaning, the fun and the possibilities, in 'everyday' experiences and relationships. I believe that embodying these things is how we can live our lives more fully.

Creative works help us each find our own clarity and our own joy. Readers bring their hearts and souls to reading, just as authors bring their hearts and souls to writing – and together we make a whole.

I read books, lots of books, and watch films. I admire art, and love theatre and music. I try to be an awesome partner, sister, daughter, friend. I live an engaged and examined life. And I strive to write as honestly as I can.

I have lived in two countries – England and Australia – which has helped widen my perspective, and I have travelled as well. I love learning, and have completed courses in all kinds of things. My careers have been in Human Resources, and in eLearning and training, so there has always been a focus on my fellow human beings and on understanding, conveying, sharing information.

Knitting gives me some down time and the chance to craft something with my hands. Coffee gives me stimulation and a certain street cred. My favourite colour has segued from pure blue to dark purple, and seems to be segueing again to marine blues.

I think John Keats is the best person who has ever lived.

And that's me! Julie Bozza. Quirky. Queer. Sincere.

If you want to know more, please do come find me at juliebozza.com and libra-tiger.com.

# Other titles by Julie Bozza

The Butterfly Hunter Trilogy:
    Butterfly Hunter
    Of Dreams and Ceremonies
    Like Leaves to a Tree
    The Thousand Smiles of Nicholas Goring

Albert J. Sterne:
    The Definitive Albert J. Sterne
    Albert J. Sterne: Future Bright, Past Imperfect

The Fine Point of His Soul
Homosapien … a fantasy about pro wrestling
Mitch Rebecki Gets a Life
A Night with the Knight of the Burning Pestle
A Threefold Cord
The 'True Love' Solution
The Valley of the Shadow of Death

Anthologies:
    A Certain Persuasion
    A Pride of Poppies

9 781925 869194